LONE WOLF

LONE WOLF

Michael Gregorio

This first world edition published 2017
in Great Britain and the USA by
SEVERN HOUSE PUBLISHERS LTD of
Eardley House, 4 Uxbridge Street, London W8 7SY.
Trade paperback edition first published
in Great Britain and the USA 2018 by
SEVERN HOUSE PUBLISHERS LTD.

British Library Cataloguing in Publication Data
A CIP catalogue record for this title is available from the British Library.

ISBN-13: 978-0-7278-8722-1 (cased)
ISBN-13: 978-1-84751-829-3 (trade paper)
ISBN-13: 978-1-78010-897-1 (e-book)

Typeset by Palimpsest Book Production Ltd.,
Falkirk, Stirlingshire, Scotland.

LIST OF CHARACTERS

POLICE OFFICERS
Captain Lucia Grossi, *carabiniere*, Special Crimes Squad, Umbria
Detective Inspector Desmond Harris, New Scotland Yard
Detective Chief Inspector Harold Jardine, New Scotland Yard

SYBILLINES NATIONAL PARK POLICE
Marzio Diamante, senior ranger (deceased)
Sebastiano Cangio, acting senior ranger (western sector)

ORGANISED CRIME ('Ndrangheta, Camorra)
Don Michele Cucciarilli, 'Ndrangheta boss
Rocco Montale, 'Ndrangheta lieutenant
Franco Carnevale, London nightclub owner, Camorrista
Jimmy Carnevale, Franco's only son, Camorrista
Vince Cormack, Franco's right-hand man, Camorrista

CIVILIANS
Loredana Salvini, Seb Cangio's girlfriend
Dino De Angelis, a farmer
Sergio Brunori, a schoolboy, aged eight
Carla Brunori, a letting agent, Sergio's mother
Umberto Bianchi, a consultant urologist
Peter Hammond, a consultant neurosurgeon

Note:
'Ndrangheta is the name of the Mafia from Calabria in the south of Italy.
One clan is an *'ndrina* (singular), groups of clans are *'ndrine* (plural)
Camorra is the name of the Mafia from Naples and the surrounding area.

This novel is dedicated to the people of Umbria and Marche who lost everything in the massive earthquakes of 2016.

UMBRIA, 1944

'It was as cold as hell that night.

'We'd pinched a hen from the last farm we'd passed, cooked it quick, then peed on the fire. Couldn't keep a fire going, could we? We knew that they were looking for us . . .'

'Who told you they were coming, Grandad?'

'You didn't ask things like that, young Sergio. Not in the Resistance.'

'Why not, Grandad?'

'They told you what to do. You did it, or they shot you. Bang! So, there we were up on the hillside, lying in ambush, whipped raw by the wind, taking turns keeping watch with these binoculars we'd picked up on the last raid. Carl Zeiss – Jena. Spectacular glasses, believe me. You could see from here to Perugia with 'em.'

'You, and who else, Grandad?'

'There was seven of us on watch that night. And all you could hear was the sound of our teeth. They wasn't only chattering because of the cold, mind. We knew we might be dead that night. Then, of a sudden, someone whispers, "There they are!"'

'The Jerries, Grandad?'

'That's right, Sergio. Down in the valley, spread out across the meadow, making for the Argenti farmhouse . . .'

'That old place on the hill near us?'

'That's the one. Twelve Jerry soldiers in leather boots and steel helmets, each one carrying a machine gun. And that was when the fog came down.'

He was telling the story for the umpteenth time.

The important thing was that everyone should know. Even Sergio, his only grandson. Sergio was old enough now, and Grandad Brunori told the story every chance he got. Most people didn't believe him, but those that did made the sign of the cross and went home looking over their shoulders in the dark.

Sergio stared at him, eyes wide, taking in every word.

'Those Jerries had orders to blast the living sh . . . well, to kill us dead . . .'

'But you're still here, Grandad,' Sergio whispered.

'We was saved by the fog. Like I said. As thick as a . . . you know, that Persian carpet in the living room? All thick and fluffy, like? And just a glimmer of a moon, no light coming out of it. We couldn't see a thing, but we heard it, all right.'

'What did you hear, then?'

'A scream in the woods. Long, and horrible. Then another one. And another one after that. Then a howl that froze the blood in your veins, and stopped your heart from beating.'

'Did you run when you heard it?'

'Run, lad? We had to stop them Jerries.'

'So what did you do?'

'We waited, didn't we? Loaded, a bullet in the breech, ready to fire. Told the others to do the same, for all the use it was. You couldn't see the end of your rifle for the fog. We stayed that way all night. On guard, in position, ready for anything.'

Sergio nodded, his face set stern and stiff, as if he was on guard with his grandad.

'Next morning, down in the woods . . . You wouldn't believe what we saw, lad. We'd heard the shooting, rat-a-tat, rat-a-tat, but it didn't last long. And they hadn't come looking for us. Where were the Jerries? That was the question. At dawn, I gave the order, didn't I? Advance! For all I knew, they were down there waiting for us . . .'

'Were they, Grandad?'

'Well . . . they were, and they weren't. They were dead, lad. Every last one of them. Twelve men torn to shreds, thrown away like bits of old paper. Arms and heads and legs and guts all over the place, the ground sopping wet with blood.'

'Was it wolves, Grandad?'

'Not wolves, lad. We saw the wolves . . . They was hiding in the wood, their eyes bright like diamonds in the gloom. They ran off when they saw us coming, more scared than we were. There'd been a massacre, but it wasn't the wolves that did it.'

'Who was it, Grandad? Who killed the Jerries?'

'I'll tell you, lad, but on one condition.'

'What's that, Grandad?'

'Don't you go telling this to your mother . . .'

ONE

Catanzaro, Calabria, June 2015

'It's the cornea, Don Michele . . .'

'You've been telling me that for three months.'

'Those rips and floaters . . . There's serious damage to the retina, too. I was hoping that the laser treatment would fix it.'

'A waste of fucking time that was.'

Professor Martini had dealt with thousands of patients in a distinguished career that stretched back thirty years, but he had never had a patient like Don Michele Cucciarilli before. The man wanted miracles. He wanted them today. They should have been delivered yesterday, if that were possible.

And talking of the possible, he wanted the impossible.

One vitreous rip had led to two, then three, and each one bigger than the one before. Laser scarring hadn't worked, and might have made things worse, putting off the inevitable until the inevitable became unavoidable. Don Michele's sight was cracking up like a car windscreen that had been hit by a brick. Unless somebody could stop the process, he'd be blind inside twelve months. Untreated diabetes type two. An insatiable appetite for sugar, sweets, alcohol, and all the other good things in life. He'd be lucky if his heart didn't stop before his eyes gave out.

'There's always cryopexy, Don Michele.'

'Cry-o-fucking-*what*?'

'Cryopexy. It's the latest thing. We freeze the torn areas, then let natural healing do the job. If nothing else works, we could always try for a corneal transplant.'

The Don turned to Rocco Montale, said, 'If nothing else works?'

The Don trusted Rocco, had to trust him now. One fucked eye was bad enough, a bit like a pirate, but you could get along with one eye. But no eyes at all? That was a problem. You needed someone who could cover your back, twist his neck like an owl and see all ways at once. Rocco Montale was a rock, all right. A solid rock in a stormy sea. And the storm was bound to get worse. There was a clan war going on – soldiers shot, cars bombed, kidnapped bodies left in baths of acid. You needed eyes in the back of your head. Drugs from Asia, drugs from South America, a price war bringing calamity all round. A war that needed stopping soon, or they'd all go down the plughole.

'What if that cropy-stuff don't do it?' Rocco asked the doctor.

Professor Martini threw Rocco a dirty look. Still, he had to answer the question. Don Michele was waiting. 'Surgery,' he said. 'Scleral buckling, vitrectomy . . .'

'What's that, then, doc?'

'They drain out all the fluid, replace it with gas to flatten the retina, then . . .'

'Who's they?' Don Michele pounced. 'Won't you be doing it?'

The professor shook his head, grateful that his medical competence had been exhausted. Advanced surgical procedures inside the *bulbus oculi* were fraught with risks. There was no going back once you reached that stage.

'I wish I could,' he said. 'It's a job for an ophthalmic micro-surgeon.'

Rocco couldn't stop himself. 'Making surgeons small now, are they?'

The professor didn't answer, reaching for the eye-pads, while Don Michele turned his face to the light, his eyes hot and itchy with the drops the quack had used to dilate his pupils.

'Right,' said the Don, when the bandages were in place. 'It's time for billiards.'

The professor laughed, thinking that Don Michele was joking. It didn't take him long to find out just how wrong he was.

A scholarly looking man in his mid-fifties, Professor Martini had fine fair hair, slender hands, intense blue eyes.

They tied him to a kitchen chair with wrapping tape.

'So,' Don Michele said, 'what's your prognosis, Prof?'

Martini looked up as if he hadn't understood the question.

'Prognosis?' he said. 'I . . . I made my diagnosis before the operation.'

'And?' the Don said, cutting in on him.

'Detached retinas, diseased cornea . . .'

'And you did the laser op, *and . . .*'

It was a question, though the grammar wasn't right.

'And it . . . I'm afraid, it didn't work out.'

'Fucking right, it didn't,' the Don said quietly. 'So, what happens now?'

The surgeon stared at him, uncertain what to say, or how to say it. Was a flow of tears going to have any effect on a mobster who was partially blind? He let out a sob, real enough, but louder than real, dramatic enough for a stone-deaf man to hear a mile away.

'I'm waiting for an answer,' Don Michele insisted.

'I . . . I don't know. You'll need to consult someone else. There are so many different causes. You need to see a retinal specialist. A man who transplants corneas.'

'Like who?' Don Michele snapped. 'Gimme a name!'

A name came out like machine-gun fire. A name meant someone else. A name meant passing the buck. That name would put the weight on another man's shoulders.

'Who's he, then?' the Don asked. 'Where can I find him?'

The professor might have smiled but he was careful not to show it. Don Michele had taken the bait, and that was the only thing that concerned him.

'He's the best ophthalmic surgeon in Italy,' he said. 'I can call him, tell him . . .'

'There's no need for that,' the Don said.

'Why not, boss?' Rocco Montale chipped in, knowing the Don was expecting it.

'Why *not*?' Don Michele said. ''Cause he'll be coming to the funeral. Rocco, kill those lights!'

The room was suddenly pitch black. No one could see a thing in the basement.

'How does it feel to be blind, Professor?' the Don asked calmly.

Professor Martini didn't answer, but he did begin to whimper, felt his bladder emptying into his best linen slacks.

Something bad was about to happen.

Whatever it was, he knew that he was going to be at the centre of the action.

Don Michele held out his hand. 'Rocco, give it here. Reds first, then we'll move up through the colours.'

Rocco handed him a red ball.

'You know what, Prof? I can see better in the dark. In a manner of speaking. When there's light, it's like a fire blazing straight into my eyes. But when it's dark . . .' He stretched back his hand, then said: 'Hey! Cry out louder, will you, Prof? So I know where to aim.'

The billiard ball flew out of his hand and crashed against the back wall with a loud *ping!*

'Gimme another . . .'

Rocco put another red ball into Don Michele's hand.

'A touch to the left, boss,' Rocco suggested.

The third ball smashed the doctor's glasses, broke his nose. The next one took his front teeth out. Every time the Don scored a hit, the doctor screamed, louder and louder, just as Don Michele had requested, and the rest of the gang went wild, yelling, *'Bravo! Centro! Colpito!'*

After a few more hits, the Don said, 'Rocco, switch on the lights.'

He didn't say it for himself, he said it for the others. They were screeching like the crowd in a Roman arena. He wanted them to see what a billiard ball could do when you put some muscle behind it.

'What's the state of the patient?' he asked, like a doctor consulting his juniors.

'A bit like a splattered melon, Don Michè.'

'Is he still breathing?'

'Out cold, but breathing, boss.'

'Sluice him down,' the Don said, 'then you can all have a go.'

As Rocco poured a jug of water on the doctor's head, Don Michele said: 'Your funeral's on Thursday, Prof.'

Then he turned to the rest of the gang, and said: 'OK, finish him off.'

Ping! – zing! – slam! – zap!

It was so much fun, they kept on going, even when the doctor was a crushed pile of meat and shattered bone.

TWO

Polsi, Calabria

The conclave of the *'ndrine* took place in Polsi, as it always did.

The first of September was the holy feast of la Madonna della Muntagna.

Rocco Montale was leaning over the first ramp of stone arches, standing high above the crowd, watching the procession down below. A ringside seat, but only people like him got a place up there. He had come to pay the Don's respects to the Virgin Mary and her Infant Child.

The Virgin Mary had appeared in Polsi centuries before.

The cult of the holy Virgin was undying in the Aspromonte mountains.

Down in the street, people bowed their heads, or knelt in prayer as the statue approached, and the procession began to slow down. Hands stretched out to touch the miraculous effigy as the statue-bearers came to a halt, wiping the sweat from their brows on the wide sleeves of their blue-and-white ceremonial shrouds, watching as the priest walked slowly from one end of the ramp to the other, collecting the offerings from representatives of the clans.

Rocco Montale handed Don Michele's envelope to the parish priest.

The priest dropped the envelope into his sack. '*Mille grazie e mille miracoli per Don Michele.*'

'*Ossequi alla beata Virgine,*' Rocco said in return, and made the sign of the cross.

Money bought miracles, and the Don had just doubled his usual donation.

The Feast of the Madonna was a time of truce, a day when all disagreements were left aside. A day of celebration, a safe place to meet and talk, a place to settle old disputes and throw out new challenges, a place where any man could demand justice, or revenge. The Feast of the Madonna of the Mountain was a day of reckoning, a day of planning, too.

The major action was taking place at a rustic villa on the edge of the town.

No guns.

That was the rule the 'Ndrangheta laid down in Polsi.

The procession over, Rocco walked into the courtyard of the villa.

Thirty-odd bodyguards were sitting at long tables laid out with food and drink in the cool beneath a big canvas sunshade.

'What's going on?' Rocco said to one of his men.

'They're still arriving,' Diego told him, as a big car pulled into the courtyard.

The driver stopped, jumped out and opened the rear door, helping out a man who looked as if he had five minutes left to live. Don Calogero Abbate's legs were swollen with chronic kidney disease. There was talk of gangrene, possible amputation. Two soldiers carried him into the villa, linking their hands to make a seat for the Don to sit on, and Rocco Montale followed them in.

It was a big room. Low wooden rafters, small windows, a big round table.

He nodded to Don Michele, then took his place by the wall.

What a gathering. All the big names were there. Old men who still ruled over their clans with an iron hand, men of the next generation standing behind them, their sons and grandsons, who would take over when the don died, or was murdered. Twelve of the richest men in Italy, the most powerful men in an empire that was in continual expansion, not just in Europe, but all over the world. That was why guns were out of bounds in Polsi. The bosses of all the different *'ndrine* were there, plus special guests from France, Spain and England. Guns were for the other three hundred and sixty-four days of the year.

Don Michele stood up, asked to speak, and permission was granted.

'Friends,' he said, looking around the room, 'I am glad to see you here once again. But what I see causes me great sadness. We are all growing old. Growing old fighting. Time will see us off, if violence spares us. I see before me a pressing problem. But I have a remedy to offer, if you will hear me out.'

Walking sticks banged on the stone floor, voices of assent were raised.

Don Michele spoke from behind dark glasses. Some wondered why he didn't take them off. It wasn't dark in the large room, but it wasn't light, either. He looked around as he spoke, but his eyes fixed on no man. Was it indifference? Arrogance? Something else?

He told them what was on his mind, how it would be organised.

'A great deal of planning and preparation has gone into this,' he was saying, 'but in Umbria we've got everything we need.'

That word rumbled round the room – *Umbria, Umbria* – like a spell or an incantation. Umbria, an unknown mythical place, somewhere in the north.

'Umbria will solve our problems, and guarantee our safety,' the Don went on.

Rocco remembered the conversation he had had with Don Michele the week before. They had been working on the details, checking the logistics, calculating the available resources, weighing the dangers.

— *Umbria, Don Michè? That ranger's still in Umbria.*

— *Sebastiano Cangio?*

— *You've let him live too long, boss.*

— *We'll settle with Cangio when the time comes. First, we need to work a miracle.*

— *A miracle, Don Michè? Your eyes, you mean?*

— *Not just* my *eyes, Rocco.*

'If you trust in me,' Don Michele was saying to the other clan bosses, 'you won't regret it, I can promise you.'

He told them again what the plan would mean in practical terms, and all of them had a reason to listen. If not for themselves, then for their wives, their children, their soldiers and their families.

'Does everyone agree?' Don Michele concluded.

Glances were exchanged.

They all said yes.

Then hands were shaken, pledges were given.

A magnificent lunch was served in the courtyard beneath the sunshades.

Aubergine meatball starters, traditional chick-pea lasagne, barbecued swordfish steaks served with capers and lemons, followed by ice-cream, coffee, chocolate-coated figs, honeyed *mostaccioli*, brandy and cigars.

Umbria was on everyone's lips, in everyone's thoughts. They all wanted to know where Umbria was, and what went on there, wondering how Don Michele had managed to seize on a territory so far from home.

Later that afternoon, the young men carried the heavy statue of the Madonna back through the narrow streets to her resting-place in the parish church of Polsi. There were people crawling on their knees, others crying, beseeching the statue, begging for a holy miracle.

A miracle? Rocco Montale thought.

The Madonna was an amateur compared to Don Michele.

THREE

1 March, Valnerina, Umbria

S eb Cangio didn't need a clock to know what time it was.

The sun rose from behind the mountain on the far side of the river, casting a pale shadow on the ancient wooden floorboards. Each strip of wood was like the marker on a sundial, though the intervals were growing shorter now with spring coming on. The sun crept into his room each morning, waking him more gently than any alarm clock.

Unlike the blinding, fiery blaze of dawn in his native Calabria, the slow infusion of light in Umbria was something that he looked forward to. He never closed the shutters, waking up early for the pleasure of seeing each new day unfold.

He'd been working the evening before, revising *Managing Survival – The Reintroduction of the Wolf in Umbria*, before collapsing into bed in a state of exhaustion. He was pleased with the way the paper was shaping up. He had emailed a proposal to *The European Wildlife Journal*, and had received a reply from the editor expressing interest. It would be the first academic paper he had published since fleeing Catanzaro and the university almost two years before.

The sun lit up his jeans and jumper.

They were neatly folded over the back of a chair.

The shirt he'd been wearing the day before had disappeared. His uniform was dangling from the door of the wardrobe on a hanger, waiting for him to climb into it.

Lori was back . . .

She'd been staying at her parents' place in Ceselli, which was further down the valley. The doctor had told her mum and dad to stay in bed. They both had flu, and Lori had spent the last three nights taking care of them.

He hadn't heard her come in, so he must already have been sleeping.

She would have been tired, too, but that hadn't stopped her from tidying up after him.

How many women would think of doing something like that for you?

Lori was the assistant manager of a supermarket in Spoleto. They'd been living together for almost a year in an old red *cantoniera* house that stood on the lower slopes of the mountainside looking out over Valnerina. Loredana took care of the house and him. And neither of them had ever once talked about marriage.

Down in Calabria, getting married seemed to be the only thing on every girl's mind.

He sometimes wondered whether Lori avoided mentioning the subject for the same reason that he did: they seemed to be rubbing along well enough without the need for a wedding ring.

He turned on his side and looked at her.

He had never known a girl who looked so mysterious first thing in the morning. She slept face down, flat on her stomach, her hair tied back with an elastic band that always came loose during the night spilling glossy nut-brown curls across her shoulders.

The mere sight of her brought his blood to the boil.

His blood boiled easily, he had to admit.

He remembered arriving in London from Calabria, finding a job in an estate agent's office in Islington, hitting the town on Friday nights. Getting laid was the easy part. Getting away the next morning was trickier.

In particular, he remembered a girl called Amanda Parsons . . .

She looked like a goddess. Had he ever been ogled by eyes so dark, touched by nails so perfectly manicured, kissed by lips so red? She'd come bursting out of a dress which had left little to the imagination.

He had caressed and kissed and probed that body all night long.

If this is London, he had told himself, it would suit him fine. Even if there were no wolves in the Royal Parks, no Calabrian sunshine to brighten the days, and food that smelled of grease wrapped up in a plastic carton. He could live with the grey skies, the stench of the Underground, the zombies munching junk food while they stared at their mobile phones and tablets and moved their heads to the racket coming out of ear-pods that, fortunately, only they could hear.

If all the girls were like Amanda Parsons . . .

In the first light of a Sunday dawn, the illusion had vanished.

On the pillow which separated him from a face that the night had treated badly, smearing lipstick on her chin, and mascara on her cheeks, he had found two revolting hairy insects that had scared him for an instant.

The goddess had shed her false eyelashes.

A hand resting on the pillow had lost two or three of the manicured fingernails which had torn into his flesh the night before as she groaned with passion into his ear.

He had rolled out of bed, and stepped on a bra containing two squashy cups of flesh-coloured silicone.

Was this what he had been making love to in beer-induced ecstasy?

The girl was as pale and stiff as a naked plastic mannequin in a shop window.

Would he need to press a button to reanimate the body with which he had been coupling so furiously the night before?

He remembered diving into his clothes and running out of there with his shoes in his hand for fear of waking her up and being forced to watch her put herself together again to face the world and him.

In that instant, Lori turned on her side to face him.

He reached out, laid his hand on her breast.

It was warm, soft, inviting.

Real . . .

Once, at the university, someone had asked him what he wanted out of life.

That was easy. He had always known what he wanted. A place to live that was full of wolves, good food and a girl with curves in all the right places. He'd been planning to live in Calabria – Soverato, maybe, somewhere by the Ionian Sea – close to the mountains, where he could specialise in wildlife biology (he was writing up his thesis on the wolves of Aspromonte at the time), go scuba diving and teach at the university.

Instead, he had found the Paradise that he was looking for in Umbria.

Mountains, wolves, great food, plus Loredana Salvini.

The problem was, you could die in Paradise, too.

He had found himself facing the nightmare which had forced him to flee from Calabria in the first place. Two years before, on Soverato beach, he had witnessed a murder, seen the distinctive tattoo on the neck of the killer. It was the trademark of the Cucciarilli clan.

'They'll kill you, Seb,' his mother had warned him.

He had caught the first plane to London from Lamezia Terme.

It was easy to lose yourself in London, but he really missed his home and Italy.

Then Umbria had been hit by an earthquake and they had started recruiting volunteers to help in the devastated national park. He had sent in an application. Next thing, he was a trainee park ranger. Umbria was a long way from Calabria, he felt safe there. Safe? He fell in love with the place. And the wolves had secured him a permanent job there. The wolf population in the park was growing, they needed an expert who would monitor the animals when the earthquake crisis was over.

Sebastiano Cangio, assistant park ranger.

Wolves, good food, and Loredana Salvini . . .

But the earthquake brought the jackals, too, criminals and thugs, the men of Don Michele Cucciarilli among them, killers who wore the salamander tattoo and waged an endless war against their enemies.

Was he supposed to run away again, go back to London, leave the wolves, and Loredana?

He had made his decision. He wasn't going anywhere.

They had tried to kill him twice already.

A bullet in the thigh had left him with a permanent limp. Six months before, they had murdered his partner, Marzio Diamante, blowing his head off with a shotgun, probably mistaking Marzio for him. The 'Ndrangheta hadn't killed him yet, but they were definitely trying to.

He felt a warm hand settle on his shoulder.

'Good morning,' he said.

'What time is it?' Lori murmured.

Her eyes opened wide as he told her.

'Five *o'what*? I need my beauty sleep . . . Hey . . . *Seb*? What the hell are you *doing*?'

He was slipping off his boxer shorts.

'*Cristo santo*,' she sighed. Then she began to giggle. 'You are insatiable, Seb Cangio. No morning nap for me, then?'

'Later,' he said, his hands beneath her T-shirt, exposing her breasts.

She arched her back, eased out of her panties. 'This is rape,' she said, falling back on the pillow, spreading her legs. He moved down slowly, nuzzling her stomach, the grooves of her thighs, then stroked her sex very slowly with his tongue.

He had learnt a lot from watching wolves.

Touching and feeling were as important as mating. If the she-wolf wasn't ready to play the game, she would snap, snarl and bite. But if she was, her mate would smell the hormones she released as she opened up to receive him.

Lori was no yielding she-wolf, though.

She let him have his way for a while, then she laid her hand flat on his chest and pushed him away.

'Now, you lie back,' she ordered, rolling on top of him, sitting astride of him, taking hold of him, guiding him into her. Her face was hidden beneath the veil of her hair, her hands sat heavily on his shoulders holding him down as she began to pump him, slowly at first, then gathering momentum.

In a moment of lucidity before he lost it completely, he knew one thing.

You fight to save the things you love.

FOUR

3 March, London, England

He was stuck in heavy traffic when the phone began to ring.

He read the name on the digital display, thought *fucking hell.*

He pressed the hands-free button: his voice sounded loud in the empty car.

'Hiya, Pat. What's up, then, love?'

Patrizia started talking, couldn't hold it in. Talking and talking. She didn't stop as he crawled onto the Wandsworth Bridge, heading for Brixton and the club. She didn't draw a breath, or so it seemed, the words pouring out in an endless rush.

The same old problem, obviously.

Patrizia was flat-out terrified as she told him what had happened.

'He fucking *what?*' He couldn't believe it, really couldn't.

Thank God the traffic was moving so slowly, or he might have run into the car in front.

'*He's getting worse,*' she was saying. '*Much worse than the last time. This can't go on, Vince. Where the fuck will it end? There must be something we can do . . .*'

'And he wasn't drinking, you say? Not a drop? So why did he take his clothes off, then?'

He listened for a while, his eyes gaping wider as she told him the story.

'*Christ knows what came over him,*' she was saying.

Her husband had gone into the garden the night before and strangled Simba.

'Simba? Jesus Christ, he *loved* that girl! He always had a lot of time for Simba . . . What a fucking turn-up! You sure you've got your facts straight?'

Patrizia swore she wasn't joking.

'Naked, too, you say?'

'*Not a stitch on him,*' Patrizia said, '*all silver in the moonlight.*'

It didn't stop there. There was more, much more. Patrizia told him everything.

'That takes the bloody biscuit!'

Simba was the family dog. A German shepherd. Getting on a bit, but still a formidable animal. Perfect with the kids, and handy as a guard-dog. Jimmy's pride and joy. Stone cold sober, he'd stripped himself arse-naked the night before, then gone into the garden and torn the family pet apart with his bare hands.

'*There was blood all over his face . . .*'

Patrizia started sobbing, the sound echoing inside the car like a wah-wah guitar.

He didn't say anything. What was there to say? He waited, let her cry herself out.

'*What am I gonna do with him, Vince? He's totally lost it. He's gonna get us all in the shit unless we put a stop to it.*'

She was right, of course.

As soon as she put down the phone, he called the boss, explained the situation.

'This won't go away,' he said. 'We've got to fix it quick.'

'*He's got a temper, everyone knows that. Who ain't got a temper?*'

'This ain't temper, Franco. This is something else. Something mental. You ain't seen nothing like it. He's like a kettle coming to the boil. He focuses on something, some*one* . . . If someone stares at him a bit too long, or answers him back, his eyes turn into two glass balls, boring into the fella like a fucking power drill. Then, he . . . well, he just explodes. An' there's no way of stopping him. You know what he can do. That girl, the slag, remember what he did to her?'

'*You're talking about my only son and heir.*'

'I'm talking about a sick boy, boss. He needs help. We gotta sort him out, before he goes too far. OK, so last night he went for the dog. Tonight, he might decide to have a go at Patrizia, or one of the kids.'

'*There must be someone who can . . . you know, put him right.*'

'I'll see what I can do about it, Franco.'

He had someone in mind, of course, someone who might be able to help.

He cancelled his appointments for the rest of the day, then he made a call.

It was funny, really, the situation turned around like this. Usually, the doctor came to him, looking to score. Now, he was in the wanker's private studio, laying a bag of powder on the table, asking for his professional opinion.

'I'll try and keep this as simple as possible, Vince . . .'

'You do that, doc. What's up with him?'

'A most unusual psychotic disorder . . .'

'His head, you mean?'

The doctor stroked his hands together as if he was washing them clean.

'That's the top and bottom of it. Fortunately, there's some literature on the subject, and there are one or two clinical studies which may prove useful. The most important thing is that we need to make a decision. We don't have a lot of time, you see. His condition . . . well, it's evidently worsening. We're faced with a choice here. On the one hand, there's the long-term solution.'

'How long would *that* be?'

'Many months, maybe years . . . We're talking about a mental institution, a padded cell, a strait-jacket, and drugs. Clorazil and sedatives for the most part. However, I really do fear that things may continue to deteriorate.'

'Why's that, doc?'

'Those cranial CT scans you showed me . . . Where did they come from?'

'The solicitor sent him to a clinic, thought he had concussion. In the end, there was no need to use them at the trial. The defence got him off on a plea . . .'

The doctor stabbed the plastic bag with a biro, took a pinch of powder, stuffed his fingers up his nose, then sniffed and licked his fingers.

'Whoa . . . Did a consultant see them? No? There's evidence of a tiny pod or nodule which may be affecting the neurotrans-mitters in the . . .'

'Simple, doc, remember?'

'There's pressure on a certain nerve that produces this kind of violent behaviour. That nodule's been there a long time, as you told me, probably from when he was a young boy. If it keeps on growing, well . . . there's no way of predicting what might happen. But if we can reduce the pressure by removing the cause of it . . .'

'When you say "we", doc, who are you talking about?'

'Well, *me*, as it happens.'

'You?'

The doctor laughed, said, 'What sort of a surgeon did you think I was?'

It took him a minute to get over his surprise.

'When would you be able to do it?'

'The quicker we make a move on this,' the doctor said, 'the better.'

Then another thought popped into Vincent's mind.

'For a job like this, what sort of money are we talking?'

The doctor smiled and rubbed his hands together again.

'A year's supply might do the trick,' he said.

He met the boss at the club that night, told him what the doctor had said.

'He thinks he's nuts, then?'

'He thinks he can help him, that's what matters, boss. The problem is, where can we take him? No private British clinic would take the risk, that's what he said . . .'

The boss held up his hand, went quiet, sipping his drink, thinking it through.

'Remember when I was away last summer?' he said at last. 'Yeah, in Polsi down in the south of Italy. There was someone there who might be able to fix us up, give us a hand. I'll give him a blow, see what he says.'

The boss lit a cigarette, blew smoke into the air.

'D'you fancy a foreign holiday, Vince? Get some decent food down you?'

Before he could answer, Franco was on his feet again, stubbing out his cigarette.

'I'll be in the office making the call,' he said. 'You wait here till I get back.'

FIVE

Two weeks later, Valnerina, Italy

There was still snow at the top of Monte Coscerno. The white crusting seemed to glisten in the moonlight like icing on a cake.

Sebastiano Cangio let out a sigh of relief as he watched them through his binoculars, outlined against the sky, then moving slowly right to left and downwards, following their progress from the summit towards the snowline.

He'd been searching for them for three nights now, and finally he had found them.

The lost wolves . . .

How could you explain a thing like that to the executive park manager?

One minute they were there, the next minute I lost track of them? He was supposed to be the expert. That was why they had given him the job. A published Ph.D. on the behaviour of *Canis lupus lupus*, and he had no idea where they'd gone, or why?

That was the thing about wolves. Unpredictable wasn't the word for them. They might stay in one place for years and years, then vanish just as suddenly as they had appeared. As if they had held a conference overnight, and voted to move on.

That was how it seemed, though he knew that that was not how it worked.

It was the breeding male who made the decisions. Wherever he decided to go, the female followed, and the younger wolves would trail after her. What had sparked the male to move on? Had he suddenly decided – *felt*, Cangio thought, hunger niggling at his own stomach – that the food supply was running short?

Or did he know, given the state of the season, that there would be richer pickings elsewhere in the park, in areas where he had hunted when he was younger, maybe, a member, rather than the head, of another pack?

Spring was slow in coming this year, food was scarce.

If they couldn't find enough to feed the female and the new cubs, they would move on.

He watched them trailing down the mountainside in single file, moving towards the snowline, heading back towards their old hunting-ground.

They must have been to Biselli or Rocchetta, though there had been no reports of attacks on sheep or other animals from either of the villages in the mountains over to the north.

He tightened the focus on the night-glasses, moving in close.

The breeding male wasn't leading the pack . . .

He was bringing up the rear. One of the first-generation cubs, now two years old, was leading them back, and he was limping badly, dragging one of his rear paws in the snow, leaving long slashing trails behind him.

Had they gone hunting in alien territory, and been obliged to fight? And having fought, had they lost?

All of them were there: the limping two-year-old, the pregnant she-wolf, the cubs born last season, the other two-year-old male, and the breeding male at the end of the line. Wherever they had been, and whatever they had fought, they'd been chased off. By something bigger and more powerful. A man with a gun, or a larger group of wolves? There were no bears this far west. Not that he knew of, anyway. A wild boar?

What else could beat off a family of wolves?

He had heard a report on the radio a few days before.

A RAV 4, one of those big sporty Japanese SUVs, had come roaring out of a tunnel at high speed heading for Camerino, smacking into a wild boar so big that it had made the national news.

'Twice the size of a baby elephant,' one of the rangers had reported.

The car had been a write-off, both passengers in hospital, and still the boar had needed shooting before it finally stopped breathing. The world was breeding monsters, and some of them were living in the national park.

The leading wolf was setting a slow pace; the others were keeping to it. They were as disciplined as a troop of Navy Seals heading back to base with their wounded.

What would have happened, he wondered, if the breeding male had been killed?

The others would have scattered, that was for sure. Some might have made it back to Monte Coscerno, though they might just as easily have separated and fled in all directions. The fate of a lone wolf was written in blood. It either starved to death, or it died fighting. Rival wolf packs were the biggest threat, though hunters and farmers came next on the list. Anyone with a gun seemed tempted to take a pot-shot at a lone wolf.

They were out of the snow now, heading for home.

Cangio put his night-glasses away in their case.

He groaned out loud as he got to his feet.

The wound in his thigh was still playing up almost a year after getting shot.

That was what happened if you played the lone wolf . . .

He glanced at his watch.

The luminous fingers told him it was 01.55.

This lone wolf was going home to bed.

Six kilometres north-east, 02.00

A cold draught ruffled the hairs on the back of his hand.

His hand had a life of its own, moved of its own accord, pulling hard against the needle which was strapped to his wrist, ripping it out, opening up the vein with a spurt of blood, cutting off the sedative flow, waking him up.

Pain throbbed deep inside his brain.

A dull ache, like drums in the distance, moving closer, closer.

His fingers followed the line of the stitches . . .

They had opened his head – taken something out, or put something in, he wasn't sure. He had heard people talking, someone saying, 'What the fuck am I supposed to do now?'

The voice was hoarse and desperate.

Then the black curtain had blanked out his senses again.

They had told him what would happen before they started. They called it intraoperative brain mapping, something like that. The anaesthetist would wake him up, the surgeon said, or put him to sleep, depending on what they were doing, or what they were about to do next. They called it 'wide-awake surgery', telling him it was for the best. He wouldn't be sleeping all the time. They would wake him up and ask him to do certain stupid things – wiggle your toes, move your left hand, say 'salt and pepper', open your right eye, now close it – so that they could see which bits of his brain were working, and which bits weren't.

They'd made him do and say these things before they put him to sleep.

'Just to make sure you can do them,' the surgeon had told him.

It was a bit like being a kid again.

Then that voice saying: 'What the fuck am I supposed to do now?'

They'd put him back to sleep while they talked about it.

He didn't know what they'd said, or what they'd done after that. Maybe they hadn't done anything, though the stitches seemed to suggest that they had. He wasn't stupid, after all. He just had these fits that he couldn't control, when things got out of hand and a part of himself that he didn't know took over.

But now he was awake.

And the air was chilling the back of his hand.

There was no reaction when he sat up on the operating table.

Nobody told him to stay still, keep quiet, or wiggle his toes. The room was empty, the tiles cold beneath his feet as the green surgical drape fell away, leaving him naked as he made for the open window, the fresh air, and the night outside.

There were stars in the sky as he walked through the grass.

Stars like tiny silver buttons spattered on a black velvet sheet.

The moon was a big silver ball hanging low above the trees.

He followed the moon.

Into the wood, going downhill, letting gravity carry him.

What am I supposed to do now?

He knew what he wasn't supposed to do, but he couldn't help himself.

He opened his mouth, and a noise came out, loud and long, a noise that seemed to tear at his throat and burn in his lungs. Then he heard the voices somewhere behind him, coming closer, the sound of something crashing through the trees and the bushes.

They were coming to get him . . .

He started running, moving his legs to the throb of the pain, going downhill.

He wasn't going back there.

Ever . . .

One kilometre north, 02.30

Dino De Angelis held his mobile phone in the air.
The signal came and went up there, you couldn't count on it.
Suddenly, he heard the dial tone, and speed-dialled his home number.
The phone rang twice, but the signal faded away before anyone could answer.
'*Cristo santo!*' he said out loud.
Next time someone said a phone could save your life, he'd tell them a thing or two.
On his own up there on the mountainside, and at his age, too. No phone, and no one to talk to. He hadn't even thought to bring a radio.
Davud, the Albanian lad who usually watched the herd, was stuck in hospital down in Spoleto. There was something wrong with his lungs, they said, some sort of liquid, an inflammation. He'd picked the right bloody time to go sick, two calves the night before, and more on their way at any time now.
De Angelis had lit himself a fire outside the hut, as much for company as for warmth.
He had sat on a rock, watching the whimsical jig of the dancing flames, the way the embers glowed when the wind caught hold of them, gusting through the mountains to some strange rhythm of its own.
He had watched the day fade slowly into night.
Most of his life had been spent up there.
As he looked down from the high pasture, he remembered when he'd been the lad who kept watch over the herd each night, then the grown man who had inherited his father's cows, a married man by that time, the proud father of two little girls. After a while he'd been sufficiently well off to stay at home at night with his family and pay someone else to watch over the animals.
Bloody Davud, malingering in a hospital bed . . .
Like it or not, he was back on the mountain, and the cows were ready for calving.
He let the fire burn down, then he crushed it out with the heel of his boot.
A car went past far below in the valley, the sound of the engine no louder than the buzzing of a fly. He followed the headlights

along the road beside the river, lost sight of them where the woods began.

It was getting dark now. Bloody cold, too.

Inside the hut, he lit the kerosene lamp, then built a fire in the stone hearth.

Fire was the only company for a man up there on the mountain, alone at night.

Well, he had his father's gun, of course. The old Rizzini twelve-bore was hanging up behind the door. He thought of the radio again, and cursed himself. Still, the animals were quiet in the byre next door. Maybe he'd be lucky, and have a quiet night.

It might seem stupid for a farmer, but that was how he felt about it.

He hoped no calves would be born that night.

He wrapped a blanket around his shoulders, settled down in the old rocker in front of the fire, and that was the last thing he remembered.

Then a noise woke him up with a start.

The fire was low, he was freezing cold.

It took him a moment to remember where he was, and what he was doing there.

The cows . . .

He grabbed his mobile phone.

It was dead, no signal.

'Bloody phone,' he growled, dropping it on the floor.

Maybe a calf was on its way. If the phone had been working, he might have asked his wife to send someone up there to help him. Davud's younger brother, Zamir, maybe . . .

'Cristo santo!'

He stood up, groaning with the aching stiffness in his bones, threw wood on the embers, then he stopped and listened.

There was no sound coming from the byre, none of the huffing and groaning that told you a cow was going into labour, that it was time to get the tools and the blankets ready.

So, what had woken him up?

He reached for the shotgun, snapped it open, checked it was loaded, then snapped it closed and pointed the two barrels at the door.

At calving time, the predators came round.

Wolves . . .

He was up there on his own, without a phone, and the wolves were at the door.

He started shaking, couldn't stop it. The gun in his hand bobbed up and down. He should go out there, fire a shot or two, and frighten them away. They might try to take a newborn calf, or even attack the mother while she was weak and stretched out on the ground, but they wouldn't attack a man with a gun.

He heard the noise again, but further off this time.

It didn't sound like any wolf that he had ever heard.

A wolf would whoop or bark, or growl and snarl when it went on the attack.

If it wasn't a wolf, what was it?

Someone playing silly beggars?

Rustlers come to steal his cows?

He couldn't decide what to do for the best. Shout out, keep quiet? Start shooting, risk getting shot? Make a fight of it, or let the robbers have what they'd come for, so long as they left him in peace?

He stood there for a long time, eyes on the door, gun in his hand.

Then he heard the noise again.

A shriek of terror, almost.

Far away now, long and drawn out.

Coming from the valley down below.

There was nothing down there apart from the woods, the old Franciscan monastery, and the farmhouse the Argenti family had abandoned years ago.

A howl of agony, like an animal that was trapped, or being tortured.

His memory jolted, remembering the tales that had circulated down in the valley long ago, the creature that had roamed the woods and mountainside above the River Nera.

Not an animal, but not human, either.

What if the story was true?

You needed a silver bullet to kill one of those, they said.

He sat by the fireside in the rocker, nursing his father's ancient shotgun, pointing it at the door, waiting for the sun to come up.

One kilometre south-west, 02.45

You could hear him a kilometre away.

Not so much a scream, more of a howl, followed by deep gasping breaths.

They'd been chasing him for ten minutes, following the noise he was making.

A wild dash through the woods in the dark, leaves and branches slashing at their faces, roots and brambles reaching out to trip them up.

They kept on running, knowing they had to find him before someone else did.

The wood was dense, the trees badly planted too close together, the ground overgrown.

No houses yet, though they were getting close.

They'd need to douse the torches soon, avoid being seen.

'Fu . . . ck . . . ing . . . hell. This . . . isn't . . . why I . . . came here.'

The yob was out of breath, short of puff, starting to fall behind.

It's all *your* fucking fault, he wanted to say. *You* let him break loose.

'You didn't sedate him,' he said, instead, not caring whether the fucker heard him or not. There'd be a time for making himself heard soon enough.

'Sedate him?' *Puff.* 'What for?' *Groan.* 'There was . . . nothing I could do.'

'There was one thing you could have done.'

'Your way,' the other man said. 'Not mine.'

'Shush!' he hissed, stopping dead.

He held up his arm, stopping the other guy, holding him back. 'There he is!'

'Shut your mouth, I told you.'

A ghostly figure staggered across a clearing in the forest.

Naked white flesh flashed silver in the moonlight, a bulging gut, fold upon fold of it, heavy male breasts, his head down, arms swinging ape-like, legs like tree trunks formed out of lard. He moved in slow motion, a fat man on the run.

Not running, though.

He couldn't manage running.

He zigzagged left, then staggered right, like a ship with no rudder, the wind picking up the sail, pushing the hull forward a bit, then letting go of it again. Stopping dead, then opening his mouth, howling at the moon like a fucking banshee.

It shook the pair of them, seeing him like that in the moonlight, naked as the day he was born, the head-wound open, face covered with blood, a grown man screaming like a baby in the dark.

'Gotta shut him up,' he said. 'There's a house this side of the hill.'

The last thing he needed was witnesses.

He took a step forward, raising his voice, not shouting though, keeping it calm.

'Hey there,' he cooed. 'Yeah, right, it's me. Come over here!'

The figure stood still then, dead on his feet. Another kilometre, his heart would have given out. With all the drugs they'd pumped into him. He'd been living on thiopental, pentobarbital, and God knows what else.

'What was that stuff you gave him?'

'Desflurane,' the other man whined. 'And he's still on his feet.'

'You should have given him more,' he said, 'a double dose.'

'And killed him? Is that what you wanted?'

The prey was standing still. The clockwork moving him forward had run right down. He didn't even turn around. Didn't try to escape.

'We'll take him back, then ship him home . . .'

'Sure thing,' he said, and made a deep slashing cut with the scalpel across the other man's windpipe. 'You fuck it up,' he hissed, 'you pay for fucking up.'

A gurgling vomiting groan erupted from the other man's lips.

He lurched down on his knees, both hands gripping his throat like he wanted to strangle himself, trying to staunch the blood tide, knowing there was no way it was going to happen. His life was leaking out between his fingers as the message got through. His eyes bloomed wide like sunflowers before he fell down flat on his face on the ground.

Turning away, he went on slowly across the clearing.

'Take it easy,' he said, getting close to the fat man. 'No one's gonna hurt you. You come along with me. Come on, that's right. I'll take you back, then I'll take you home. You've had a bit of a run, that's all, a bit of fresh air. You must be knackered.'

The big lump of blubber looked at him, tried to say his name, couldn't get it out. 'V . . . v . . . – V . . . v . . . – V . . . v . . .'

There was blood on his face, a gaping wound in his head where the stitches had split.

'You've come a long, long way for sweet fuck-all,' he said gently to the fat man, walking him slowly through the forest till he saw the place that he was looking for, an old farmhouse he had spotted the day before, talking quietly, keeping him calm.

As they reached the path, he put his arm around the naked man's shoulder, pulled the scalpel across his throat, digging in deep, giving it muscle, pushing him away as the blood began to spurt.

He watched him die, then he pulled out his mobile phone and made a call.

He hated giving this sort of news. Everything fucked up, and two bodies to get rid of.

'Jesus H,' he muttered as the call was answered.

He kept it simple, tried to explain, listened to the voice at the other end of the line.

'Yeah, yeah, I'll get it sorted,' he said.

The silence stretched out.

He waited, listening, the line wasn't dead.

Then the voice said quietly, *'We'll talk it over when you get back.'*

It took him half the night, dragging the body through the trees, the big one first, a short distance only, then going back for the other one, half killing himself with the effort. He had made a mistake there. He could have made it easier on himself and walked them both to the farmhouse before using the scalpel. Abandoned, out of the way, it was a perfect place to stow unwanted meat. He could sleep on the plane tomorrow going home.

It was sorted now, over and done with.

That was the important thing.

SIX

The next day, Stansted Airport, UK, 14.15

He was sitting outside Arrivals in a Mercedes C.
It had taken a bit of wrangling to hire a decent black car.

'We got loads of white ones,' the snotty kid behind the rentals desk had told him. 'OK, they're only Es, but they're half the C Class price. It's a special offer, long weekend.'

'Black,' he'd said, slipping the kid a tenner. 'One day only. Cash on the nail.'

A black Mercedes was the only car to use when you were picking someone up. No one noticed a black Merc waiting outside an airport, except the passenger who was looking for the car and the driver he'd been told to expect.

There were other cars parked up in front of him. Three of them were Mercs. All black with smoked-glass windows, just like his.

He glanced at his watch again.

Twenty-five past two.

The mark was taking his time.

Fifteen minutes later, a man came out of the revolving door.

He recognised him straight away. He had his photo on his phone, but he would have guessed, in any case. He had that travelled look about him, a black leather tote bag hanging from his shoulder.

The guy stopped short outside the revolving doors, popped a fag in his mouth, struck a light, then pulled out his mobile phone, and started tapping the keyboard.

His own phone rang inside the car.

He let it ring three times before he answered.

'Where the hell are you? I've been waiting here for ten bloody minutes.'

'I've just pulled in, sir. A black Mercedes. If you cross the road and turn sharp right, I'll flash my headlights for you.'

He watched the guy come strolling towards him. A snazzy, silvery-grey suit, a nice black canvas mac thrown open, zip-up Belucci alligator boots. Flash, but not too flash.

He jumped out of the car and opened the rear door.

The passenger handed over his luggage, and left him to stow the tote bag in the boot alongside the humble Nike sport sack he had brought up on the train from London before hiring the car at the airport.

He'd caught a whiff of G-and-T as the guy got into the back seat of the Merc. That was why he had had to wait. The fella had gone through Customs, then walked into the nearest bar for

a drink or two. He was talking on the mobile now, the rear
window rolled down, blowing out smoke in both senses.

'Yeah . . . yeah, it's all dusted. What a fucking caper, Jesus
. . . Yeah, sure . . . I'm on my own . . . What a shitty job . . .
Thank God it's over. Yeah . . . right, then . . . sure thing. Yeah,
yeah, I'm on my way.'

A tap came on his shoulder.

'Let's get this motor moving.'

He turned round, touched the peak of a chauffeur's cap he
wasn't wearing, said, 'They told me to take the A10, sir. There's
road-works on the motorway. Is that OK with you?'

The guy smiled, looked him in the eye. 'Take any route you
like,' he said. 'Just take me home, and make it slow. Been up
all night, working my fucking balls off. I need to kip, if you'll
excuse me.'

'Certainly, sir,' he said, as he pushed the automatic shift into
drive, checked the wing mirrors, then pulled away, checking the
rear-view mirror every so often to see what was happening on
the seat behind. The guy was checking his messages as they
drove across the motorway flyover and joined the A120. There
was traffic, but not a lot of it, more cars heading for the airport
than coming away from it.

By the time they drove around Bishop's Stortford, the passenger
was fast asleep.

Next stop, Little Hadham.

He turned off the A120 onto a lane called Horse Cross.

After collecting the car that morning, he'd sussed the area for
a couple of hours, picking out places that would suit him along
the route. This one was perfect, a dense wood at the end of a
forgotten cul-de-sac. There were rooks in the trees, not a soul
on the ground. It stood to reason. You live in the country, you
don't need to go out for a walk.

As the car moved into the shadows, he reached the chosen
spot, a kind of sheltered bower with bushes pressing in on three
sides, the sort of place that poachers, courting couples, and people
of the night would use.

You wouldn't find anyone there at three o'clock in the
afternoon.

He pulled off the road, and switched off the engine.

Nice engine, he thought. On or off, you couldn't hear it.

He grabbed a bottle of fizzy water from the passenger seat, got out of the car, and opened the rear door.

'Hey!' he said, tapping the guy hard on the noddle with the plastic bottle.

'Hey?' The guy opened his eyes, and looked around. 'Where are we?'

'Piss stop,' he said, and he liked the sound of it.

'Pit stop?'

'Something like that.'

He turned away, unscrewed the cap of the bottle, took a swig.

He heard the passenger get out of the car, murmuring something, getting pally maybe, saying, 'Yeah, why not?' or something like that as he rambled over to the bushes, unzipped his trousers and let fly. 'Oooo, *yes*, I needed that,' he called back over his shoulder. 'Ryan-bloody-air, the fucking cheapskates. You know what it's like. Queues for the loos, you give up in the end.'

He turned around, zipping up his trousers, and saw the bottom of the plastic bottle pointing at his face. His mouth started to form a question, when the bottle went *pop* and the bullet hit him square in the forehead, knocking him flat on his back.

The Bersa Thunder 9 was a nice gun, but a bit of silencing always helped.

OK, there was a strong breeze, but you never knew where you were with the wind. Sometimes it deadened the sound, other times it carried it a long way.

The passenger looked so peaceful lying there on a bed of grass. As if he'd gone straight back to sleep, except for the big red hole in the centre of his forehead. His eyes were open, fixed and staring, blood trickling out of his nostrils, running down his cheeks.

'Painless, what?' he said, as he turned to the car.

He raised the boot-lid, unzipped his Nike bag, took out the two large bottles with glass stoppers and placed them carefully to one side. He dropped the remains of the plastic bottle into the Nike bag, then turned back to the corpse, dragging it into the bushes. There was a tiny clearing where the peepers probably hung out after dark, ogling what was going on inside the cars through night-glasses.

He dropped the body among the empty fag packets, used paper tissues, dead johnnies. Then he took a deep breath, unknotted the passenger's tie, unbuttoned his jacket and shirt, unzipped his pants and alligator boots, then proceeded to strip him naked.

Everything went into the big Nike sports bag.

Not everything, though. The wallet with four credit cards, his passport, and all the other things that might identify him went into the plastic carrier bag he'd picked up at the airport shop when he'd bought the bottle of water . . .

Something fluttered away on the breeze like a butterfly, disappearing into the trees.

'Shit!' he said.

He thought about chasing it, but what did it matter?

A bit of paper?

It was probably the receipt from the airport shop where he'd bought the water. No one was ever going to trace that back to him.

He tried on the Eberhard Chrono 4, slipping his own watch deep into his jacket pocket. The alligator boots were his size, too, brand new as well.

Some things were just too good to dump.

'Loot,' he said out loud, as he stuffed the boots into the carrier bag.

Once they'd emptied the leather tote bag, he'd ask them for that, as well.

There was just one last thing that needed doing.

He went to get the stuff from the car.

He took one of the glass bottles from the boot, removing the stopper as he went back into the trees. He bent close, poured sulphuric acid over the dead man's face, then he stood well back and listened to the hissing noise it made. The crater in the centre of his forehead started to bubble and spit like a volcano getting ready to blow, then everything just sort of caved in as the flesh and bone dissolved.

The stench was something else.

The white smoke burnt his eyes and made his nose feel itchy.

He went back to the Merc for the other bottle, covering his nose and holding his breath as he poured more acid onto the dead man's hands, making sure to bathe all the fingers, taking extra special care about that detail, stopping before the bottle was empty, looking down at the body that was laying on the ground.

'Will anyone recognise this stupid prick?' he said out loud.

There wasn't much acid left, but there was more than enough.

He poured it over the guy's dick, watching the way it shrivelled up, then disappeared in a pall of white smoke.

Now, all he had to do was find a waste bin somewhere, ditch the stuff he didn't need, then head back to the airport and drop off the car.

SEVEN

Three days later, Borgo Cerreto, Valnerina

'Me! Me! Me!'

Two hands shot up in the air.

Both kids hoped to win the book that he had brought along as a prize.

One hand belonged to a tubby little girl, the other one to a tiny, skinny boy.

It wasn't an easy question for such young schoolkids, asking them to remember what he had told them the month before about how the she-wolf chooses the den for birthing the cubs.

Cangio would have pointed to the boy. His hand had gone up a fraction faster. He was the smallest cub in this particular litter, too, so small he had had to jump up to be seen. The girl beside him had not only raised her hand and shouted out, she'd elbowed the boy in the ribs as well. If there was a prize, she was going to have it. The boy's hand sank as he reeled from the blow, but it was still there, hanging in the air.

'So, what is the correct answer, Roberta?'

Mother Wolf, as Cangio had christened the teacher the last time, showed off her clean white teeth and smiled encouragement at the girl. The teacher was the Alpha-wolf in this pack, and Roberta was her tubby little pet. Out in the wild, the little girl would have had a tougher time of it. The other wolves would have taught her not to lord it over the weaker members of the family.

Roberta twitched a smug grin at the little boy beside her, then repeated almost word for word what Cangio had told them about the den being hidden, but not too well hidden, the she-wolf marking off the area with her urine so that other wolves would know they were entering forbidden territory.

'That's very good, Roberta,' the teacher said, glancing at Cangio for confirmation.

He had to nod approval.

Roberta had carried off the prize.

He moved closer to the little boy who had taken the jab in the ribs without complaining. 'Would you like to say something?'

The kid's eyes shifted sideways to the teacher. First, he shook his head. Then he took a deep breath, and nodded. 'I know a story.'

'Sergio is *always* telling stories,' Mother Wolf informed Cangio in a way which made the other kids laugh. 'He has such a *wild* imagination.' She shook her finger at the little boy. 'Now just remember, Sergio, the subject today is wolves. W-O-L-V-E-S. Facts are what we're looking for, not silly stories. Roberta won the prize by sticking to the subject.'

'Maybe Sergio knows something we don't know,' Cangio said.

'We'll see about that,' the teacher said.

Clearly, Sergio's stories didn't go down well with Mother Wolf.

Nor did Cangio's enthusiasm go down any better. Mother Wolf pulled another tight smile. 'Sergio's tales are often a trifle *eccentric*, let's say,' she said. 'They don't always hit the nail on the head.'

And that sorts Sergio out, Cangio thought.

'Who knows?' he said, smiling back at her. 'Maybe this time he'll be on the ball.' Then he looked at Sergio. 'Is it a story about wolves?'

Sergio nodded, then wiped his nose on the cuff of his shirt. ''Bout men that turn into wolves when the moon comes up. They . . .'

'Goodness gracious! What did I tell you?' Mother Wolf muttered aloud. 'Lycanthropes again, Sergio Brunori?'

There was something that rankled between the teacher and her skinny little charge. Maybe Sergio mucked up her plans, taking her lessons into places that she didn't want to go, into places she didn't want the other kids to go. There was one in every class, he knew, a rebellious kid, quite often intelligent and hyperactive, who distracted the others.

Give Sergio a couple of years, thought Cangio, he'll eat Mother Wolf for breakfast,

He had been a bit of a Sergio himself at school. A lone wolf. A ball-breaker. He winked at the kid. 'Come on, then, Sergio, tell us about these werewolves.'

Sergio told his story in a voice that sank in pitch as he ran out of breath, punctuated by gasps as he dragged oxygen deep into his lungs. He seemed to realise that he didn't have much time before the teacher told him to stop wasting what remained of the lesson.

'. . . you hear them howling, then they show their teeth, and the bones go *CRRRR-ACK . . .*'

The class held its collective breath.

Roberta frowned, and covered her ears.

Other kids covered their mouths to stop from crying out, all of them hanging onto every word that came from Sergio's lips.

The kid might well be eccentric, but he was a natural storyteller.

There was one in every village in Valnerina. *Cantastorie* was what they called them. Old men mostly, who knew the history of the towns and villages where they were born, all the tales of dark deeds done, of saints and sinners, and heroic resistance to natural disasters – storms and floods and earthquakes.

Maybe the kid had learnt the art from someone in his family. If he had set out to take revenge on Roberta for digging him in the ribs he couldn't have been more successful. He didn't see the look of fright on the girl's round face, the glistening eyes and the downturned mouth. Sergio wasn't telling the tale, he was living it.

'Grandad and his friends had heard it, they saw what had happened. Next day, it was . . .' There was a long pause. 'A lake of BLOOD, that's what they found! As if the sky had been raining blood all night long. Those Jerries had been torn to bits by the werewolf.'

There was a void, a silence.

'Werewolves don't exist, Sergio.'

Mother Wolf's voice was sharp and final, her eyes moving from face to face, daring anyone to challenge what she had just said. Finally they came to rest on the big brown eyes of little Sergio.

'Yes, they *do*,' the kid said defiantly.

He was on his feet now, hands braced on his desk, as he stared back at the teacher. 'Grandad's dead and gone now, but *they* don't die. Mam and Dad heard one the other night. *I* heard it, too, but I didn't tell them. Mam was really frightened, see? That scream . . . Like someone's heart was being ripped out of his body.' His voice sank to a growling whisper. 'Here in Valnerina, the Werewolf – has – come – *back!*'

Had the rebellion started? Was the tiniest pup challenging the pack leader?

'Sit down, Sergio. That's quite enough for one day,' the teacher said. 'Werewolves and monsters do *not* exist, as I am sure Ranger Cangio will tell you.'

She turned to Cangio, fixing him with a look that said: *Please get us out of this mess.*

Cangio shrugged as if to say, *They're only kids.* As if to admit that she was right, and that he had made a mistake by turning the spotlight onto little Sergio.

'I've never seen a werewolf, to be honest,' he said.

A voice piped up from the back of the room. 'Sergio's grandad did. Maybe you will, too, one night in the park.'

A couple of boys in the front row nodded their heads.

The little girl had won the book, but Sergio now had a fistful of followers.

Next time he spoke to a school group, Cangio thought, instead of blandly defending the wolves, telling the kids that they only attacked when they were hungry, he should spice up his talk with a bit of blood and horror. His wolves sounded like bank-clerks doing a routine inventory, while these kids wanted wolves that would thrill them and terrify them.

You could teach them the truth when they got a bit older . . .

He felt his phone vibrating against his thigh in his trouser pocket.

He'd been getting messages all morning. Now, with the lesson nearly ended, he pulled out his phone and glanced at the list of calls he had missed. Three from Lucia Grossi, four from Loredana.

Was something up?

He raised his hand, holding up the phone to the teacher like a kid who needed urgently to go to the toilet. 'You'll have to excuse me,' he said. 'People are looking for me.'

'Maybe it's about the Werewolf,' Sergio said.

Mother Wolf waved her hand towards the door and raised her chin in a gesture which seemed to say, *Go on then, you've caused enough trouble for one day.*

'Thank you for coming, Ranger Cangio,' she said, turning her attention to the children, dismissing him in an instant.

Cangio wanted to thank her for the opportunity to talk to the kids about the wolves in the park, but the woman was already telling the class to take out their maths books.

He turned and waved his hand to the kids as he reached the door.

Only Sergio waved back.

Out in the corridor, he pulled a bottle of water from his back-pack and took a long drink, washing away the taste of chalk and acidity on his tongue. Then he called Loredana, whose number was top of the missed calls on the list.

'Seb?' Lori's voice was barely a whisper, which meant she was busy at work.

'Sorry to disturb you,' he said, 'but you called me . . .'

'That bloody woman's been ringing me all morning. Wanted to know why you weren't answering your phone.'

He thought he knew who she was talking about.

'I'm at the school in Borgo Cerreto,' he said. 'I told you . . .'

'The manager didn't like it, obviously. She's in a right bloody mood. You call her right away, she sounded like she'd blown a fuse.'

Everything was bloody that morning. Sergio's stories, Lori's boss, Lucia Grossi. He had caught Loredana at an awkward moment, obviously. And all the time, one thought kept rattling through his mind.

'Did she say why she was looking for me?'

He hadn't heard from Lucia Grossi since the press conference in Perugia six months before, the day she'd been promoted head of the Special Crimes Squad.

'Do you think that I've got time to waste on her?' Lori's whisper was growing harsher. 'She said to get in touch right away. Something important, she said, OK? So do it!'

Who was giving the orders, he wondered, Loredana or Lucia Grossi?

He closed the connection, and called the other number.

The phone rang five times before it was picked up. Lucia Grossi wasn't sitting over her phone then, waiting for him to ring her. Still, he thought he heard a note of relief in her voice.

'Cangio! Did you get lost in the woods today?'

'Lost in a deep, dark forest full of strange little creatures,' he said. 'I was talking to a class of schoolkids in Borgo . . .'

'I've got a job for you,' she cut him off sharply. 'Can you get here right away?'

'Where's here?' he asked.

'My office in Perugia. In an hour, let's say?'

Lucia Grossi in all her splendour.

Bossy, brash and totally unfeeling.

All the reasons for which he had been so carefully avoiding her.

The same day, Catanzaro, Calabria

Don Michele was smoking a cigar, but he wasn't celebrating.

'What a fuck-up,' he said to Rocco. 'A right proper fuck-up . . .'

Rocco Montale made the right noises.

It didn't do to make the wrong ones.

'He was recommended, boss,' he said. 'It was their decision. What could we do?'

Don Michele chugged on his Montecristo, sending clouds of blue smoke into the air like a tribe of Comanches on the war-path.

'We need to tighten up security for a start,' the Don was saying, talking to himself more than anything, going over the details, trying to put the situation into perspective. 'We guarantee the staff, we find the right man for the job, we pay him on the nail, and everyone's happy. What could be wrong with that?'

'Like I was saying . . .'

'No, Rocco. Like *I* was saying, they had to go and do it their own fucking way. *Dio santo*, fucking foreigners! They won't listen, won't take advice. We should have said no, should have left them in the shit. Instead, we did that goon a favour. And what does he go and do? He sends me a package with a babysitter, and the sitter goes and tops the fucking baby! He flew out first thing the morning after, and no one even tried to stop him. We need a tighter checkout routine, Rocco. If anyone tops anyone around here, I decide who gets the fucking chop and who does the chopping. Right?'

He glared at Rocco, maybe seeing him, maybe not, his elbow propped on the table, holding his cigar.

'So, Rocco,' he said, 'what's up, then?'

'Carlo Piscitelli called me, Don Michè.'

'What does he want?'

'He's got a batch of fresh fruit coming in . . .'

Don Michele let out a sigh, then he stubbed out his cigar.

'Hmm,' he said, though he didn't sound keen. 'Yeah. Maybe . . . just maybe, we'll take a look when it gets off the banana boat . . .'

Perugia, Umbria

Traffic was heavy on the ring road, but that was nothing new.

Every motor vehicle heading north, south, east, or west, had to skirt around Perugia.

The medieval town on the top of the hill was pretty enough, but a new town had sprouted all around it like an ugly fungus. Development had started in the '60s, and it was still going on. Speculators would buy a run-down farmhouse, knock it down, then build a 'luxury high-rise residence' for a hundred families. The result was a sprawling suburban mess. Driving to the town centre was a nightmare.

Fortunately, he was heading to Elce, a residential suburb on the northern edge of town. With all the urban planning going on, he thought, wouldn't it have made sense to park the *carabinieri* command headquarters closer to a major road?

Lights flashed up ahead.

Hazard lights came on as drivers stepped on their brakes.

Cangio sighed, and did the same thing. A major hold-up by the look of it, a tailback disappearing inside the Prepo tunnel. An accident maybe. Or major roadworks that no one had been warned about. Repair work went on day and night on the busy ring road, beacons channelling four lanes into two lanes of traffic, or reducing two one-way tunnels into one two-way tunnel, while gangs of navvies tried to patch the road or prop up the tunnels.

The work never ended because the traffic never ended.

The poet Dante would have written an epic about the Perugia ring road.

As the traffic edged forward, he sent an SMS: *Traffic jam – going to be late.*

Late for what? That was the question.

It was a quarter to eleven by the time he reached the Elce turn-off. At eleven o'clock he was circling the block for the second time, looking for a place to park. Twenty minutes later, he walked out of the lift on the second floor and knocked on a door marked *Special Crimes Squad – Comandante.*

Special Crimes was bureaucratic double-speak; the politicians didn't like to mention the word *Mafia.* No one wanted to admit that the 'Ndrangheta had taken hold in Umbria. The Squad had been cobbled together immediately after the shoot-out at the Marra olive-oil factory six months before.

'Come in!'

The *comandante* was sitting behind her desk.

Her hair was shorter than he remembered it. Not a single luxuriant black curl was left. Lucia Grossi looked like a kid who'd been expelled from some tough orphanage, though the gleaming silver braid on her shoulders told a different story.

Getting shot and saving Cangio's skin had helped her career, no doubt.

'Talk of the Devil,' she said to a man who was sitting in front of her desk.

The man stood up and turned to face Cangio, a worried smile on his lips.

'This is Sebastiano Cangio,' Lucia Grossi said, indicating him with her hand like an exhibit in a zoo. 'He's the ranger that I was telling you about.'

Inspector Harris was from Scotland Yard's Organised Crime Unit, Lucia Grossi explained in Italian. Evidently, Harris spoke enough Italian to understand her. He held out his hand. 'Please, do call me Desmond,' he said, as Cangio took it.

A high forehead, a narrow face, a shy smile pulling at his lips. Intelligent eyes, thought Cangio, as those grey eyes studied him. What was Harris doing in Umbria? Then another thought bubbled up into his mind. *The ranger I was telling you about.*

What had she been saying about him?

'Perhaps we ought to sit down,' Harris suggested, speaking

English now. 'There isn't much to tell you, but . . . well . . . I understand from Captain Grossi that you have lived in London, Ranger Cangio.'

'That's right. I lived there for a while.'

Harris nodded. 'I imagine you know Stansted Airport, then? I flew in from there this morning. It's a rural area apart from the airport complex. I was amazed at just how empty the countryside is when you see it from the air.' He paused, and stared at Cangio. 'Not the place for violent crime, you might think . . .'

'No, it isn't,' Cangio said, wondering where this was leading.

Harris reached for a battered briefcase on the floor beside his chair. 'This is what was discovered near there last week.' He glanced at Lucia Grossi. 'May I?' he asked.

Lucia Grossi waved her hand. 'Go ahead,' she said.

Harris took out a green cardboard folder, and handed it to Cangio.

'I hope you've got a strong stomach,' he said.

Cangio opened the folder and found a sheaf of large photographs. The first one showed a naked corpse lying face up in long grass.

'The place is called Horse Cross,' Harris said. 'It's popular with courting couples, according to the local police. They received an anonymous tip-off, telling them to go and take a look. Other people may have seen the body and failed to report it.'

The next few pictures showed close-up views of the face and the hands.

'Doused with acid, then left to rot,' Harris murmured. 'We don't know who the victim was. Male, relatively young, mid- to late thirties. But that's about it. He was shot at point-blank range, so it's probably a professional hit. A nine-millimetre bullet straight into his forehead.'

Lucia Grossi was hovering behind Cangio's shoulder.

'A bit like putting down a sick horse,' she said.

The pictures made Cangio's stomach roll.

The acid had burnt a hole through the dead man's face, eliminating the eyes, nose, and mouth, taking out the back of the skull and everything in between.

'There are some minor dental remains,' Harris said, 'but they won't be much use unless we can tag a name to him.'

The hands were blackened fingerless stubs of bone poking out of acid-stained palms.

'No hope of checking his prints on IDENT 1 . . .'

Cangio looked up, and the Englishman smiled. 'The UK Print and Palm database,' Harris explained. 'Whoever did this knew exactly what to destroy. A pro, as I said before. We ran our results through the NDNAD system, as well, but it's relatively new. DNA from a man without a recent criminal record wasn't going to turn up anything there, either.'

'Is he a criminal?' Lucia Grossi asked.

'We don't know who he is,' Harris said. 'That's why I'm here.'

Cangio held up the last photograph.

'They really made it hard for you, didn't they?' he said.

Acid had been poured into the Y where the dead man's legs met his stomach.

'They tried to cancel everything, even the genitals. It seems so gruesome . . . even senseless. A warning to others, perhaps, though there's just no way of knowing.'

Cangio looked to Lucia Grossi, asking silently for help.

Why should he be interested in what had happened near Stansted Airport?

'I'm a park ranger,' he began to say.

'A possible clue was found near the body,' Lucia Grossi said.

Harris reached into his briefcase again, took out a sheet of paper in a nylon sleeve, and handed it to Cangio.

'This is a computer-enhanced image of a restaurant bill,' he said. 'There's no name, unfortunately, and the original was very dirty. It was found in a pool of mud near the corpse. There'd been a lot of heavy rain in the area the night before. But, as you can see, it appears to be from an Italian restaurant.'

Cangio strained his eyes to read a few words, and a € symbol.

'It's all we've got to go on,' Harris ploughed on. 'The corpse was found late on Saturday afternoon, the 17th of March, not far from Stansted Airport, as I said. A pathologist examined the remains that evening. He estimated that the murder had taken place about forty-eight hours before the police were called to the scene. There was a Ryanair flight from Perugia airport to Stansted on the 15th of March, which arrived at lunchtime. We are working on the assumption that the victim was on that flight.'

'The assumption?' Cangio asked.

'That restaurant bill,' Harris said. 'Traces of partially digested food in his stomach included, among other tasty things, truffles and trout. We presume that he ate them for dinner in Italy the night before he was killed.'

Tasty things? Did the man have a sense of humour?

'And that's where you come into it, Cangio,' Lucia Grossi said.

She smiled a smile which seemed to say: *You still owe me a favour.*

'I sent the UK pathologist's report to the Parks & Forestry Commission laboratory in Norcia,' she said. 'And this is what they had to say . . .'

She returned to her desk, sat down, and referred to a sheet of paper.

'There are two species of trout in the River Nera,' she said, 'the *fario* variety, and the *iridea*. The *fario* is specific to the River Nera, while the *iridea* is produced in greater quantities. If you went fishing in the Nera, you might catch a *fario*, but if you went to a restaurant, you'd find an *iridea* on your plate. There are fish farms producing *iridea* trout throughout the area, as you certainly know, Cangio. Not long before he died, this man ate an *iridea* trout and truffles of a variety known as *scorzoni*, which are also commonly found in Valnerina. Chemical analysis revealed the presence of both of them, as well as various other minerals which are peculiar to the waters of the River Nera . . .'

It all boiled down to this: Lucia Grossi wanted him to take Inspector Harris on a tour of restaurants serving trout and truffles in Valnerina.

'There must be hundreds of them,' Cangio protested.

'In that case,' Grossi said with a tight smile, 'you'd better get started.'

EIGHT

Padova, Veneto

Professor Bianchi was always wary when the telephone rang. He checked the digital display, didn't recognise the number.

The area code was 0961, which was somewhere down south, he thought, though he couldn't say exactly where.

That was one of the problems with being the president of a national association: calls could come from anywhere, though they rarely came directly to him. One of his secretaries handled the preliminary contacts, as a rule.

He ignored the phone call, let it ring itself out.

Of course, it might be an invitation of some sort . . .

The bigger companies were never short of cash for junkets and conferences, sometimes quite sensational ones. On the last occasion, he had cruised the Norwegian fjords for five days in exchange for three one-hour illustrated talks about the latest developments in TUR, TURP, and more traditional BPH procedures.

He unbuttoned his trousers, pushed his undershorts to his ankles, and sat down.

The phone rang again.

He smiled and thought, *If they could see me now!*

Indeed, it was the fun aspect of it that broke his resolve not to answer.

He reached for the phone, pressed the button, and said: 'Bianchi here. May I help you?'

'It's about your daughter, Professor,' a deep voice said. 'Your only daughter.'

Bianchi felt his bowels cramp. 'What about my daughter?'

'Marisa's doing well, I hear.'

'She's . . . she's . . .'

'She's doing well. Like I just said. She could do even better, that's the thing. And only you can help her.'

The accent was definitely from the south, a low nasal growl, staccato sentences, the vowels drawn out.

'Do I know you?' Umberto Bianchi asked.

There was a rumble of a laugh at the other end of the line.

'Not yet, you don't,' the voice said. 'But we know you. Your reputation, anyway, Professor. Now, about this daughter of yours. She's been making regular progress at the university. And now there's a chair coming up. Somebody died, we hear. They'll need to fill his shoes, no kidding. And you can help her, like I told you before. Just you, and no one else. Now, that really is a *big* responsibility for a father.'

He wasn't used to being spoken to like this. Talked down to.

The opposite was true. He had his band of acolytes and hangers-on, assistants and protégés, people who looked up to him for patronage and favours. That was the way of things, of course. You didn't get anything for nothing. Not in this world. Not in the circles in which he moved.

The circles in which Marisa moved . . .

'What . . . exactly are we talking about?'

'This weekend, or next. You decide. A car will pick you up on Friday night. A three-hour drive. Sleep all the way, if you feel like. The job will only take you a couple of hours. We've got everything you need. We'll put you up in a five-star hotel if you want to rest when you finish, or we'll drive you straight back home. It's up to you. There and back in ten hours. Ten thousand euros, cash in hand. Per hour, of course, including the travelling. That's one hundred thousand euro for a bit of uncharted overtime. Think about it. I'll call you back this time tomorrow.'

'And Marisa?'

'She'll get what she wants, I guarantee. There's only one condition . . .'

'What's that?'

'Mum's the word.'

The phone went dead.

Professor Bianchi's bowels opened with a rush.

Valnerina, Umbria

They'd been driving for ten minutes, and Desmond Harris still hadn't said a word.

They might have been two strangers sitting side by side like deaf, blind mutes on the Underground, which was one of the many reasons Sebastiano Cangio had been glad to leave London behind him.

The first thing the Englishman had done was to reach for the seat belt. Then he had spent a couple of minutes adjusting the strap, making sure that he was safely harnessed. As Cangio pulled away, the cop had set his briefcase carefully on his knees like a kid being driven to school, then he turned his head away and looked out of the window.

No questions, curiosity apparently zero, no spark of a conversation.

Cangio had tried, of course.

Did Inspector Harris live in London? Was he married? Did he have children?

The answers came back pat: yes, yes, and no. He lived in London, but he didn't say where. He was married, but his wife was either nameless or unnameable. And as for having kids, the answer was just a flat no.

Cangio wondered whether Harris and his wife might have separated.

Having fired off his bullets, he fell silent, concentrating on his driving as they headed for the ring road. Harris murmured a hushed *sorry* as Cangio brushed his arm, turning left onto the approach road, then he smiled ironically as Cangio swung hard left again to avoid a Fiat 500 that shot in front of them without signalling, the driver too busy shouting into the mobile phone he was holding in one hand while gesticulating wildly out of the window with the other hand. As if that smile confirmed everything the English copper knew, or thought he needed to know, about Italy and Italian drivers.

Cangio felt his irritation mounting.

The driver of the Fiat had pissed him off, but you learnt to live with Italian drivers. Lucia Grossi had dragged him into something that had nothing to do with him, and there'd been no way of avoiding it. And now that smile from the mummy embalmed in the seat beside him confirmed every prejudice he had ever held against the British.

I'm doing you a favour, he felt like telling the guy. This was Scotland Yard's affair, not his. Why had Lucia Grossi let herself get caught up in it? Hadn't the British voted to leave the European Union? What the hell did Italy owe them?

Lucia Grossi's ambition had a lot to do with it, no doubt. The fact that she had saved his life meant that he couldn't simply refuse to help her. Desmond Harris was lucky not to be driving around Valnerina in a rented car with a tourist map and whatever scraps of Italian gibberish he might happen to know, looking for a restaurant he would probably never find.

But as they were passing the exit signs for Assisi, the atmosphere changed.

'Is that *the* Assisi?' Harris asked him.

'It's the only one that I know of,' Cangio said.

'It looks so beautiful up there on the hill. Stretched out like a sleeping leopard.'

Had Harris got used to the cars and the traffic? Or maybe it had finally clicked that they were going to have to work together?

'Sebastiano,' he said suddenly, his eyes fixed on the road ahead, as if he savoured the sound of the foreign name.

His awkward pronunciation made Cangio smile. He could have used *Seb*, after all, and saved himself the embarrassment. Cangio waved his hand in the air, as if to say, *I'm here. I'm listening.*

'We'll need to visit quite a few restaurants before we find the right one, I suppose?'

'There aren't so many, but it may take time.'

'What I wanted to say,' Harris glanced at his wristwatch, 'I usually eat far earlier than this. If you take into account the two-hour flight, the one-hour difference, and the hours that I've spent messing about in Perugia this morning. As a rule, I would have eaten a couple of hours ago.'

Cangio was silent, unsure what he was supposed to say.

'I suffer from chronic gastritis,' Harris went on. 'I try to keep it under control by sticking to a regular diet, and regular meal times, but . . . well, if I miss a meal, I start to feel bloated. It's something to do with pepsins in the stomach, apparently. It begins as a slow burn that just gets worse and worse. If I start belching, you'll have to forgive me. Once or twice the attacks have been so bad, I ended up in hospital.'

Cangio had a vision of himself in hospital forced to sit by Harris's bed and deal with the doctors as another great belch ripped through the night.

'The fact is, Sebastiano, I need to eat . . . What I mean is . . . If you have in mind a restaurant that might have issued that bill, could we start there, please? We could sit down like two normal customers, order some truffles, and ask some questions while we're eating. It might seem odd after those photos that we were looking at,' he chuckled aloud, 'but I can't help wondering what the attraction is. You know, truffles? They look so . . . well, so awful, so unappetising, but what do they actually *taste* like? That's what I was thinking. I ran a check on the Internet . . .'

'You've never eaten truffles?'

Harris settled his briefcase more comfortably between his feet. 'Never,' he said. 'And Scotland Yard will be picking up the bill, of course. We'd be killing two birds with one stone, so to speak. I'd like to offer you lunch, if you have no objection?'

Would he ever understand the way the English mind worked?

Desmond Harris was in Italy with a difficult investigation on his hands, but he was thinking about his stomach. Why not make a holiday of it with a decent meal or two thrown in at the expense of the British public?

'No objection,' Cangio said. 'I haven't eaten a thing since six o'clock this morning.'

Let him put his gastritis to rest with something he'd seen in the stomach of a dead man in some pathologist's laboratory in London.

For a moment, he tried to imagine Harris standing over a gutted corpse, asking a man in green scrubs and blue rubber gloves, 'What's that revolting black stuff? It looks like fresh mud.'

'It's anything but mud, Inspector. His last meal must have cost a fortune. Black truffles, I'd say, by the gritty look of them.'

'Not English, then?'

'The tuber grows in the hilly parts of France and Italy. It's a subspecies of the potato family, but hellishly expensive, highly thought of in foreign culinary circles. Can't you smell it, sir? That delicate perfume beneath the stench . . .'

Then the inspector would have run a check through the computer and put two and two together. A couple of words of Italian on the remnants of a restaurant bill, direct flights to Perugia from Stansted Airport, a dead body stuffed with truffles. Bingo, the dead man had come from Umbria! Then, having been ordered to fly to Italy and check out the story, he had made up his mind to taste some truffles while he was going about the business.

Inspector Harris stretched out his legs, and seemed to relax.

'We'll have something to eat, then see if anyone remembers our man being there. How does that sound?' He said it as if they had suddenly become friends, and might enjoy a couple of hours having lunch in each other's company.

'It sounds like a holiday,' Cangio said, trying not to sound too harsh.

'We'll be working while we're eating,' Harris countered. 'It isn't often you get the chance to do that, is it?'

He tapped his knuckles against the window, indicating the vegetation streaming past the car like a solid green wall beyond the glass.

'What do the people actually do in Umbria? How do they live, I mean? What happens here . . . well, when anything happens?'

'There's not a great deal in the way of work in Valnerina itself,' Cangio told him. 'A lot of people commute to the larger towns, like Perugia in the north, and Terni in the south. They work in shops, banks, hotels, and restaurants in Spoleto and Norcia. You'd be surprised how many people work in local government administration. The rest are farmers, though they don't all work the land. Many people make a decent living looking for mushrooms, truffles and nuts, while others run trout farms, or grow olives. Umbria is all about food. Truffles, trout, pigs, and olive oil.'

'So what would a foreigner be doing here?'

'He might have come on holiday. Or on business. Then there's Francis of Assisi, art and religion. And there are lots of pretty towns to visit. We get a million tourists every year. Many of them visit the national park where I usually work.'

'And what do you do in the park exactly, Seb?'

Cangio told him about the wolves, the wildlife, the day-to-day assistance to farmers and tourists, working with schools and so on. He didn't mention the alarming things that had happened since he'd been in Umbria. He said nothing about getting shot and nearly killed by the 'Ndrangheta, nor the rapid infiltration of the Calabrian mafia in the region, bringing drugs and guns and danger.

And then it started raining.

Harris warmed up and told him about the weather in England.

Bari, southern Italy

Marisa Bianchi was about to leave for the university when the phone rang.

'*Marisa?*'

'Papà?'

Her father called her every Friday. Today was Tuesday.

'Is something wrong, Papà?'

'*No, no, my dear. Everything's as right as rain. It's just that . . . well, I've been thinking . . . you know, about the appointments commission. When are the members due to meet?*'

'Within the next few weeks. They want to fill the post by the end of the month.'

He hesitated for a moment. '*Your name is on the list, isn't it?*'

'Of course it is, Papà.' His daughter sounded amused at his concern. 'Now listen here, *please* don't start worrying about me. You've got quite enough on your plate, and you'll only make me jumpier than I already am.'

'*A bit of moral support never hurt anyone, my sweet.*'

'Of course not, Papà. I am grateful, I really am. It's just that . . . well, you know, I . . . I'm going to have to stand on my own two feet on this occasion. I will accept the decision of the commission, whatever it may turn out to be.'

He was quiet for a moment, seeking the right words.

'*You'll be the top runner, I imagine.*'

Marisa made a noise, and he tried to visualise the expression on her face.

'Well,' she said, 'if I have to be really honest . . . There are seven names on the list, and they're all highly qualified . . . well, *recommended* might be a better word. We've all got decent research papers to our names. It's the . . . well, it's that extra bit of *push* that makes all the difference in these matters.'

There was silence, an unspoken conversation between them. – *Please, help me, Papà.* – *I wish I could, my dear.*

'*Just keep your chin up high,*' he said, '*and see what happens. I'm sure you'll make it.*'

He put a lot of force into the word *sure*, trying to tell her that it was a cert.

'I do hope you're right,' she said, though she didn't sound very convinced.

She didn't know that he was holding a trump card, and that he was ready to play it, but there was no way that he could tell her about it.

Not now. Not ever.

'*Oh, by the way, my dear, the other reason I rang . . . I won't be phoning you this Friday. I have a speaking appointment, and a dinner afterwards. I shall probably leave my phone at home that night. I don't want it ringing at the wrong time.*'

His daughter laughed and said, 'Is there ever a right time?'

In other circumstances, they would have told each other stories about phones going off at inappropriate moments, but he was in no mood for joking. '*Just wait until they call to tell you that you've got the chair,*' he said.

He ended the call, then sat for some moments staring at nothing.

Then he rang a different number.

The phone rang and rang, and he was about to give up, take it as a sign of destiny.

It might be better to let things run their natural course. After all, Marisa might just get the chair at the university without any help from him. And if she didn't, well, perhaps that was how things were meant to be . . .

'*Yes?*'

The deep, southern voice at the other end of the line took him by surprise.

'It's . . . it's me,' he said.

This announcement was greeted by silence.

'I'm ready to do what you asked me to do,' he said into the phone.

'*I'm sure you won't regret it,*' the voice came back at him. Then there was a pause, a long one. '*Still, there is one thing you'd better do some thinking about.*'

He hardly dared to ask what the something was. 'Wha . . . what's that?'

'*A celebration present. Have you decided what to give her when this is over?*' He heard a sharp intake of breath, then the sound of a throaty chuckling. '*No sacrifice is too great for the sake of a child. Isn't that right?*'

The conversation ended with a click.

He *was* right, of course.

Was there anything he wouldn't have done to help Marisa?

Valnerina

When they drove out of the Sant'Anatolia tunnel, rain was tipping down.

'Not long now,' Cangio said, turning north on the SS 209.

The road followed the winding course of the River Nera, which had cut a wide gorge through mountains that rose fairly sharply on either bank. Dark clumps of trees and bushes covered the lower slopes, while swirling clouds obliterated everything above.

'It looks just like a painting,' Harris said as they rounded a bend and the picturesque walled fortress town of Vallo di Nera came into view.

Cangio slowed down, indicating to go left, pulling off the road before they reached the town at a sign which said 'Il Tartufo Nero'.

'The Black Truffle?' Harris said. 'That sounds right, doesn't it?'

'The food's pretty good here,' Cangio said. 'In the summer it's one of the most popular restaurants in the valley.'

'What makes you think that this is the place?' Harris asked.

Cangio killed the engine. 'That piece of paper you showed me. The one that they found near the corpse.'

'Did you recognise the name or something?'

'Not the name, but something that was written there.'

'A smart-looking place,' Harris said, as they walked towards an ancient mill which had been beautifully restored and done up as a restaurant.

'We may be out of luck,' Cangio said, as they reached the entrance.

A sign had been pinned to the door: *CHIUSO PER FERIE.*

'*Chiuso* means closed,' Harris chipped in, 'but what does *ferie* mean?'

Cangio had shaded his eyes with his hand and was peering through the glass door.

A man was standing by a huge open hearth, a broom in one hand, a dustpan in the other.

Cangio pushed the door, a cow-bell rang, and the man in front of the fireplace glanced over his shoulder. 'Can't you read, son?' he said. 'We're still closed. I'm just putting the place in order.'

Then he stood up straight and turned around, noting Cangio's uniform.

'I'm sorry, officer,' he said quickly. 'Like I told you . . .'

'Do you mind if I ask you a couple of questions?'

The man chuckled humourlessly.

'There's no harm in trying,' he said. 'I'll answer you if I can.'

'Is this the only restaurant that does truffles with Parmesan?' Cangio asked him.

The man stared at him for a moment, surprised by the question. 'Well, like I said, we're . . .'

'Closed for the holidays, I read the sign,' Cangio said. 'But that's not what I'm asking. I know that you do truffles with Parmesan cheese. Does anyone else do that dish?' He waved his hand towards Harris. 'My friend here is English. Someone recommended a restaurant in Valnerina, but he forgot to get the name

of it. I thought of you, straight off, of course, but if you're closed
. . . Do you know of anyone else that serves truffles and cheese?'

The man propped his broom against the wall, and set down
the dustpan.

'We used to have a monopoly on it, just us, you know,' he
said. 'It was a roaring success, especially with the foreign visitors. Truffles and Parmesan, the best of the best, and all on one
plate. It was Edna's . . . my wife's idea.' He blew a raspberry.
'Last season someone else decided to have a go. Bloody thieves!
It's not a scratch on ours, of course, I'm telling you.'

'Naturally,' Cangio agreed. 'His English friends were over
here last week, though. There were two of them. Two men.'

The man scratched his ear. 'We've been closed the last six
weeks,' he said. 'My only daughter's living in Australia, see. Just
had a baby. Me and the missis just got back. We'll be opening
up next Monday if you'd care to come back?'

'We're too hungry to wait till Monday,' Cangio smiled. 'What
did you say the other place was called?'

It was raining even heavier when they got outside.

'What was all that about truffles and cheese?' Harris asked
him.

'That bill of yours. You were looking at truffles and trout, but
I spotted part of another word that was written on the paper . . .
parm. Parmesan cheese, that's my guess. Truffles and Parmesan.
Not many restaurants offer that combo here in Valnerina.'

As they got into the car, Cangio glanced in the direction of
Monte Coscerno.

You could hardly see it now for the clouds. The weather would
be savage up near the summit, he thought, wondering about his
wolves as he turned the key in the ignition, and they drove north
on the SS 209 again.

Valnerina

The rain was pelting down near the summit of Monte Coscerno.

The young wolf lay in a sheltered hollow behind the den,
licking his wound.

The den was built into the side of a mound, beneath a slab of
rock that the earth had thrown up.

He couldn't go inside the den, though.

The female was resting, waiting in there, gathering her strength. Her time was nearly up.

If he tried to go inside, she would tear him apart.

He couldn't move, couldn't stand, and water was beginning to pool all around him. He had fallen into a stupor the night before in the hollow where he usually slept, but he didn't feel safe there any more. He hadn't been able to mark his terrain, had been obliged to urinate on the spot where he was lying, and that was a sign of weakness.

Maybe the rain would wash it away before the others could smell him.

He had woken during the night and found one of the younger wolves licking the blood from the gash in his stomach and thigh. They were starving, desperate now. The pack had gone off hunting again, searching for food. They hunted at night as a rule, but the day and the night were equal now. They needed fresh meat, especially the female. If they brought back meat, he might be safe for another night.

There would be no food for him, though.

They would never feed him now that he was unable to hunt.

The end was drawing near, closing in on him like a heavy weight.

He closed his eyes and tried to sleep, despite the cold, persistent rain, willing the end to come soon. He would have crawled away to die, but he didn't have the strength.

The water was slowly rising in the hollow, but he couldn't lift his head.

NINE

Valnerina

Il Covo del Pescatore was practically empty.

The rough stone walls were hung with nets and fishing gear that might once have been dipped in the Bay of Naples, but had never been used in the trout stream on the other side of the main road. The gnarled wooden beams above their heads had been painted white, which showed off the cobwebs to perfection. Every bit of space was crammed with junk that you might have found in a flea market. A spruced-up cellar, Cangio thought, the sort that drove the foreign tourists wild. They came into the country looking for country, and this was what they got.

It seemed as though progress had given the Valnerina a miss.

They sat at a table next to the picture window, though there wasn't much to see. A mist swirled over the river, and the mountain beyond it was capped with clouds.

'It really is a beautiful area,' Harris said. 'You're lucky to live here.'

'If I'm really lucky,' Cangio said, 'I'll probably die here, too.'

He wondered whether to mention the fact that things were not as idyllic as they might appear. There'd been two attempts on his own life in the last eighteen months, after all.

Desmond Harris smiled, seemed to think that he was joking.

Cangio stared out of the window again, leaving Harris to look at the menu.

He was worried about the wounded wolf, and would have gone to check on it if Lucia Grossi hadn't called him that day. If things had looked bad, he would have called the vet, stunned the wolf with a tranquilliser dart, then taken it into care at the wildlife recovery unit in Norcia. That was what he should have been doing, not ferrying a visitor around the park to save Captain Grossi the bother.

Harris was still busy scrutinising the menu.

'Did you spot it?' Cangio asked him.

'My Italian's not so hot . . .'

Cangio pointed it out to him. 'Truffles and cheese. That's blasphemy in these parts. But foreigners like Parmesan with everything, including truffles, and lots of them stop off in roadside restaurants like this one when they're cruising through the area.'

A man in a waistcoat came bustling over, bright-eyed and smiling.

'Are we ready to order, gentlemen?' he asked.

Cangio smiled back at him. 'We'd like to try something from your tourist menu,' he said. 'Scrambled eggs with truffles and Parmesan cheese. We were told that it was excellent.'

'It's the house special,' the waiter said. 'Our very own invention.'

'That isn't what they told us at the Tartufo Nero,' Cangio said.

The waiter seemed to stiffen, then glare at Cangio. 'Did he send you here?'

'That's right. They were closed, he said.'

The waiter pursed his lips. 'Been closed a month, they have. To be honest, I thought they might have gone out of business. You know, given up, the competition being too hot. He tells everyone that he invented the recipe, but my missis got there before him! Cristoforo Colombo discovered America, but they named it after that Vespucci fella, didn't they? Being first means nothing. It's being the best that matters. And *we* do the tastiest *uova strapazzata* in Valnerina.'

'Good,' said Cangio. 'We'll start with that.'

Five minutes later, the man appeared from the kitchen, plates in hand.

'*Uova strapazzata con tartufo e parmigiano,*' he announced, as he set them down on the table.

Harris tasted a mouthful, a look of caution on his face, as if he feared he might be eating poison. Suddenly, his eyes lit up. 'Hm, that's delicious,' he said. 'Maybe this is what he came to Italy for.'

'How do you mean?'

Harris patted his stomach. 'Our man. The victim. For the food. *Mangiare.*'

'You think they beat him to death at Stansted for the recipe?'

He was being droll, but Harris didn't seem to notice.

'What comes next?' he asked, as he cleared his plate.

Harris's truffled trout and Cangio's grilled chops came next.

'The trout really *is* tasty,' Harris said. 'I like the truffles, I must say.'

'Now comes the hard part,' Cangio said when they had finished eating. 'We don't have a picture of the dead man. Not one that we can flash around in public, at any rate.'

'If the place is usually quiet at this time of year, they may recall a foreigner.'

'If he was foreign,' Cangio warned him.

Harris took another sip of wine. 'Will you do the talking, please?'

Cangio waved his hand and called the owner over.

'We need to ask you a couple of questions,' he said, as the waiter reached the table. 'This gentleman here is . . .'

'Health and bloody hygiene, I thought as much.' He held up his hands in surrender.

Cangio laughed. 'You've got it wrong,' he said. 'I was about to say that he's a British policeman from Scotland Yard. He enjoyed his lunch, by the way, especially the scrambled egg with truffles and cheese. *Complimenti!* The thing is, he's looking for an Englishman who may have got himself into trouble, let's say. Inspector Harris was wondering whether the man has ever eaten here.'

The waiter's brow uncreased, and his jaw relaxed, but he didn't remember who had eaten there the day before. The previous week was lost in the Dark Ages. 'You'd better ask Nora. She serves table normally, though she's working in the kitchen today. I'll send her in,' he said.

He walked away across the room, and disappeared into the kitchen.

'What's going on?' Harris asked.

'He thought you were a food inspector.'

'Me?' His eyebrows shot up on his forehead like Stan Laurel's. 'Eating all day? That does sounds fun.'

'It's the suit and tie you're wearing. He felt less threatened when I told him you're a cop.'

'Really? It would be exactly the opposite in London.'

'Let an Italian food inspector loose in a restaurant kitchen,' Cangio explained, 'and you're talking about fines, big ones, too. He might even close the place down—'

'The boss said you wanna see me.'

Nora was the size of a wardrobe. Arms like cured hams bulged out of her XXL T-shirt. Plump cheeks and multiple chins had pushed her snub nose, blue eyes, and pert mouth into the centre of her face. The green and white striped apron she was wearing was spattered with flour.

'Please, have a seat,' Cangio said.

The girl looked at him and frowned. 'I gotta cut the *strangozzi* before the dough dries out,' she said, showing her hands which were dusted with flour. 'We make all our pasta fresh every day.'

She served at table, but helped in the kitchen, too. A Jack-of-all-trades, Cangio guessed.

'Just a quick word,' Cangio said. 'Last week, Tuesday, maybe . . .'

'We're closed on Tuesdays.'

'Monday, then.'

'It was pandemonium,' she said. 'A wedding lunch and a bike club. Run off our bloody feet, we were.'

'Were there any foreigners in the restaurant that day?'

Nora didn't need to think. 'Two men,' she said, and a smile curled her lips.

'Two?' Cangio glanced at Harris. 'At separate tables?'

'Naw, they were sitting together,' she said, 'British, I think. One of them was sitting just where you're sitting now.'

Cangio felt his heart go up, then down. Thanks to the truffles and cheese, they had struck lucky.

'Do you remember what they ate?' he asked her, just to be sure that they were talking about the right men.

Nora glanced at him, then squinted. 'You must be joking,' she said. 'The place was chock-a-block. The same thing as you, probably. One of them foreigners stuck in my mind, 'cause he was a good tipper.' She leant close and dropped her voice. 'Wedding guests! I can't stand 'em. They aren't paying the bill, so why leave a tip?'

'What did he look like, the man who left the tip?'

Nora's cheeks bunched up in a smile. 'You're pushing it now,' she said. 'They're all just faces to me . . .' Then she tapped the tip of her nose with her forefinger. 'Hang on a bit,' she said, and pulled out her mobile phone.

Her fingers were large, the phone seemed tiny. It might have been the Book of Destiny, as she scrolled through it, a look of concentration on her face.

'Here we go!' she said. 'I knew I hadn't cancelled it. This lot were cyclists up from Rome. What a bunch of jokers! One of them asked me to take a snap, but I couldn't get his phone to focus, so I took a pic with my phone, then I texted it to him.'

She handed the phone to Cangio.

A group of men in cycling kit, all in their forties, all dressed in fancy synthetic colours, were holding up their wine glasses to the camera.

'You see them two there?' Nora said, plonking a white finger on a table in the background of the photo. 'That's him,' she said. 'Him, and his mate. They were here together that day, then he came back a couple of days later.'

'He was alone?'

'That's right. That's when he left me the tip.'

Cangio looked at the display, then handed the phone to Harris.

One man was looking straight into the camera, frowning at the rowdy cyclists, maybe. The other man was frozen in the act of turning away, as if he didn't like the thought of being photographed.

'Which one came back the second time?' Cangio asked.

'The one who's facing the camera,' Nora said.

Cangio used his thumb and forefinger to blow the picture up to full-size. He stared at the narrow face and greasy, slicked-back hair. Over thirty, under forty, maybe. 'Is this a good likeness?' he asked the girl.

'It should be,' Nora said. 'That phone cost me four hundred euros. I wanted one that took good photos, see.'

'Can you forward that picture on to me?' he asked her.

'No problem,' Nora said. 'What's your number?'

A few seconds later, Cangio's phone gave a *ping*. He checked the screen, then sent the picture on to Harris, who immediately stood up, took out his wallet and gave the girl a fifty-euro note.

'Is that enough?' he asked Cangio.

'More than enough.'

Then again, he thought, Scotland Yard was paying.

Nora asked if she could take a photo of them. 'Just so I'll remember who gave me the best tip of the year,' she said.

Out in the car park, Harris told him where he wanted to go next, then he pulled out his phone again. 'I'll just let Captain Grossi know how things are shaping up,' he said.

'How's the gastritis?' Cangio asked him, as he got into the car.

'Gastritis?' Harris said, and this time he was smiling.

Catanzaro, Calabria

Rocco Montale's phone trilled.

Gino's report from the hospital mortuary.

'Three today, Rocco. I'll have a look, then let you know.'

A couple had died in a head-on car-crash, the driver over the limit in every sense, speed, drink, and maybe drugs, while the other one had been knocked off his bike by a hit-and-run driver.

Two men and one woman. Sex made no difference, that's what they'd told him, anyway. Man or woman, it didn't matter.

Fresh was more important . . .

He pulled the handle and the drawer rolled out with hardly a sound on well-oiled bearings.

He shone the torch inside.

The man on the bike was a mangled mess.

There'd been an item on the local TV news that morning, describing the accident. He'd been knocked off his bike on his way to work, and the body. . . .

Body?

It had taken the traffic police and forensics ages to find all the pieces scattered along the road for over a kilometre. There were still bits missing, apparently, but that was par for the course, and nobody was complaining too much. They had enough to put in the coffin, so the family would be happy enough in the tragic circumstances.

There were several witnesses to the accident. At the moment it was still being listed as manslaughter, though the word 'murder' was now being used in cases where the driver hadn't stopped. The cyclist and his bike had been trapped beneath the vehicle for more than a minute. It must have been like being caught up inside a meat-grinder. They'd shown the dead man's wife a mole on his wrist when she came to do the identification, couldn't show her the face or the body, not in that state.

They'd catch the driver, too. He'd be going to jail. It wouldn't take them long to find him. Let's face it, how many people in the Catanzaro region were driving a bright red Seat SUV with an F registration? Two or three max.

The dead man's head was like a punctured rugby ball, all out of shape, black and blue, though the mortuary staff had washed off the blood. The right eye was crushed. He lifted the dead man's left eyelid with his thumb.

Empty . . .

They needed two in any case, so this corpse was no use.

The couple were in an even worse state. The woman had gone flying through the windscreen, not wearing a seat belt. They hadn't got around to cleaning the man up yet, his face still a pulped mass where he'd slammed up hard against the glass. There was a shard of crystal poking like a spear into his left eye.

He slid the drawer closed, took out his phone, and made a call.

'*Rocco? It's me again.*'

The voice at the other end growled the same old question.

'*No use at all. Still, it's only a question of time.*'

'Call me when you've got something,' Rocco said, and closed the call.

Assisi, Umbria

Lucia Grossi was sitting at a table in the airport concourse.

She smiled and waved, calling them over like the hostess on a TV show.

Cangio wondered what she was doing there. No one could drive from the *carabinieri* command post north of Perugia to St Francis of Assisi Airport in less time than it had taken them to drive there from Valnerina. Not even the head of Special Crimes in a souped-up squad car with blue lights flashing and sirens blaring.

'I ordered coffee,' she said, waving her hand in the air, A waiter came bounding over with an espresso, a macchiato, and a cappuccino. 'I hope that I got it right,' she said, taking the espresso from the tray.

Another party trick, Cangio thought. She had drunk coffee with both of them before.

Harris was still in the throes of confusion as he reached for the cappuccino. 'How did you guess that we'd be coming here?' he asked.

'Shall we call it . . . female intuition?'

She was putting on a shameless performance for the Man from the Yard. Still, he wasn't quite the guileless lamb that Cangio had taken him for. Harris's face turned to stone as he asked, 'Who exactly did you speak to in London?'

Cangio saw a hint of a blush as Lucia Grossi ran her fingers through her hair. 'It was a . . . Mr Jardine, I believe.'

'Detective Chief Inspector Jardine,' Harris corrected her. 'My section leader.'

'I thought I'd better bring him up to speed. I told him I had designated someone to help you in your search,' she said with a nod in Cangio's direction.

Cangio swallowed his coffee, and ignored the burning in his throat.

He had no name, no role, he was just someone that *she* had designated.

'Mr Jardine said you had sent him a photo of a possible suspect, and that his team would be doing their best to put a name to the face. That *was* fast work, congratulations.' She beamed a smile at Harris. 'I was already halfway here when you phoned me. They'll check the airport, I thought, it's the next logical step. A little official help will speed things along, as I'm sure you'll appreciate.'

An Italian cop would have called it 'interfering with an investigation'.

Cangio asked himself what Harris would have to say about it.

Harris ran his hand through his stubbly hair. 'So, you thought you'd give us a surprise?'

'That's one way of putting it,' Lucia Grossi said. 'I called the airport on the way, and spoke with the security manager. I told him that I . . . that *you* would like to see the video footage of the boarding of last Thursday's flight – there was only one flight, as you know – to Stansted Airport. He was so impressed when he heard that you're from Scotland Yard.'

'*New* Scotland Yard,' Desmond Harris corrected her.

'He's expecting someone dressed as Sherlock Holmes,' she joked.

Cangio watched Harris, silently egging him on. Go on, Desmond, put her in her place. Weren't the English supposed to be masters of sarcasm? A nasty word or two would do no harm. And if she pretended not to understand, he was ready to provide an exact translation, and maybe rub a bit more salt in the wound.

'I can only thank you,' Harris said with a shrug. 'I'll be sure to inform DCI Jardine of the invaluable assistance I've received from you and Ranger Cangio.'

'Jardine thanked me when I spoke to him,' she said. 'And we managed to sort out a minor problem at the same time.'

'I'm sorry?' Harris leant forward, glancing to see if Cangio had guessed what was coming next.

Cangio concentrated on the coffee left at the bottom of his cup before he drained it.

'I told him that a formal note from Scotland Yard requesting our assistance would be appreciated.' Lucia Grossi's red lipstick seemed to take on a glossier hue. 'As you know, the United Kingdom has recently opted to leave the European Union. Well, I mean to say, if we are obliged to divert manpower from our own investigations, Scotland Yard can hardly expect us to simply fall in and cooperate any more. I need a signed request for help to pass on to my superiors. They'll have to justify the time and expense which is involved, as you can imagine. We are pleased to share information, but only within reason. There are limits, you know.'

Lucia Grossi laced her fingers and sat back comfortably in her seat.

Was this a full-blown diplomatic stand-off? Cangio asked himself.

'Well, Mr Jardine saw my point. I'm expecting a fax from London at any moment. With everything in order, I don't see any black clouds on the horizon.' She stood up. 'The security manager will be waiting for us, I imagine. His name is Lorenzo Duranti. By now, he ought to have located the tapes that I asked him to find.'

Cangio tried to imagine what it meant for Lucia Grossi and her career, the chance to show off a request for assistance from Scotland Yard in an investigation that she was personally coordinating.

It reminded him of the motto one of his workmates in London – a salesman who would have slit every throat in the office to make a big deal – had printed on his visiting-card: *Quo non ascendam?*

How high can I go?

Did Lucia Grossi have the legend tattooed somewhere on her body?

Valnerina

Rain lashed down on Monte Coscerno.

The soil was thin, the grass sparse, streams formed everywhere.

The wolf was still lying in the hollow, couldn't move out of it, though he hadn't drowned.

The pool of water had quickly turned to mud, then a tiny dam had burst, and the level had stopped climbing.

The rest of the pack still hadn't come back.

Perhaps they had found food . . .

The rain rolled over the mountainside, filling the air like thick smoke, obscuring everything, dampening down every sound.

There was nothing beyond the pool of mud and his own helplessness.

Cold and shivering, weak from loss of blood, exhausted now, indifferent to its fate, just waiting for a death which wouldn't come, the wolf must have closed its eyes, then fallen into a stupor . . .

He woke with a shock, and tried to move.

His vision was blurred, the rainwater running off his muzzle and into his eyes. He bowed his head, then lifted it, looked into the fog that clung to him like chicken down when they raided a henhouse.

He shuddered with fright, unable to move a limb.

There was something there.

In the fog, so close, invisible.

He could smell it . . .

A stink of something earthy – sweaty and rancid.

Then something moved in the swirling fog, coming closer.

He raised his eyes, saw two bright lamps glare in the fog above him . . .

Then claws swiped through the mist – CRRRACK! – and he was dead.

TEN

Catanzaro, Calabria

Don Michele knew that someone was there.

He'd heard the door move on its hinges, felt the displacement of air in the room.

His hearing seemed to be getting better as his sight got worse and worse.

They'd given him glasses, but that didn't really help. He was seeing double, even triple sometimes. *Keratoconus* was what they called it. It was like looking through a prism, the image all fragmented into shards. And then there was the endless itching and burning. Fucking shite!

'Rocco?'

Rocco Montale flopped down on the sofa.

'We need to spread the net wider, boss,' he said. 'Gino called me from the mortuary. The quality of corpse down there isn't up to much. They only get a dozen stiffs a week, and half of them are geriatrics who've died in the hospital. It's standard procedure, he says. You die in a hospital, they have to give you a post-mortem, make sure you ain't the victim of some mercy-killing medic. Most of them were half-blind, anyway – cataracts, diabetes, old age . . .'

'What about the others?'

'Motor accidents. Not much left to play about with. Faces splattered all over the windscreen or the road.'

Don Michele was wearing his glasses, looked a sight, his corneas turning into protruding cones that seemed to fix on you like some unblinking nutcase in *Kung Fu Panda* or *The Penguins of Madagascar.* Rocco watched the animations with his kids.

'So, what now, boss?'

'This fucking truce,' Don Michele said. 'We could have walloped someone from a rival clan . . .'

'We could pick up someone off the streets. Some useless motherf . . .'

Don Michele shook his head. 'Not on,' he said. 'A kidnapping with murder thrown in? Some innocent Joe, his family kicking up a rumpus? The coppers would go wild. They couldn't let something like that slip by. It's not an option . . .'

'There is *one* option, though. We talked about it the other week, Don Michè. Let me have a word with Carlo Piscitelli . . .'

'Come off it,' Don Michele said. 'I told you, didn't I? How the fuck would *you* feel looking out at the world through the eyes of one of them? It's got to feel *right*, you know what I mean? I mean, if it don't feel right, then . . . then, fuck me!'

Rocco knew he was going to have to talk seriously to the man. He didn't like it, but he knew he had no option. If the boss went blind they were finished. But if he saved his sight, they might have a chance. Still, if he saved his eyes and didn't like what he got, that would be a problem. He might decide to take it out on whoever had made the suggestion.

Rocco knew that no one else was close enough, or trusted enough, to say what he was going to say.

'Look at it this way, Don Michè,' he said, and regretted his choice of words immediately.

'Look at it *what* fucking way!' Don Michele growled. 'I can't see a fucking thing.'

'It would just be temporary,' Rocco said, getting into his stride quickly, speaking with conviction. 'It'll give you the time to find a better solution. To be honest, boss, I've . . . I've had a word with Carlo Piscitelli already. Word's passing down the line. When the right one arrives, he'll give us the word, then you can have a . . . a think for yourself.' He bit hard on his tongue. He'd almost said 'have a look for yourself'. 'Then, when something better comes along . . .'

'Gimme a whiskey,' Don Michele said.

He was drinking heavily these days, morning, noon, and night.

As Rocco handed him the cut-crystal glass, the boss took a drink, swallowed it in one, said, 'OK, OK. Let's see what Carlo can come up with.'

He didn't sound convinced, but that didn't matter to Rocco.

The important thing was that Don Michele hadn't said no.

Monte Coscerno, Valneria

The wolves emerged from the mist.

Suddenly, the leader stopped in his tracks.

The others pulled up short and raised their noses in the air.

There was a strange smell, a foul stink, that clung to the turf.

Their territory had been invaded.

The leader sank down, stretched forward, pointing his nose at a divot.

Something had slipped or slithered on the grass, turning up the damp earth.

He began to growl, a deep earthy guttural sound that began in his throat and vibrated through his body, raising his hackles. He bared his teeth, flattened his ears along the sides of his skull.

The others watched him, imitating his stance, growling, too, knowing something was wrong, not knowing what it was, ready to attack if he did, ready to run if running was the right response to the danger.

The female nudged him aside, sank her nose into the divot. She started growling, too.

This was her domain, the den so close. There were no pups yet, but soon there would be. She would decide whether they would leave or stay.

She raised her muzzle, and smelled another smell.

She weighed the smells one against the other. The smell from the divot was strong, but it wasn't so fresh. The fresh smell drew her forward. Hunger pushed her onward. The leader and cubs fell in behind as she edged forward, one paw at a time, a brief quivering hesitation between each step.

There was blood, she was sure of it . . .

And the vile smell grew weaker as they moved towards the empty den in the fog.

The smell of blood grew stronger, bones appeared, a carcase stretched out on the ground. The injured cub was dead. More than dead. Torn to pieces. Tatters were scattered in the mud where they had left him when they went out hunting.

The cubs began to whimper and cry.

Not for the dead.

It was the sight of blood that set them off, and hunger that drove them on.

The sight of blood and fresh meat.

As the lead wolf dug his teeth into the haunch of their dead brother, the she-wolf and her family began to jostle and tug at what was left.

The wolf they had left behind was dead.

Killed . . .

He wasn't rotting carrion.

His blood was wholesome, fresh.

But most important, he was meat . . .

Assisi Airport

'Call up that snap, Duranti.'

Grossi tapped the screen to show him where she wanted the photo which had passed from phone to phone, and a moment later it opened up as a separate window. From the way she ordered Duranti about, and the way he went along with it, Cangio wondered whether she might have saved *his* life at some point, too.

'Action!' Duranti murmured to himself as he pressed a button, and the video began.

Passengers were queuing with their luggage, tickets, and passports, preparing to board the 11.30 flight to London the previous Thursday.

They were crammed in the tiny office of Lorenzo Duranti, four people cooped up inside a tiny plastic cubicle. The video ran on for almost twenty minutes until the face of the man in Nora's photo cropped up: 'Unknown One,' as Desmond Harris called him.

Unknown One was standing in line behind a man who was wearing a large blue turban. Unknown Two, the man who had eaten with Unknown One at Il Covo del Pescatore, was nowhere to be seen.

'He probably took a different flight home,' Lucia Grossi said.

'He may have decided to stay in Italy for some reason,' Cangio suggested.

'In that case, my staff will find him,' Grossi said quickly.

Unknown One did not remain unknown for long.

Duranti called up the on-board checklist, identified the only Indian passenger on the flight, then came up with the name of the man who had followed him into the departure lounge.

'We follow all the standard EU checking procedures,' Duranti boasted.

Kit Andrews had been born in Ipswich, UK, in 1977, the passenger list revealed.

Desmond Harris put through a call to London, gave someone the name and passport number.

Five minutes later, his phone rang.

Harris answered, staring at Lucia Grossi, then he shook his head. 'Kit Andrews died in a car accident four years ago,' he said. 'A false name, and a false passport.'

Duranti made a point of defending the good name of the security staff. 'Our employees are carefully selected and expertly trained. OK, we're only a small provincial airport, but the anti-terrorist regulations are strictly adhered to.'

Lucia Grossi stood up, and patted him on the shoulder. 'Not to worry, Duranti, spotting him was the hardest part. No doubt Scotland Yard will come up with a name. Now, is it possible to find out when "Kit" arrived in Perugia?'

Of course it was possible. Mortified with humiliation for the gaping hole which had just shown up in the security measures for which he was responsible, horrified by the loss of face, not only in front of Captain Lucia Grossi, commander of the SCS, but also in the eyes of Inspector Harris of Scotland Yard, the passenger list for Monday 12th flashed up on the screen in a matter of seconds.

It was printed out and handed to Lucia Grossi.

Would she read it first, Cangio wondered, or would she pass it on to Harris?

A glance was all she needed to find what she wanted, before handing it on politely to her foreign colleague.

Harris didn't bother to look at it.

'We still don't know who the other man was,' he said. 'Duranti, do you have a video of Kit Andrews arriving in Italy?'

'Certainly,' Lorenzo Duranti replied, typing the date and flight number into the computer. 'We keep all video records for six months.'

Within minutes, they were watching the scene in the arrivals hall as the passengers on flight FR4593 from Stansted presented their passports at the security booth. Kit Andrews was one of the first to go through the checkpoint, carrying hand luggage only, a big black leather tote bag. He looked relaxed, less tense, than the day on which he had flown back to London. As the official handed back his passport, Kit Andrews raised his eyes, looked into the camera, and gave a two-fingered salute, the way an off-duty soldier might have done.

Was it a sign of relief? Cangio wondered. Knowing now that the passport was false, it was easy to think of Kit as a hardened criminal, who had just got away with whatever deception he had had in mind.

A man ten places behind him in the queue looked nervous.

'Bushy eyebrows, and black hair. Could he be Unknown Two?' Desmond Harris said, pointing him out on the screen.

Unknown Two looked like someone who needed urgently to go to the toilet.

Duranti checked the list again, and came up with the name of Barry Farrington.

While Harris made another call to London, Grossi asked Duranti to run the sequence through again.

Cangio edged closer to the screen, watching carefully as Barry Farrington approached the desk with his passport in his hand, glancing at it before he handed it over to the policeman on duty. Was he making sure that everything was in order? While the border guard leafed slowly through the pages, glancing at the passenger, then checking again on his computer screen, Farrington shuffled his feet and moved his head.

'If this is Unknown Two,' Lucia Grossi said, 'then the man who called himself Andrews went back on his own three days later.'

'They're pretending not to know each other,' Cangio said.

Lucia Grossi pounced on him. 'Why do you say that?'

'Farrington glanced beyond the passport barrier four times in less than a minute. Andrews had got through safely, remember. This man kept looking in his direction to make sure that nothing was happening out in the arrivals hall. Are there video cameras on the other side of the passport barrier? If we're lucky, we might see them team up.'

'I'm sorry, there aren't,' Duranti said. 'Once passports have been okayed, the passengers aren't our business any more. However . . .' He flashed an oily grin at Lucia Grossi. She was the boss so far as he was concerned, and to hell with New Scotland Yard. 'I can check the car-park security cameras. They're only single photographs shot at one-minute intervals, but there may be something. It may take a bit of time to go through them.'

Lucia Grossi nodded, and Duranti turned his attention to the keyboard again.

'Could they have met for the first time on the outward flight, sitting next to one another by chance?' she said to Duranti.

'With Ryanair, it's definitely possible.'

'They ended up in a restaurant together,' Harris reminded her. 'Would you go out to dinner with someone you had met on a plane?'

Lucia Grossi looked at him for a moment too long.

'It all depends, don't you think?' she said with a hint of a smile.

'These are the outside shots that day,' Duranti said, calling her attention back to the computer screen as he shuffled the photographs forward. 'This is twenty minutes after the flight landed. Twenty-three, twenty-four. There he is!'

'Kit Andrews' appeared on the pavement outside the exit door. In the next still he was lighting a cigarette. He remained on the same spot for five or six shots, as other people walked into the frame, or walked out of it.

'And here's Farrington,' said Lucia Grossi. 'Freeze it, Duranti.'

The sequence froze, the two men only two or three metres apart. The first man was smoking, the second one trailing a suitcase behind him, head down, his face a blur.

'Now, move ahead one frame at a time,' she said.

Duranti obeyed.

'Andrews is still there, but Unknown Two has disappeared.'

'They didn't know each other,' Lucia Grossi said. 'Not a word or a glance passed between them. Did you see anything to the contrary, Cangio?'

She sounded so dismissive, and the visual evidence certainly backed her up.

'It would be a hell of a coincidence if they met by chance in the same restaurant.'

'Oh, I don't know,' Lucia Grossi said. Then her voice turned plummy as she acted out the scene. '"What a small world! You were on the UK flight this morning. Do you know a good spot to eat? We could share a table. What do you say?"'

A coincidence? It could well be.

Cangio's eyes were fixed on the screen, the pictures flipping forward minute by minute in an unending sequence. Kit Andrews disappeared just as a man in a sports cap stepped into the picture. He, too, had a cigarette in his mouth, as if he couldn't wait to get out of the airport building to light up.

'And that's it,' Duranti announced.

The picture blipped, and next frame came up on the screen.

Cangio smothered a cry in his throat as Duranti froze the picture.

Desmond Harris's phone blared out in that instant, a sound that filled the tiny room.

Harris listened for a moment, holding up his hand for silence. 'Barry Farrington is a false name, too,' he said. 'They were on the same plane, both using false passports. That is no coincidence. Those two men were together.'

Cangio leant close to the computer screen.

The man in the cap had been bending forward to light his cigarette.

It wasn't possible to see his face from that oblique angle. It wasn't easy to say how young or old he might have been, though he wasn't too old, Cangio thought, given the baseball cap he was wearing. But a dark mark on the side of his neck was partially visible.

Was it a salamander tattoo which started behind his left ear and ran inside the collar of his jacket?

Salamanders were immune to fire, the legend said.

By fire they meant flames, but fire meant *fire* to some people.

Salamanders were supposed to be invincible, indestructible, symbols of strength.

Now, younger members of the 'Ndrangheta clans had laid claim to the creature.

He had seen a salamander tattoo on the neck of a killer as he smashed a rival gang leader's head against a rock on Soverato beach two years before. A killer with a similar tattoo had blown the head off his partner, Marzio Diamante, just six months ago, then chased him halfway across Europe with just one thing on his mind: kill Cangio!

The salamander often darted through his nightmares.

The salamander always nestled in his darkest thoughts.

He saw the creatures everywhere, even when they weren't there.

Was he seeing one now in the pixelated b/w photograph on the video screen?

He played with the idea of telling Lucia Grossi and asking Duranti to run through the photographs again, then go through all the videos which had been made that day at the airport when Unknowns One and Two arrived.

But he knew what Lucia Grossi would say.

He was making mountains out of molehills, courting attention, seeing his name in lights, imagining headlines in the newspapers. 'The ranger who whipped the 'Ndrangheta.' *Fame has gone to your head*, she would tell him. *You cry wolf at every opportunity, Cangio, and no one's listening.*

And maybe she was right.

What had he seen, after all?

A birthmark, a scar? Or was it just another stupid tattoo? So many people had them nowadays, apeing their pop idols and their football heroes. There were millions of fancy dragon designs out there, it took an expert to tell one from another.

He clicked the button and the frame advanced one minute.

Other passengers were leaving the arrivals building now.

But there were some things caught in the frame that might be important.

A man was standing at the kerbstone by a vehicle with a sliding door.

He has only visible from the knees down, but Cangio recognised the leather boots he was wearing.

And from behind the sliding door, a name poked out: *Francesco.*

As he called up the next frame, the man stepped inside the vehicle and disappeared from view.

ELEVEN

North Africa

The boatmen in Zuara didn't bother with masks.

They only wanted to see the back of your left hand.

A red spot meant that you went to sea in a wooden boat, while the others were squashed into rotting old *gommoni*, rubber boats that sank, or barely made it out beyond the coastal limits, heading north towards Pantelleria, where the Italian navy was waiting to take you in tow to a safe port in Europe.

Italy was Europe, the Boko Haram had told him.

The Italian sailors all wore white masks and plastic hygiene suits with hoods as they threw out life jackets, bottles of water, blankets the colour of gold but made of a tinsel that kept you warm and dry when the waves got rough and the night got cold.

There were more masks in Lampedusa, green ones this time, worn by the soldiers, doctors, and nurses, as the migrants were given injections, something to eat, and a bottle of water, a pair of plastic sandals and a tracksuit, then moved out of the security area and onto the ferry that would take them on the next step of the journey.

The tracksuits were all the same colour, so the red spot came in handy.

And all the while, every time that they were searched and checked, someone was there, looking out for the big red spot that wouldn't wash off. He hoped the spot would never fade, because it got you special treatment, the treatment you had paid for in cash to the Boko Haram.

There were more face masks at the refugee camp in Sicily.

And now, in the hospital, there were more people wearing green masks, and long green cotton gowns. They all smelled strange, like they'd been brewing the moonshine that everyone called Man Powa in a copper still.

Like the one who was pushing the needle into his vein now, saying a word he didn't understand that sounded like *rilassati . . .*

Catania Airport, Sicily

The refrigerated carrier boxes were blue.

They looked like reinforced plastic with four big locks, two on each side of the lid, and large printed labels, red on white, that said *Not To Be Opened In Transit.*

There were a half a dozen boxes, each one containing two packs of ice, and the consignment number.

The ambulance drove out of the compound with its sirens blaring, a man in the back making sure the boxes didn't roll around or fall off the stretcher gurney on the way to the airstrip.

The private jet was waiting on the tarmac, its engine thrumming.

Within ten minutes, it would be winging its way to the north.

A flight plan was required, of course, but there were no international customs to deal with when the plane was scheduled to land in Umbria in one hour and thirty-five minutes. There would be no customs controls at the small provincial airport of St Francis of Assisi.

A helicopter would be waiting on the tarmac for the plane to land.

A private helicopter from a private clinic, where a private patient was already being prepared for the procedure.

Valnerina

'What do you mean, Don Michele?'

'You heard me. I don't want to go ahead.'

'Not go ahead?'

'That's what the Don just said,' Rocco snapped.

'I . . . I don't see the problem,' the doctor was saying.

He was a smart little man, prim and neatly dressed. Now, he looked puzzled and slightly amused, a dumb grin on his face, as if he didn't know what to make of this reaction. He pulled on his collar, straightened his white coat, then said: 'I mean to say, the goods have . . . arrived, and they're as fresh as can be, I promise you. And, well . . . *you* are here, too, Don Michele, and so am *I* . . . This opportunity is just too *good* to throw away. We can't just stop everything *now*, can we?'

Rocco bit his lip, and shook his head.

You didn't speak like that to Don Michele.

If the Don wanted something stopping, it stopped.

The Don was sitting up now. 'You need me to explain it to you?'

Instead of saying no, thanks, there was no need for an explanation, the doctor said yes.

Maybe he thought he could bring Don Michele around.

He was wrong again.

If the Don had decided, you were never gonna bring him around.

'You know where this material comes from, do you?'

'As I told you, Don Michele, it comes from Lampedusa . . .'

Don Michele's finger stuck up like a metronome in front of his nose, left-right, no-no.

'Don't give me that,' he said. 'We both *know* where it comes from before it *gets* to Lampedusa, don't we? What I'm asking you – and I want a straight answer – is which bit of fucking Africa does it come from? Can you tell me that?'

The doctor looked desperately at Rocco, sending out messages.

We need to get him thinking straight on this issue.

Rocco carefully looked the other way.

If the Don had made up his mind, thinking straight didn't come into it.

'These replacements are . . . they're perfect, Don Michele.

They've been removed and prepared by experts, and carefully maintained in transit. They are worth . . .'

'They ain't worth shit,' Don Michele said.

The doctor opened his mouth, then closed it again.

'They come from dead blackies,' Don Michele said. 'They're no fucking use to me. Just look at this one!' Don Michele picked an eyeball out of the tray and stuck into the doctor's face. 'What colour do you see?'

'Colour? Colour's got nothing to do with it.'

Don Michele held the eyeball up to his own eyes. 'They're fucking green. And as for fresh,' he sniffed hard, 'I smell stale fish.'

'I'd stake my reputation . . .'

'You ain't got a reputation,' the Don reminded him. 'You're working for me.'

'You couldn't be more wrong, Don Michele. Let me explain . . .'

Rocco wondered whether the doctor was trying to save face, or hasten his own end.

'Eye colour has nothing at all to do with the cornea. The colouring is caused by mineral pigmentation inside the iris,' the doctor went on with a patronising smile. He might have been lecturing to a group of students, Rocco thought. He didn't seem to realise that he was dealing with a man who was going blind. And not just any man. He was shining his bright little light into the dilated pupils of one of the most powerful 'Ndrangheta bosses in Italy.

The Don's face was a mask of disgust. 'You wanna make me look like a freak?'

The doctor laughed.

Another mistake, Rocco thought.

No one laughed when the Don asked a question.

'They look green *now*,' the doctor explained, 'because his irises were green, but the layer that you need is colourless, translucent, and almost transparent, allowing the light to pass straight through it, dispersing the rays . . .'

'Don't give me that crap. If I say they're green, they're fucking green.'

The doctor wouldn't learn, wouldn't keep quiet.

Give the Don his way, Rocco was tempted to tell him.

There was no other way to handle the boss.

'What Don Michele means . . .'

'Shut it, Rocco. He knows what I mean. He's got ears, right?'

'Right, boss.'

For the first time that day, Don Michele smiled.

'Wrong, Rocco,' Don Michele said.

He reached across in front of the doctor, lifted a scalpel from a kidney tray of surgical instruments, grabbed the doctor by the lobe of his left ear, then slashed down hard with the scalpel.

The ear and half of the doctor's face came away in his hand.

'He *had* ears,' Don Michele said. 'He didn't use them.'

The doctor opened his mouth, then froze with shock. Rocco rabbit-punched him in the throat before he could scream, and he hit the floor like a heavy wet sack, blood pooling immediately on the white tiles.

'Rocco, cut the other one off,' Don Michele said, 'then dump the fucker. Because you've got money, they think they can spin you any old shit.'

Was this the third or fourth ophthalmologist whose patter hadn't convinced the Don?

While Rocco was slicing off the other ear, Don Michele said, 'And that can of worms . . .' He pointed to the blue refrigerated plastic box containing eyes that had seen African forests, Saharan deserts, the Mediterranean Sea, and all the rest. 'Get shut of that lot, too.'

Next thing the Don was on his feet, ripping off the medical gown.

'Take me home, Rocco,' he said, waiting while Rocco helped him on with his shirt and his jacket. 'This fucking clinic gives me the creeps.'

Fifteen minutes later, the chopper lurched up into the air.

Don Michele seemed in a better mood than on the journey up. Suddenly, he was chatty.

'What can you see down there, then, Rocco? Umbria's got a lot going for it. Woods and mountains, sheep and olive groves . . .'

Rocco looked down.

They were still pretty low, the pilot not bothering to gain altitude, riding straight out towards the Nera valley, which they would cross on the way to Assisi and the waiting jet. You could see everything . . .

He could see everything, Rocco corrected himself. The Don

couldn't see a thing, and often asked him to tell him what he could see when they were flying or driving around.

Rocco laughed. 'There's an old Jeep down there on the track below . . . No, hang on, it's more of a Land Rover. Belongs to the park rangers by the look of it.'

Don Michele grabbed hold of his arm. 'Can you see who's in it?' he said.

While the Don was speaking, a face had poked out of the side window, looking up at the helicopter. 'A fella with a young face,' Rocco said.

'Could it be that Cangio?' Don Michele said. 'There can't be many of them rangers knocking around here now, can there?'

Rocco laughed. 'If we had a hand grenade boss,' he said. 'What a lark!'

Don Michele was quite excited now. 'I reckon it is him, Rocco,' he said. 'Who else could it be? We blew the head off the other one six months ago. Cangio's the only ranger left in this neck of the woods.'

Don Michele squeezed up against the window, sheltering his eyes with his hands, trying his best to see the man down below in the Land Rover.

'I bet you it's him,' the Don said with a tremor in his voice.

'I wish I'd brought my shooter along,' Rocco said.

Don Michele pulled back from the window, settled himself against the seat.

'We're keeping him on ice, Rocco. Nice and fresh, until we meet him right up close. You'll have plenty of opportunity to use your shooter, I promise you.'

TWELVE

Monte Coscerno

Cangio glanced at his watch, then made a note of the time in his notebook.

He switched off the torch, slipped on his gloves again.

Such total darkness – no moon, no stars – made the night seem even colder than it was.

It was three or four degrees above zero, though it felt like four or five degrees below.

It was twenty-seven hours since the last sighting, and he didn't like what he was seeing.

No, it was worse than that. It wasn't simply that he didn't like the way they were behaving, it was the fact that he couldn't *explain* their behaviour that he didn't like.

The pack leader seemed to be driven mad by fear, or fright.

But what was he afraid of?

Wolves don't become paranoid for no good reason. They react to danger. A danger presents itself; the wolf reacts. But that was not the order in which things were happening. The pack leader, the dominant male, was constantly looking around him, behaving as if he expected to be attacked. To all appearances, his behaviour was erratic. Though no threat was evident, he clearly felt himself to be in danger. It made no sense at all. There were no other wolves in that section of the park, and wild boar would never come up that high, knowing they'd find nothing to eat at that altitude.

What else could be the cause of it? Stray dogs?

He would need to monitor their behaviour more carefully, and that would take a lot of time that he didn't have. Not with Harris and the investigation into the murder at Stansted Airport. Not with Lucia Grossi getting so deeply involved in it, dragging him away from his job.

He had written the time, 23.35, in his log.

If Lori was staying down at her parents' place that night, that would give him a bit more time. Another hour would be useful, though it might be worthwhile grabbing a blanket and a ground-sheet from the Land Rover if he was going to be there for another hour. Only one thing was certain: it wasn't going to get any warmer.

He fished out his mobile phone, brought it to life. The screen lit up, throwing pale light on the leaves of the clump of grass behind which he had taken cover.

The wolf let out a low, grumbling howl, acknowledging him, perhaps.

The wolf didn't often show it, but it was more than probable that he always knew when Cangio was there. It was almost an honour, Cangio thought, to know that though he wasn't exactly welcome, he did not represent a threat.

He pressed himself closer to the ground and covered his mouth with his hand, waiting for Loredana to answer the call.

'Seb, are you OK?'

She sounded worried. She always did when she was at home alone at night, and he was out on the mountainside or in the woods.

'Are you at home?' he asked, though there was no need to ask.

'I would have told you if I was staying down at Mum's,' she said.

She didn't bother asking him where he was. She knew. If he was whispering into his mobile as midnight approached, then he was on the mountain watching his wolves.

They were both silent for an instant.

'When are you coming home?' she said, her voice building up to battle-cry. 'I . . . I haven't heard from you all bloody day. I was going to phone that Captain Grossi, but I thought it probably wouldn't have been appreciated.'

'I'll be home in two ticks,' he said.

He cut the line, and the display light died.

He picked up the night-glasses, took a last look at the den.

The outline of the lead male was constantly on the move. Prowling round and round the den, then climbing up on top of the earth mound, twirling around to left and right, as if he might catch sight of something by surprise.

Why was the leader on guard? he wondered.

Why had the others stood down?

He watched and waited, feeling the same paranoia mounting in his breast.

He would have fought to defend them, though that was not his job.

His job was to watch over them, keep tabs on them, and nothing more.

And if a predator came along while he was away, then so be it.

The *cantoniera* house

It was a quarter to one by the time he finally slipped into bed.

Loredana was fast asleep. She opened her mouth and let out

a moan, turning away from him. She didn't react when he whispered her name. He stretched out his hand, resting it against her flank, feeling the warmth. It was better than a cast-iron stove.

'I'm home,' he whispered.

He fell asleep thinking about the wolves, their senses and their perceptions.

Did they only see what was there? Or did they have 'feelings' about their territory, 'suggestions' and 'intuitions' which might lead them to do things for the wrong reasons? Could wolves imagine the existence of things that they couldn't see?

Could they fear things that didn't exist in Nature?

Like men who fear their own fears . . .

Next morning

He was shaving when the phone call came in.

It was 6.23, they'd just said on the radio.

The man's teeth were chattering.

'C . . . can you . . . c . . . come up n . . . now?'

'Just give me time to get in the car,' he'd said.

Then Cangio had asked again, just to make sure. 'Are you all right?'

Dino De Angelis had cut him short, teeth still clacking, saying, 'I'll be waiting.'

As if he didn't like being up there alone any longer than was necessary.

It had taken him almost thirty minutes to drive there in the Land Rover.

Once he crossed the river and left the road behind, climbing the gentle slope of Monte Galluro with Monte Cavogna to the north, the view of Valnerina opened out before him. Bathed in early morning sunlight, the mountains were densely forested with pines and holm oaks. Rocky outcrops soared into the sky, or fell straight down into the valley below. Tiny villages spotted the mountains on the other side of the river gorge, cottage windows flashing as they reflected the light.

Idyllic was the word for it, though Dino De Angelis didn't seem to think so. He was living on top of a mountain in a hole that was as deep and dark as Hell. Was the hole of his own making? That was what Cangio was asking himself as he drove through the village of Rocchetta, saw the signpost, and turned left.

The farmer lived at the end of a track that was rutted by winter run-off. Large stones and jagged flints littered the track and made for a bumpy ride, the Land Rover bucking and jerking as it climbed the gradient. As snow melted off at the top of the mountain, water came trickling, then cascading, down into the valley in a thousand streams and rivulets which swelled the River Nera.

If you wanted isolation, this was the place to look for it.

Maybe De Angelis had lost his mind living up there on his own.

You met some odd characters in his job, Cangio was thinking, when a man jumped out in front of him, waving an ancient double-barrelled shotgun.

Dino De Angelis had hair like a lion's mane, white like his straggly long beard. He was wearing a weathered army combat jacket with a torn, ragged sleeve, and knee-high rubber boots. He looked as if he had no wife or family to tell him that he looked a mess, though it wasn't so, as Cangio would discover later.

He checked the *Parks Police* logo, then waved Cangio out of the LR with the shotgun.

'I hope that isn't loaded,' Cangio said.

The man looked at the gun in his hands, then lowered it.

'Thanks for coming,' he said, his voice rough, as if his throat was parched.

Did he always narrow his eyes and clench his jaw when he met a stranger?

'Follow me,' he said, not wasting words, turning away and heading up the track past a rough stone hut to a byre of perforated bricks with a rusty corrugated-iron roof.

'The cows are in here,' he said, as he pushed the byre door open.

The stench of mulch hit Cangio in the face.

'Just look at this!' De Angelis said, his anger lending strength to his voice. 'In forty years, I've never seen nothing to match it.'

A full-grown black-and white-cow lay disembowelled on straw that was soaking with her blood. All that remained of a new-born calf was the head and spine and part of the ribcage.

'You've had visitors,' Cangio said, trying to keep it light.

It wasn't the sort of thing you saw every day of the week, though he had witnessed the mass slaughter of sheep by wolves on a number of occasions.

'You can claim compensation,' he said. 'The State pays for damage caused by wolves.'

'Wolves?' The man snorted with disgust, waving his hand at the dead cow and calf. 'Is that what you think, ranger? Wolves?'

Cangio ignored the protest. 'Did you leave the door off the latch, by any chance?'

The farmer turned and looked at him, wide-eyed, amazed.

'D'you think I'm mad? Leave the door open? That's asking for trouble.'

Cangio dropped down on his haunches beside the carcases.

The throat of the heifer had been ripped wide open. There were deep claw marks on the pale pink, hairless flesh beneath the animal's jaw, slashing cuts, quite unlike anything a wolf might do.

Though if it wasn't a wolf . . .

He was careful not to voice his doubts.

Dino De Angelis swore, a constant stream of obscenities.

'When they're starving,' Cangio started to say, 'they'll go to any lengths . . .'

'Like opening closed doors? Come off it, will you?'

Cangio stood up, then turned to face him.

Before he could speak, De Angelis said, 'I did NOT leave the door open!'

It wasn't quite a shout, but it was more than a denial.

Was he making a scene? Was that it? The authorities wouldn't pay him a euro if they thought he hadn't closed his animals in for the night. Judging by the state of him, Cangio got the impression that De Angelis might have been lost to the world at the bottom of a bottle the night before.

And yet what the man had said made sense. The rest of the herd was closed up safely in the byre. And that was where the heifer and calf had died. What if De Angelis *had* closed the door, as he said? Who could have opened it? Not wolves, that was for sure.

'This isn't the first time,' De Angelis was saying. 'There's strange things going on up here.'

Cangio pulled out his mobile, started taking photographs of the dead animals.

'Are you saying that this has happened before, and you didn't report it?'

'I've been up here for almost week now,' De Angelis said. 'The lad who watches over the herd, he's sick in hospital.' He wiped his forehead with the back of his hand as if he were sweating.

Cangio breathed on his hands, then rubbed them together. It was cold in the byre.

'Five or six nights ago, I heard a noise,' De Angelis said. 'I was in the hut, sitting by the fire. There was something . . . a noise outside, something scratching at the door. Trying to get in, that's what I thought. *Dio santo!*'

'A dog?' Cangio suggested.

'I don't keep dogs,' De Angelis said. 'Not with the cows.'

'So, what was it?' Cangio asked him.

'You tell me,' the man said, his voice sinking low. 'Then, later on, I heard this . . . What would you call it? Not a scream exactly, more a wailing noise, as if someone was in pain. It sounded as if it was coming from those woods further down the hill.' He waved his hand over the dead heifer and the remains of the calf. 'I should have shot it then, when I had the chance.'

Cangio let him finish, watching as the man caught his breath. '*It?*' he asked.

De Angelis nodded. 'That's what I said.'

'In the woods, you say?'

'That's where the noise was coming from.'

'An owl out hunting, probably. Hares often squeal . . .'

'That weren't no owl, no hare,' De Angelis said, and he cursed again. 'There's talk of a . . .' The farmer closed his eyes and shook his head, as if afraid to put the idea into words. 'If you had heard about it, ranger, you'd know *what* I'm talking about.'

The way he said it took Cangio by surprise.

Not you'd *know* what, but you'd know *what* . . .

'What's that, then?' Cangio asked him, curiosity leading him on, though good sense told him to keep his mouth shut.

'Ask anyone down in Valnerina,' Dino De Angelis said.

He glared at Cangio, challenging him, daring him to deny

what everyone knew, or was supposed to know down in the valley.

Were they all going mad? Cangio asked himself. First, the kid at the school in Borgo Cerreto, now a grown man. They saw these things on television and thought they were true. Witches, ghosts, and werewolves . . .

He took another photo of the scene, then put his phone away.

'Thanks for calling me, Signor De Angelis. I'll submit my report, saying that your cows have been attacked by wolves . . . Let's keep it simple, shall we? It doesn't matter how they got in, it's what they did that matters to you. Put in your claim as a wolf attack, and it will be dealt with. I'll make a point of saying that the byre door was securely shut, all right?'

He hoped the concession would calm De Angelis down.

'It *was* shut,' De Angelis said defiantly. 'And that was no fucking wolf.'

'If you want compensation,' Cangio said, insisting, 'it *was* a wolf.'

He walked out of the byre and left the man to it.

It was either that, or call an ambulance and have him carried off to the funny farm.

As he was driving back down the track, he heard a pulsing, throbbing sound above his head.

At first he thought there was something wrong with the Land Rover, then he heard a *swoosh*, a rush of air, and the chopper cut across the sky a hundred yards in front of him.

Flying low, much too low, he thought.

The helicopter was white with red stripes, a four- or six-seater, similar to the ones they used in Castelluccio for mountain rescue, emergency services, and tourist jaunts, though the colours were all wrong.

Another private helicopter, probably.

It circled above the trees, as if the pilot was looking for something. Then it reared up in the air, and disappeared from sight. The woods on the right of the road were dense, wild, and untended, with an air of long abandonment about them. Were they the woods that Dino De Angelis had been talking about? A rough stone wall marked the right-hand side of the road, closing off the estate.

He saw a sign as he passed a stone gateway, a lane leading up into the trees.

Villa San Francesco.

He stood on the brakes, jerked to a halt, then sat there staring at the sign.

Villa San Francesco?

There must be a house in the woods. A grand old house if the fancy name was anything to go by. It might be anything at all, of course. A private retreat, a new hotel, a business of some sort, with rich guests, or top executives flying in and out by helicopter to overcome the isolation of the place.

Francesco . . .

That name had been written on the side of the vehicle at Assisi Airport. Was there something similar about the way the name was written? The same type of lettering, maybe?

He drove in through the gates, and started heading up the lane.

If anyone stopped him and asked what he was doing there, he could always say that he was following up on the report that Dino De Angelis had made.

Had they seen wolves, or heard strange noises at Villa San Francesco?

THIRTEEN

Villa San Francesco

The road wound through dense woodlands.

A real road, Cangio realised suddenly, a narrow ribbon of slick black tarmac, not the usual unpaved gravel track that served as a private road in most parts of Italy.

Whoever was living out there was treating themselves well.

He drove for more than a kilometre, the trees and bushes closing in on either side. And as he rounded the final bend, the building came into view.

Villa San Francesco wasn't a villa at all. It was a convent or monastery, some sort of religious foundation. There were hundreds of them scattered all over Umbria. Monasticism had taken root in Norcia over fifteen hundred years before with St Benedict, and St Francis had fuelled the fire five hundred years later.

Unlike most of the other monasteries in Umbria, this one showed signs of recent and extensive renovation. The red-tiled roof was new, the copper drainpipes burnished and gleaming, the ancient stone walls pointed to perfection.

There was a car park, too, three cars standing on the wide expanse of sand-coloured pebbles. The cars were newish, relatively up-market, a boxy-looking Audi, a Japanese model that he didn't recognise, and an F-reg Fiat 500 Sport.

Guests, or workers? he wondered.

He put it down to the earthquakes.

There were lots of these properties knocking around, most of them empty. Such buildings were too big for ordinary people. It stood to reason. Anything old would cost a fortune to maintain. Most religious buildings were Grade A-listed, filled with frescoes, sculptures, and other works of art. State subsidies were offered to help with the upkeep, but it would take more than an occasional handout or a tax rebate to keep them in order.

That was the trouble with Umbria; there was almost too much art and too many old buildings that had to be preserved.

The only people who really benefited were the builders and restorers.

A lot of them had grown rich as a result. Every time there was an earthquake, they rubbed their hands with glee. If something fell down, they knew it would have to be put right again. The local tourist industry was the only real industry. And if all the churches fell down, why would anyone bother to visit Umbria?

He pulled up on the gravel, and climbed out of the car.

A vast amount of cash had been used to put Villa San Francesco back on its feet.

The chapel with its two-bell tower and Romanesque facade was probably the oldest part of the complex. New stained glass gleamed brightly in the large rose window high above the stone-framed door. But the building was vast, by the look of it. How many monks or nuns would have lived in such a place? It was laid out around a cloister, he imagined, with cells and dormitories, kitchens and workshops, and maybe a scriptorium where the monks had worked, illuminating manuscripts. There must be barns and outhouses for keeping animals, a hostel for pilgrims, a hospital for victims of the plague.

There were few real monasteries left now.

They were just big, draughty places that no one wanted. Not even the Catholic Church. There was a crisis in religious vocations, everyone said. All the monks and nuns appeared to come from the Philippines, Africa, or South America these days. Most of these buildings had been converted into luxury hotels, health spas, time-share holiday rentals, or cultural centres which offered just about everything from gongs and yoga to belly dancing.

What was Villa San Francesco offering? he wondered.

Two stone lions slept on either side of the entrance gate. A marble plaque boasted a sculptural relief of St Francis administering the holy sacrament to a kneeling pilgrim. Next to the sign was an electronic panel marked *Santuario di Villa San Francesco* and a red plastic button which activated a microphone/speaker. A TV camera peered down at him from the wall. Close up, it looked more like a fortified bunker than a monastery. Was it now a private sanctuary for some multi-millionaire rock musician?

He pushed the button, and waited.

A minute passed, and nothing happened.

Was he disturbing someone's meditation, or someone's sleep?

He pushed the button again, and a microphone crackled into life.

'*Yes?*'

'I'd like to visit the convent,' he said.

'*That isn't possible, I'm afraid.*'

The voice was metallic, unyielding, providing no additional information.

Whoever was monitoring the conversation must have seen that he was wearing a uniform, yet they didn't ask him who he was, or what he wanted. Maybe they didn't care. Perhaps they had nothing to fear.

'May I see the church, then?' he asked.

'*The church is no longer open to visitors.*'

Could it be that they were really monks, a closed religious order?

'May I speak to . . .' He hesitated for a moment. What did you call the top monk? 'To the person in charge?'

'*Please make an appointment by referring to our website.*'

Website?

'Can't I telephone and ask?'

'*We do not accept phone calls from an outside line.*'

'Is this a closed convent, a silent order, prayer and meditation only?'

'*Information is available to the public on the website.*'

He had run out of uncompromising questions.

'Thank you,' he said.

Nothing came back.

The metallic hum died away as the connection was cut.

And God bless you! he thought as he turned away and wandered back to the car.

The monks in Umbria had always been renowned for their hospitality, but this lot seemed to be giving nothing away.

The gravel car park was laid out on a slope. As he swung the car in a wide circle, he caught sight of something at the rear of the convent that he'd been half-expecting to see, though he didn't quite believe that he was seeing it.

A helicopter landing pad. Was that where the aircraft had come from? Or had the Pope dropped in for morning coffee and a bite to eat?

Was that why they were being so cagey?

Anything was possible in Umbria, the 'mystical' heart of Italy.

He turned right at the gate in the direction of Borgo Cerreto and drove for ten minutes, stopping off at the first roadside bar he came to.

'What can I get you?' the barman asked him.

Cangio ordered a bottle of mineral water.

'Large or small? Fresh or fizzy?'

'A small one, please. And make it still water.'

Then he ordered a coffee.

'Can you add a drop of cold milk to the coffee?' he said, as the barman turned to his Gaggia, wondering how to get a conversation started, how to bring it around to a question that was puzzling him.

'No problem at all,' the barman said, taking in his uniform, then looking at his face for the first time. 'Hey,' he said, 'haven't I seen you someplace?'

Cangio's picture had been splashed all over the newspapers

and on the local TV after the shooting at Marra Truffles just six
months earlier. Before he had the chance to reply, the barman
said, 'Yeah, I saw you on the telly!'

The conversation went easily after that.

The barman knew of the truffle-merchant who had died when
police had raided the factory where he was processing cocaine.
'Antonio Marra dropped in here occasionally,' he said in a hushed
voice. 'A real wide boy, that one. He got what was coming to
him, if you ask me.' The barman seemed excited by the fact that
the Calabrian mafia had been moving into the area. 'What do
they call them fellas?'

'The 'Ndrangheta,' Cangio specified.

'Now, *they* might shake things up a bit round here,' the man
said, leaning over the counter. 'Build a few factories, you know,
create a bit of work for the youngsters. Fresh blood, a bit of
investment and development. Big money, that's what we need.
Without the tourists, this place is deader than a cemetery at four
in the morning.'

'Talking of fresh blood,' Cangio said, 'you'll need a bigger
cemetery if the 'Ndrangheta moves in. They'll get the kids to
build it, then the mafia will bury them in it.'

The barman had a laugh about that, seemed to think it was a
great joke.

Then the conversation drifted naturally to business and the
economic crisis.

'Are things looking up at all?' Cangio asked him.

The barman sniffed with disgust, then shook his head. 'It's
getting worse with every day that passes,' he said. 'I'd sell up,
if anyone would make me an offer. I'm making fifty euro here
on a good day. It's passing trade mostly, people on their way to
work in Spoleto or Terni. A coffee, a packet of fags, a ham
sandwich if I'm really lucky.'

'Still, a lot of building seems to be going on,' Cangio said.

'Thank God for earthquakes!' the barman laughed. 'If things
fall down, you've got to put them back in shape. There isn't
much else to keep the wolf from the door.'

'I passed a place called Villa San Francesco on the road to
Rocchetta,' Cangio said. 'Do you know it? Recently restored,
by the look of it. They must have spent a fortune doing it up.
I bet the builders brought you loads of business. I mean to say,

you're the closest bar. Breakfast, lunch, a beer or two before going home . . .'

He drank some water from the bottle and waited.

'The builders? Yeah, they were up there for a few months. And not just the local lads. They had loads of specialists and fitters in, too. Technicians, like. They came from Rome, Milan, all sorts of places.'

'What were they fitting?'

The barman shrugged. 'No one talks about their work, do they? And you can't really blame them. I mean to say, if I went home and told the wife what I've been doing in here all bloody day, she'd have me put down.'

'So, what is it, Villa San Francesco?' Cangio asked. 'Now the work's done, I mean.'

The barman pursed his lips, then sniffed loudly again.

'Is it still a monastery?' Cangio suggested.

'Nah, I don't think so. I thought our luck was in, though,' the barman said, confiding now, one elbow on the counter. 'When I saw those helicopters coming and going, d'you want to know what *I* thought?'

Cangio waited.

The barman lowered his voice, looked left and right in the empty room.

'Bunga bunga,' he hissed across the counter. 'Silvio B, you know? Orgies, and that. I thought he might have bought the place. Out there in the woods. A millionaire like him. It's as private as you like. It would be a great place for . . . well, you know, the old bunga bunga.'

'And did he buy it?' Cangio asked.

The barman shrugged his shoulders again.

'How should I know?' he said, ringing up the bill. 'That's one euro eighty.'

Cangio paid, and turned to leave.

'I'll tell you one thing, though,' the barman called after him. 'I haven't seen too many half-dressed bunga-girls in *my* bar recently.'

FOURTEEN

Loredana was in the kitchen when he got home that evening.
'Hi, there, stranger,' she said, glancing over her shoulder.
He moved in close behind her, put his arms around her waist, kissed the back of her neck.

'Had a good day?' she asked him.

'It's looking better now,' he said. 'I've been running around, getting nowhere.'

'Lucky you!' she said, turning to face him, planting a kiss on his lips. 'I've been stuck in the shop all day. And now you've got me slaving in the kitchen, too.'

'What's on the menu tonight, then, chef?'

'Salad and steak,' she said. 'We're eating too much pasta.'

'It sounds good,' he said, sitting down to take off his work boots and woollen socks.

He padded through to the bedroom in his bare feet, put on a clean pair of socks, then slid into his 'slippers', a pair of Timberland moccasins he had bought ten years before while still at university. They fitted him like a glove, and were far too comfortable to throw away, though Lori often threatened to do just that. He would have grabbed those shoes if the house had been on fire.

Lori favoured her five-inch stilettos for getting out of a burning house.

'I'd wear those, and nothing else,' she always said. 'Can you imagine the fireman fighting to save me, naked except for my high heels?'

Cangio had no doubt the firemen would fight over her even if she were wearing rubber wellies and a shopping bag over her head. Loredana was a firefighter's dream.

'Can you start the barbecue?' she said, turning back to the salad bowl.

He took a bottle of red wine from the rack, carried it outside, popped the cork, then left the wine to breathe while he cleaned the barbecue grill with a wire brush, sprinkled charcoal nuggets into the tray, added a squeeze of lighter fuel, then struck a match.

Running around all day, and getting nowhere?

It was worse than that. He was like a truffle dog on a leash. Only one thing on his mind, and it wasn't truffles. That photograph he'd seen at the airport. The man in the cap stopping to light his cigarette. The mark on his neck . . .

Was it a tattoo, or wasn't it?

And what about that name written on the side of the van?

He hadn't seen a minibus with a sliding door in the car park at Villa San Francesco, though the lettering on the sign outside the gate had been . . . well, similar. Which proved nothing. Lucia Grossi would have wiped the floor with him if he'd told her what he thought he might have seen on that blurry airport photograph.

Until he laid his hands on something more solid, he decided, it would be best to keep quiet and say nothing.

But those thoughts would not go away. It was like a video-loop running through his brain, the man in the baseball cap coming out of the airport, a cigarette in his mouth, bending forward to meet the flame, exposing a tattoo – well, a *mark* on his neck – before he climbed into a waiting vehicle.

If it *was* a salamander, did it mean that something was going on in Umbria?

'How's the barbecue coming?'

Lori was laying the table under the porch.

'It'll be ready by the time we down a glass of wine,' he said.

It was early in the year to eat outside, but Loredana usually got what she wanted. If a romantic meal on a chilly evening was her idea of heaven, then he could go along with it.

He poured two glasses of wine, then sat down opposite her.

She dipped her finger in the wine, then licked it dry.

'Montefalco red,' she said. 'You like it?'

He took a sip, watching as she raised the glass to her lips.

'I see a lot of things I like,' he said.

She arched her eyebrows. 'Like what?'

He loved the way she was looking at him for a start. He knew what she was thinking, too. She wanted him to take that glass from her hand, plant his lips on hers, suck the soul out of her, carry her inside, then rip off her clothes like a kid unwrapping his Christmas presents.

That was what he *should* have done.

He wanted to do it, too.

But then the moment passed.

She looked away, and Cangio heard the words he was saying, almost unable to believe that they were coming out of his mouth.

'Have you heard of Villa San Francesco, Lori? It's an old monastery out near Ponte on the way to Rocchetta.'

She frowned at him. She hadn't been expecting a question like that one.

'*Dio santo*, Seb! You're sipping a wine the Gods would kill for, and you haven't even said it's good. What's going on inside your head?'

Yes, he could go along with it. What *was* going on in there?

He shrugged. 'Curiosity,' he said. 'I drove past there today, and wondered what it was.'

'What did you say it was called?'

'Villa San Francesco.'

Lori took another sip of wine. 'It sounds like the place where one of my mum's friends tried to park *her* mother. The old lady's ninety-eight, and drooling. They can't take care of her. She thought it might be a nursing home for OAPs.'

OAPs with a helicopter pad?

'Does anyone know of an OAP who's actually in care there?'

'How should I know?' Lori said offhandedly. 'You'd better turn those steaks over before they burn.'

Blue smoke was streaming out of the barbecue.

'Isn't it the old Franciscan monastery?' she said. 'When I was a kid, we used to picnic in those woods at weekends. The place was totally abandoned then.'

'Now it's looking good. They've put a lot of money into it.'

'Good for them,' she said, pouring more wine for both of them.

'It's quiet up there,' he said. 'A bit too isolated, though.'

'Why do the rich buy islands? Isolated's what they want.'

'These people come and go by helicopter . . .'

His voice trailed away like the sounds of the rotors passing over his head.

'That friend of your mum's . . .'

'What about her?'

'Did she send her mother to Villa San Francesco?'

Lori laughed. 'I doubt it very much. I mean to say, this woman's husband is a retired plumber. Do you know any plumbers with a helicopter? Keep an eye on that meat,' she warned him. 'I like mine rare.'

'Ask your mum if she's heard anything else, will you?'

She turned on him then, suddenly worried. 'Why are you so interested?'

He should have known it was coming. Every time he wanted to know something, and she didn't see the reason for it, she got worked up about it.

'I'm just curious,' he said as he speared a steak and laid it on a plate. They were big, fat Florentine steaks, five centimetres thick. This one was oozing blood. 'I think I'll wait a bit longer for mine,' he said.

'Are you thinking of sending me to Villa San Francesco when I'm past it?'

'I haven't got a helicopter, either,' he said. 'Still, maybe when the prize money arrives . . .'

'Which prize money?'

'You know, the Nobel . . .'

Lori raised her eyebrows at him, but she grinned as well.

'You'll walk off with it,' she said. 'There's no one else in your category.'

'Which category are we talking about?'

She bit into her steak and didn't reply.

Padova, Veneto

The black Mercedes C picked Professor Bianchi up at ten o'clock.

The driver in a dark suit opened the rear door without a word.

There was a glass partition between him and the chauffeur, but he was used to being ferried around in luxury vehicles. There was a bar cabinet – stocked with refrigerated water only. They weren't taking any chances, were they?

The windows were dark smoked glass. So dark, he could hardly see out of them. Lights and signs whizzed past in a faded blur as the car accelerated, and then they got onto the Mestre–Padova motorway, the spaghetti junctions throwing his sense of direction.

Were they heading north or south, east or west?

He settled down in the corner and read through the draft of the paper on shockwave treatment he was planning to give in Malaysia at the end of the month, forgetting all about the road and the drive. He made notes in the margin with his favourite fountain pen, the one the association traditionally presented to a new president, a platinum Mont Blanc engraved with his name.

He only spoke to the driver twice.

The glass partition came down with a subdued electronic *ping-ping-ping*.

'You left your phone at home, sir?'

'Of course.'

An hour later, the glass came down again.

'Do we need to make a rest stop, sir?'

'How much further?'

'Just over an hour, sir.'

'I'll be all right, thank you.'

After that, he closed his eyes and slept for a while.

It was a strange experience, like being carried off by kidnappers, not knowing where they were taking you, or whether they would be bringing you back. More like a dream than any reality he had ever known.

Valnerina

Lori's head settled heavily on his shoulder.

Cangio kissed the tip of her nose, then pushed his mouth against hers.

'Don't start messing about,' she warned him, though she didn't pull away.

He ran his hand along her jaw, nuzzled her neck, then kissed her throat.

'I've been working hard all day while you've been gallivanting.'

'Gallivanting? I've been working, too,' he protested, his hand on her breast.

'You call what you do work? Walking around in the woods all day?'

He didn't answer, pulling the sheet away, reaching down towards her . . .

That was when the phone rang.

'Let it ring,' Lori whispered in his ear.

Cangio thought of Dino De Angelis. Had something else happened up there?

'I have to answer it,' he said. 'It might be an emergency.'

He rolled away, sat naked on the edge of the bed, picked up the phone.

'Cangio here.'

'Have you heard from Desmond Harris?'

There were no preliminaries, no apology for disturbing him at home at such a late hour. Lucia Grossi sounded nervous, edgy.

He glanced at Lori, mouthed the word *work*.

'Why would Harris phone me?' he said.

'I haven't heard a word from London. I'm in and out of the office all day. I hoped he might have called you.'

'I would have let you know, wouldn't I?'

Lucia Grossi was silent for a moment, taking it in.

Lori watched him, drawing a question mark in the air with her finger.

'Which means he hasn't bothered getting in touch with you, *either.'*

'That just about sums it up, Captain Grossi,' Cangio said, naming her for Lori's benefit.

'They're up to something . . . I wonder what it is.'

Was this the paranoid side of her character coming out? Hey, babe, he felt like telling her, if you want to be paranoid, try doing it when I'm not in bed with my girlfriend, OK? Instead, he kept quiet, wondering where this was leading.

'Cristo santo! They should have identified him by now. They've got the pic from Nora's phone. They've got the airport videos. What else do they need?'

Cangio looked at Lori again, rolled his hand helplessly in the air.

'We're pretty certain that he didn't go back to England. Not from Assisi, that's for sure. He may have left from some other airport, of course, but my men haven't turned up a thing. Do you know what I think?'

She left him hanging, waiting for a response.

'What do you think?'

'He's still here. He's still in Italy.'

OK, he thought, the guy's still in Italy, but where do I come into it?

'We need to find him.'

You need to find him, Cangio thought.

'They must have been sleeping somewhere. Probably in Valnerina, or why go to that particular restaurant? They were staying somewhere close by, that's my take on it. We need to drop a brick in the pool, then work our way outwards, following the ripples. I want you to draw up a list of places where they may have stayed. You know the area better than anyone, Seb. I'm thinking of bed-and-breakfasts, holiday flats, caravan sites . . . Oh yes, the letting agencies, too. My men will be checking all the hotels, sending out faxes with photos and descriptions, but I think it would be a better strategy if you took care of the Valnerina scene. Do you think you can handle it?'

'I've got so many things to do in the park.'

'I've already cleared it with the park director, Alberto Bruni. You'll be seconded to me for the moment, so put everything else on hold, OK?'

I'm the boss, that's what she was saying, you take orders from *me.*

And then the final order came.

'Meet me by the Sant'Anatolia tunnel at noon tomorrow. There's a bar with a car park, according to the satellite. That should leave you plenty of time to come up with that list. All clear?'

'All clear,' he said. 'Tomorrow at noon.'

Captain Grossi put the phone down, and Cangio turned back to Lori.

'What the hell does she want?' Loredana asked.

'She needs a hand,' Cangio said, playing it down.

Lori looked at him, reaching out to caress him.

'So do I,' she said.

Arrival, 01.20

A short, plump man in a white coat was waiting at the front door.

'So glad that you've arrived,' he said, offering his hand. 'Just follow me, please.'

The man turned away, walking straight into a wall of darkness.

Smart lighting flashed on, illuminating a long, wide corridor as they went along it.

He felt as though the past – his own professional life, his international reputation, his only daughter, Marisa, and all the other things that he held dear in life – were disappearing in the darkening void that he left behind him.

He was confused already, had no idea where he was.

He could have been anywhere in Italy.

Everything had looked the same through the smoked-glass windows of the car.

'Did you have a good journey? Not too much traffic? Not too long?'

The man didn't stop, turn around, or seem to expect any answer to his questions.

Were they questions?

Above their heads, the heavy stone vaulting was like the ceiling of a church, though the walls on either side of the corridor were plastered, recently painted, a smooth expanse of marble floor stretching away beneath their feet. A number of doors opened off to left and right, but all the doors were closed, and what lay behind them was a mystery.

Framed posters hung at intervals on the walls, sepia photographs of vintage racing yachts in modern red frames. There were no names, no titles, no indication of where or when or why the pictures might have been taken. Everything was bright and new, the air lightly tinged with perfumed disinfectant, with red fire extinguishers dotted here and there along the corridor like Grenadier Guards on parade.

It was more impressive than he had expected, a model of organisation and cleanliness.

Suddenly, the man stopped in front of a door.

'You'll find everything you need in there. The item was delivered half an hour ago by helicopter. You may have seen it while you were driving up.' The little man suppressed a titter, as if he might have just said something very funny. 'The helicopter, I mean,' he said by way of explanation. 'Did you see it?'

He had seen only trees and bushes in the night coming up the
drive, and then only dimly from behind the darkened windows
of the Mercedes.

'I didn't see a thing,' he said.

It seemed wiser to say nothing.

And yet, there were things that needed to be said.

'Will I be seeing . . . anyone else while I'm here, apart from
yourself?' he asked.

'That won't be necessary,' the man said, as he opened the
door and stepped aside like a valet. 'The staff are ready and
waiting for you. You'll find all the documentation on your desk.
Now, that's everything, I think. If you should need anything,
anything at all, just pick up the phone, and I'll be along in no
time.'

He nodded towards the door and waved his hand, inviting him
to enter.

'Your room, sir,' he announced.

Your room . . .

As if he were an honoured guest who had been there before.
A guest who was likely to return. Well, he had already come to
a decision on that score. This would be the one and only time
he would ever come to this institution. If all went well, he would
never see it again, nor even know the name of the place.

If all went well . . .

That thought frightened the life out of him.

He knew what he had been promised if everything went
according to plan.

But what would happen if something went wrong?

He dared not allow himself to even think of that possibility.

As soon as it was done, he would phone Marisa, tell her that
his speaking engagement had been cancelled, make some excuse.
More than anything in the world, he wanted just to hear her
voice, and know that she was safe.

What a party they would make of it when she got what she
was hoping for! How proud he would be of his only daughter
who had climbed to the top of the dung-heap at the tender age
of twenty-nine! And all thanks to him . . .

He would have to be careful. He would need to clamp down
on his joy, make sure he didn't give anything away. One careless
word said in anger – 'Don't be so ungrateful, my dear,' or 'You'll

never know how much it cost me, Marisa' – was all it would take to bring the house of cards tumbling down.

Ungrateful for what, *Papà? How much did* what *cost you?*

Everything must go without a hitch. Marisa would be no wiser. And he would cancel all memory of this night, the telephone calls which had brought him to this place, and led him to do what he was about to do.

'Is the room to your liking?'

Spot-lamps let artfully into the ceiling threw a cone of light on a dark modern desk, which seemed to float like an island on a calm marble sea. An ultra-slim computer, a phone sitting next to it, a series of folders neatly arranged like a fan of cards. The room was large, the walls a delicate shade of pastel green. A back-lit monitor for viewing large transparencies hung on the wall immediately behind the desk and chair.

'You'll find everything you need in those folders.'

There were four or five folders, each one a different colour.

He had never worked this way before. Trusting other people's data, using other experts' documents and appraisals, without actually seeing and examining the subject and reaching his own conclusions.

'How long do I have?' he asked, slipping off his jacket.

'Just lift up the telephone, as I said before, and I'll take you into the arena, so to speak, the place of combat . . . Will half an hour be enough, do you think? In the meantime, we can start the preliminary procedures.'

'Half an hour . . . that should be fine.'

The place of combat, the arena . . .

Those expressions rattled his nerves. He felt like a gladiator being oiled and greased before the fighting began. He would need to prepare himself, be on his guard, know exactly what to do, and what to avoid doing. One false move and a gladiator bit the dust. What was it they said when they entered the arena and bowed low before the Emperor and the Senate?

Ave, Caesar, morituri te salutant.

He would be the one who must die if anything went wrong.

'I'll leave you to it, then. Just call me as soon as you are ready.'

The door closed.

For an instant he was tempted to call the man back, demand

to be taken to the nearest railway station. He would make his own way home, go on foot if necessary, find his way through the woods and over the mountains. Anything just to get out of there. To be as far away as possible from that place.

Morituri te salutant . . .

They would kill him, and he knew it.

Would they kill Marisa, too?

He sat down at the desk, switched on the computer, opened the first paper folder while the computer was booting up, then took out his Mont Blanc. He would take all the time that he needed, he thought defiantly. He would examine all the documents, make extensive notes, and fully assess the situation. Then, when he was ready, he would do the job with all the skill at his disposal, with a steady hand and without fear.

For Marisa, he would have done it with his eyes closed.

Forty minutes later, he was ready, more or less.

He didn't realise that his Mont Blanc fountain pen was nestling in the fluffy carpet beneath the desk.

FIFTEEN

Monte Coscerno

The wolves came loping down the hill.

There were only five of them.

The second-generation cub had been left behind.

The wound had started to stink.

He couldn't stand on his left hind leg any more, couldn't run or chase or hunt.

The young wolf was dying, and they all knew it.

By the time they returned, he would probably be dead.

It was the start of the warm season, but food was still scarce.

The female was going to need meat, and plenty of it. She was heavy and slow now, her movements hampered by the weight of the cubs she was carrying in her womb. Within a week or two there would be more hungry mouths to feed.

Three or four mouths, maybe even more.

They were heading further into the valley in search of food, steering clear of farms and hen houses they had raided during the winter, spreading the net wider and wider with each hunting expedition. The male, the female, and the second-generation cub had been that way the year before. The dense wood that cloaked the lower slopes of Monte Galluro was alive with badgers, voles, rats, field mice, sometimes deer. There would be wild boar, too, but it was better to avoid them. Boars were formidable enemies, well-armed with short, sharp tusks and long, sharp claws.

The light ground mist was perfect for hunting.

They entered the wood with caution, taking a meandering path through the trees, staying upwind, closing in on any possible prey. There was a rabbit warren down near the empty farmhouse, and no smell of humans.

Despite their hunger, they went forward slowly.

There might be other prey to satisfy their needs.

There could be other dangers – hunters, or the traps that hunters left behind them.

They were spread out in a half-moon formation, ready to move in on anything which fell inside the trap, the order hierarchical, the male in the centre, the younger wolves on either side, the female on the left point. He would give the signal, he would attack, and the others would close in like a pincer, cutting off any avenue of escape. The only hope would be to turn and run, and there weren't many animals that could outrun a pack of hungry, hunting wolves.

As they moved through the wood, the male scented something.

He slowed his pace, ears held back, eyes narrowed, tail stretched out behind him.

The rest of the family followed him instinctively, all muzzles pointing directly ahead.

There was something in the air, a stink which drew him on, though it held him back, as well. There was also an odour that he knew.

Fresh blood . . .

Suddenly, he stopped, his hackles raised, his ears erect, growling deep down in his throat.

The others stopped, too, the young ones looking left and right, learning the meaning of fear.

The growling went on and on, for minutes on end.

The blood was fresh, the smell was strong.

But there was that stink as well, something sour and sweaty . . .

He turned and ran, his tail between his legs.

The others scurried after him.

If they found nothing going back, there'd be fresh meat waiting at the den.

Wolf eat wolf . . .

It was the only way to survive.

Cangio was up at first light, working on his laptop, chasing addresses.

He drank a pot of coffee and cursed Grossi frequently as he put together the list that she wanted. Who would have imagined that there were so many people in Valnerina offering overnight or short-term accommodation? The area was dotted with bed and breakfast places, hostels, farm-holidays, and country houses, to say nothing of caravan and camping sites.

Plus the letting agencies, of course.

When he had finished, he checked the Villa San Francesco website, as well.

Not that there was very much to see. A single page, a slideshow of photographs. One side of the building slowly dissolving into a similar view of another wing. Four similar slides, then the first one came round again. There was nothing about the history of the building, nothing about the church and its restoration, and the Franciscan monks didn't even merit a mention.

The home-page overlay never changed, either. Villa San Francesco. *Contacts*. Little flags offered a choice of languages: English, French, Spanish, or Italian.

He clicked on the Italian flag, then *Contact*.

A new page appeared.

It was spartan, monastic, the colour of aged whitewash.

There were three rectangular boxes marked *Nome, Email, Messaggio*.

He returned to the home page, chose English, then clicked *Contact* again.

The same page appeared, the same three empty boxes: *Name, Email, Message*.

There was no telephone number, no name, no way of contacting Villa San Francesco except by means of an email message.

He went back to the Italian page, wrote Lori's name and surname in the box, her Gmail address in the second box, then composed a message: *Villa S.F. was recommended by a dear friend. My husband and I wish to book a double room for 2 nights (Fri & Sat, 24 & 25) at the end of this month? Can you send the current rates, please?*

He hit the *Send* button, wondering what would come back.

The request for information sounded innocent enough.

With a couple of hours to kill before meeting Lucia Grossi, he drove through the Sant' Anatolia tunnel to Spoleto, and called in at the Land and Property registration office down by the station.

'Innocent' was not the word he would have used to describe the woman behind the desk.

She was in her forties, going on twenty-one, wearing a low-cut flowery dress with a push-up bra. Squashed together like two large plums, her breasts looked primed to attack any man who walked in through the door. A pageboy haircut and dyed red hair didn't help. A diamond button gleamed in her nose. Matching diamond studs sparkled in her ears. She had a teasing smile, and a certain wanton look in her eyes.

'Nice uniform,' she said, and he felt uncomfortable.

Was she imagining what he would look like without it?

'Park ranger?' she asked.

'That's right . . .'

'Out in the woods all day, helping damsels in distress?'

She goggled at him, as if expecting witty repartee in exchange for this gem.

It brought back memories of flirtatious chatter on quiet afternoons in the estate agent's office on Islington High Street when he'd been working in London.

He took out his mobile phone, checked for messages, found none, as he had expected.

'Well, then,' she said, sounding a bit like Jessica Rabbit, 'what can I do you for?'

'I'm here about a property,' he said, refusing to play. 'A monastery in Valnerina. They call it Villa San Francesco.'

'Thinking of buying it, are you?'

He ignored the question. 'It's outside Borgo Cerreto on the road between Ponte and Rocchetta.'

She pulled a form from a wall-rack. 'You don't belong to a professional association, do you? Surveyor, architect, that sort of thing? No, I didn't think so,' she said. 'You've got that fresh air look about you. The dust gets stuck in their wrinkles, know what I mean?'

She laid the form on the counter, pointed a painted fingernail at it.

'You'll need to fill this in.'

As he pulled out a pen, rested his elbow on the counter, and started to answer the questions, he heard her breathing somewhere close above his head. He lifted his eyes, caught sight of those breasts, and tried to write faster. He could imagine an army of junior clerks fighting for the chance to go to the L&P registration office.

'All done?' She turned the paper around, propped her elbows on the counter, and read what he had written. 'Sebastiano Cangio? That's an unusual name . . .'

'I'm from the south,' he said. 'We have a lot of unusual names down there. Provenzano, Riina, Denaro. You may have heard of them.'

They were the names of the three most notorious Mafia bosses of the decade.

'Can't say I have,' she said with a pout. Then, with a show of lifting a great weight, she stood up straight, and flashed another smile at him. 'I'll see what I can do for you.'

Five minutes later, she came back with a copy of the *visura catastale*. In the name of transparency, the Ministry of Finances had made it easy for any interested party to verify the ownership of a building. All buildings were registered for tax purposes, which meant that just about anyone could obtain a copy of the most recent layout of any building in the whole of Italy. Breaking-and-entering was on the increase. More important from his point of view, the *visura catastale* contained the name of the registered owner.

'International Enterprises S.p.A.,' he read. 'A limited company. Can you tell me anything about them?'

'I wish I could,' the woman said, 'but I've never heard of them. You'll need to check their name with the local Chamber of Commerce. There's one in every town.'

'Which Chamber of Commerce?' he asked, turning the paper towards her.

She glanced at the details, frowned at him, then looked down at the paper again.

'It should be written here,' she said, 'but it isn't.'

'So, who can I ask?'

'You could start with the people at Villa San Francesco,' she said. 'Otherwise, you'll need to ask the police.'

Was *he* the police, he asked himself?

He'd been seconded to the *carabinieri*, according to Lucia Grossi, but he wasn't sure that being seconded gave him any effective police power.

'Thanks for your help,' he said as he folded the paper and put it in his pocket.

'Any time, my sweet,' she said. 'I'm always here.'

Padova, Veneto

His daughter rang that morning.

'*Papà! Papà!*'

Marisa was so excited, she began to sob. She couldn't get the words out, couldn't tell him what he already knew.

'You got the job, then?'

'*How did you guess, Papà?*'

He had been paid in cash before they sent him home. A large padded envelope waiting on the rear seat of the Mercedes. He had counted out the notes more than once on the return journey. How often did you get to touch a hundred thousand euro? Having kept their word on that score, he had known that they would keep their word on this score, too.

'Oh, a hundred thousand reasons, my dear,' the Professor laughed. 'Though one reason stands out above all the others.'

Marisa sniffed. '*Which reason, Papà?*'

'What other reason could there be?' he said, dallying with her now. 'Why, because you're the best, of course! I knew you'd beat the others into the dust, no matter how well qualified or well connected they might have seemed.'

Marisa laughed. '*You did have a word with someone, didn't you, Papà?*'

'Me? A word? What use are words?'

Powerful friends were far more useful.

'Go out and celebrate, my dear,' he said. 'I'll call you on Friday.'

'*As usual*,' she said.

'As *always*, Marisa,' he said, putting special emphasis on the word, just in case he ever needed to use her as an alibi. 'As *always* . . .'

He hoped – no, prayed – that *that* was the end of that.

He had been very lucky, and he knew it.

The slightest hitch, and Marisa might have been attending his funeral.

Only one thing was niggling him now.

A minor nuisance, but a nuisance all the same.

He couldn't find his platinum Mont Blanc . . .

Valnerina

Seb Cangio had been waiting for ten minutes in the Sant'Anatolia car park.

Then a gleaming, new Alpha Romeo V6 pulled in beside his battered Land Rover.

Midnight-blue with go-faster streaks and *CARABINIERI* written on the flank, the Alpha announced the fact that Captain Lucia Grossi, head of the Special Crimes Squad, had finally arrived in Valnerina.

What surprised him most was that she had come alone. She had no driver, no junior officer to bully. Except for him, of course. Was this his new job? Was this his foreseeable future? Running around after Lucia Grossi?

He held the door open as she climbed out of the driver's seat.

'That's quite a car,' he said, uncertain of his role, deciding on chummy informality.

'Zero to a one-twenty in four-point-three seconds,' she said, running her hand along the bonnet the way she might have petted a prized greyhound. 'To be honest, Seb, the best thing about it is the way that other drivers skedaddle to make space for you.'

She was calling him Seb, not Ranger Cangio.

Maybe it wasn't going to be too bad.

'By the way, did I thank you for looking after Inspector Harris?' she said.

He could have told her that she hadn't, but he skipped it, and she didn't thank him anyway, as if mere mention of the fact that she might have thanked was more than sufficient.

'On that note, is there any news from London?' he asked her.

She pursed her lips and looked unhappy. Clearly, Scotland Yard was not living up to her expectations. Was that why she was taking such a personal interest in the case of the missing Englishman, hoping to come up with something which she could slap triumphantly in Harris's face when he did decide to give her a call?

If he ever bothered, Cangio thought.

Having got its pound of flesh, Scotland Yard might never be heard from again.

'We had no luck with the hotels this morning,' she said. '*I* would have phoned you if we had found something. Which leaves us with alternative forms of accommodation . . . This list of yours?'

He patted the note in his breast pocket. 'There aren't as many as I thought.'

'That is good news,' she said. 'But there's something we need to do first.'

A captain's rank sat well on her shoulders. She handed out orders and compliments in the same breath. He recalled how irritating she had been when she was still trying to make her mark. She seemed less aggressive now, more confident, almost likeable. And she had taken a bullet that was meant for him. He could never forget that.

'What have you got in mind?'

'We need to take a formal statement from the witness that you found,' she said.

'Which witness?' he said, though he knew who she was on about.

'The waitress, Nora. You didn't ask her anything, didn't take any notes. No surname, address, or phone number. You seem to have missed a lot of things. Desmond Harris told me all about it. He had a wonderful time, he said. You walked into a restaurant, played at being customers, ordered a meal, and struck gold. Now that's not what *I* would call grilling a witness.'

'We asked the right questions, and Nora gave us that picture. We didn't need to "grill" her.'

He had been about to say: *What more do you want?*

'She might remember more if she saw someone in a decent uniform. Shall we get moving? My car, of course.'

Ten minutes later, they drew up outside Il Covo del Pescatore.

There was no one on the premises apart from Nora, who was working in the kitchen, ironing tablecloths. 'Our day of rest,' the girl explained, grimacing ruefully at the ironing-board.

As they sat down at a table in the dining room, Cangio smiled to himself, recalling what Gross had said about 'decent' uniforms. All three of them were wearing uniforms. Lucia Grossi's was dark blue with red stripes running down the sides of her trousers, while he was sporting the slate-grey cotton combat-suit of a park policeman. Nora, in a blue-and-white striped apron, stared morosely at Lucia Grossi across the table.

'I gave him the photo, told him everything I remember,' she said.

'I'm sure you did,' Lucia Grossi nodded, 'but memory's a funny thing, Nora. It's often much sharper as time passes. I was wondering about one thing. Are you absolutely certain you had never seen them around before?' She twirled a finger in the air. 'Not just here in the restaurant, but somewhere else in Valnerina.'

Nora drank some water from a bottle.

'Nah,' she said. 'I only saw them in here.'

'One of them had been here twice, you told my colleague. What about the other one?'

'What about him?'

'You must see lots of people every day,' she said. 'You probably notice things without even realising you've seen them. So, let's try a little experiment. I'll ask you a question, and I'd like you to answer me with the first word, or words, that come into your head. Do you understand me?'

Nora looked at her as if she was mad.

'OK,' she said with a shrug. 'Whatever.'

'Those two men, the Englishmen. Which one was the boss?'

'The boss?'

'Who was in control of the situation, in your opinion?'

Nora gave herself a moment to think.

'The thin one,' she said.

'Why do you say that, Nora?'

'Well, he did all the speaking. The other one just listened.'

'Did he speak Italian, then?'

Nora smiled. 'He thought he did, but I didn't get a word of it. I made him point out what he wanted on the menu.'

'The one who . . . tried to speak Italian. How many times did he come here?'

'He was the one who came back the second time,' she said. 'He gave me the big tip.'

Lucia Grossi nodded, cutting in on her. 'OK, Nora, that's good. But now, we need to talk about the other man. The one you only saw once. The first time that they came in here, did you noticed anything special about him?'

'Special?'

'Something which seemed odd to you.'

Had Grossi been attending a special course on interrogation, Cangio asked himself. The interview was getting stranger by the minute.

Nora looked at her and smiled again. 'It's funny you should say that,' she said. 'There was something. I noticed it while I was serving him. He had this . . . well, this . . . funny smell. You know, the way some men always use the same deodorant or aftershave?'

'A brand that you can name, is that it?'

Nora shook her head. 'Nah, it wasn't a perfume, nothing like that.'

'What was it, then?'

The waitress pursed her lips. 'You know . . . like cleaning fluid. A *clean* smell, not soap exactly, but sort of a . . . chemical smell. It was that kind of smell. As I was going through the menu with him, I could smell it on his hands and clothes.'

They got no more from Nora after that, nothing that Cangio hadn't heard already

'A chemical smell?' he said in the car park.

Grossi shrugged. 'It's more than we had before.' Then she laughed. 'You don't think he's an undertaker, do you?'

'There are plenty of those in every town in Umbria,' Cangio said.

'Or someone who does a job where they have to wash their hands a lot?'

'Maybe he'd used the soap dispenser in the toilet, and hadn't rinsed his hands properly?'

'Thank you, Cangio,' Grossi said, a note of irritation creeping into her voice. If questions had to be asked, then she was going to ask them. 'Now, let's make a start on your list of B&Bs.'

Cangio waited while she phoned Perugia and issued orders.

He didn't like being seconded to the *carabinieri*. The idea of being ordered about by the likes of Lucia Grossi for the rest of his life was a definite turn-off. Parliament had voted to reduce the number of Italian police forces from five to four, so park rangers would soon be members of the *carabinieri*. Would they – would *she* – leave him in peace to watch over the wolves, or would his job turn into nothing more than chasing illegal immigrants and guarding regional borders?

'OK, I'm ready,' she said, putting away her phone.

Cangio hesitated, as an idea flashed through his mind.

'Can I make a proposal?' he asked her.

That raised a smile. 'But we've only just met, Seb,' she said.

'Usually, I only ask on a second date,' he shot back.

She stared at him for a moment. 'OK, so what's this proposal?'

'Can we look at a place that isn't on my list? It's not far from here.'

'What sort of place are you thinking of?' she asked him with a frown.

'A place where your uniform may work some wonders.'

Monte Coscerno

The younger wolves were starving now, mulling over the bones.

They had picked them raw, and now they were cracking the rib cage, snapping the vertebrae, crunching gristle, sucking at the meagre marrow.

They knew they should go hunting – the female, their mother, was growing dangerously weak – but they were too afraid to leave the open ground near the den, the gaping hole in the mound that would hide them.

Cangio would have puzzled over what was troubling them, but he wasn't there to see it.

The lead male snapped at the younger males, growling and lurching at them, feinting bites and baring his teeth.

They needed fresh meat, or all of them would die.

And yet the hungrier they were, the less they seemed to heed him.

He had tried by example a number of times, turning away, showing them his tail, pointing his nose in the direction of the valley, trotting a few steps, then stopping, looking back, but none of them would follow him.

Not one.

They carried on crunching bones, as if the bones would fill their empty stomachs.

He tried again, head down, ears back, showing them his teeth again, growling fiercely.

They huddled close together, pulling back from the scattered remains of their brother, but still they ignored him.

In the end, he turned away in despair and went off hunting alone.

A lone wolf on the mountainside.

He would need all of his resources to survive.

SIXTEEN

Lucia Grossi skidded to a halt on the gravel.

The car park was empty that afternoon, Cangio noted. Grossi donned her cap with its flaming gold torch badge and silver braid above the gleaming black peak as they approached the door.

'They wouldn't let you in, you say? Let's see how they react to a *carabiniere* in full battle dress.'

She pressed her finger on the call button, and held it there.

'*Yes?*'

'*Carabinieri*,' Captain Grossi announced.

There was a moment of silence.

'*What can I do for you?*'

'I wish to see the director,' she said, her mouth close to the speaker. She was wearing a bright red lipstick that wouldn't take no for an answer.

'*I'm sorry, but the director isn't here today.*'

Grossi darted a glance at Cangio, then looked up into the

surveillance camera. 'No matter,' she said. 'The person in charge will do.'

There was another drawn-out silence.

'I'll call the administrative secretary, in that case.'

'That's very kind,' Lucia Grossi said, and a smile played at the corners of her mouth.

They hadn't been standing there a minute when there was a sharp electronic click and the door swung back. A small, plump man in a white hospital coat was standing in a cone of neon light.

Lucia Grossi took three steps forward.

The man in white stepped back two paces.

Cangio followed her in, content to leave the invasion to the heavy brigade.

'Captain Lucia Grossi,' she said, clicking her heels, and touching the peak of her cap. 'The admin man, I presume?'

The man looked uncomfortable, but nodded yes.

'We're making enquiries about a person who seems to have disappeared.' Her eyes took in the man's clean white cotton overall, looking for a name badge, perhaps. 'And this is a . . . a hospital, something of the sort, or so we've been told. Isn't that correct, Cangio?' She turned to him, playing the part. 'We were wondering whether he might have been admitted as a patient.'

The man took in her uniform. He might have felt like pushing her out of the door, but it was too late now. 'Villa San Francesco is a . . . a private clinic, let's say. Not a hospital, as such. Our patients are referred to us by outside consultants. We don't cater to the general public, and . . . and no one's undergoing treatment at the moment. This is a very *exclusive* facility . . .'

'Offering what?' she asked him bluntly.

The man was twenty centimetres shorter than she was, twenty centimetres wider, too.

He peered back at her. 'Well, we offer a wide variety of services,' he said. 'The sort of thing the national health service won't handle. You know, regenerative and preventive therapy. A health spa with heated pools, a Turkish bath and sauna, hot stone therapy, a fully equipped rehabilitation centre. We also offer reconstruction . . .'

'What's reconstruction?' Cangio asked.

The man smiled, more sure of himself with the man in the

less intimidating uniform. He lowered his voice, as if the female *carabiniere* might be offended by what he was about to say. 'You know, facial enhancement, breast implants, liposuction, laser surgery for the removal of moles, unwanted hair. That sort of thing.'

'Cosmetic surgery,' Lucia Grossi said.

Not a question, though the man said yes again.

'May I see your register?' she asked. 'I'm sure you keep an up-to-date list of the poor unfortunates that you cut and snip.'

The man looked down at the tiles. 'I'd be happy to show you,' he said, 'but that . . . well, it's beyond my power. You'll have to speak with the director.'

'I may be back with a search warrant,' Grossi warned him.

The man looked up. 'I'd show you if I could, *capitano*. The registers, the patients' files, the surgical permission slips, and so on, they're all kept under lock and key. The privacy laws are very strict on that score.' He looked apologetic. 'I'm sorry, really, but I don't have access to the personal or staff records.'

Lucia Grossi waved her hand as if to say that it didn't matter. She turned away, looking around the entrance hall. 'It's nothing like the austere monastic setting that I was expecting. No hint of prayers, or meditation, no Franciscan asceticism. It may look like a church from the outside, but in here it seems almost *too* modern.'

Coming through the front door was like stepping out of a distant past into a distant future. With the aid of plasterboard moulding and suffused neon lighting, the reception area had been transformed into an oval model of startling design with multiple mirrors which gave a sense of infinite vastness.

'It looks better than the most exclusive spas in the south of France,' Lucia Grossi said.

'The sanitation regulations are very demanding, as I'm sure you know. It was easier to totally renovate the interior than to patch up what was here before. This monastery was a total ruin before we took it over. Now, of course, everything conforms to the very highest medical standards.'

'Could you show us quickly?' Lucia Grossi cut him off in full flow. 'We won't take much of your time. It's just . . . well,' she laughed, and patted the breast of her uniform jacket, 'you never know in this bloody job. Stodgy food, irregular hours, sitting around all day in the most uncomfortable cars and rickety office chairs. I may be back for a bit of a lift myself before you know it.'

Cangio had to admire her pluck. She was ready to play down her authority and belittle her looks if it helped her to find what she was looking for.

The man gave a weak smile, but he buckled.

'Well, I . . . I can't show you much,' he said, waving his hand to the corridor behind him. 'The surgical wing and the spa are strictly off-limits for obvious reasons. Outside clothes carry germs . . .'

'What about the medical staff?' Cangio put in.

'We work with top consultants in the field,' the man said. 'Top-class patients, too. You know, film stars, TV personalities, people like that.'

'Is there anyone that we would know?' Grossi asked him with an innocent smile.

The man looked startled. 'I . . . well, I can't really mention names. It's more than my job is worth. You know, privacy, professional standards. Whenever we have a patient list, we call in specialist nursing and technical staff . . .'

'So you're a sort of caretaker, are you?' Lucia Grossi asked.

'That's right.'

'And your name is?'

'Alfredo,' the man replied. 'Alfredo del Buono.'

'We won't waste any more of your time, Signor del Buono. As I told you, we're looking for a missing person, and it's obvious that he isn't here.' She turned to Cangio. 'Next stop, the hospital in Norcia.'

Wasn't she getting out of there a bit too quickly? Cangio wondered. All they'd seen was an empty reception area, and a long corridor studded with closed doors to rooms that were off-limits.

She took his arm, and turned towards the exit.

'Many thanks for your help, Signor del Buono.'

The door closed behind them when they were halfway across the car park.

'Did you notice, Seb? There was no one else in the reception area. There's a smart desk, computers and monitors, an intercom for speaking to whoever rings the bell. Mr Don't-Know-A-Thing looks after that massive place all by himself.'

Instead of heading for the car, she suddenly cut left off the gravel and onto the grass.

'Let's see what's around the back,' she said.

It was a long walk in the cold shadows beneath the high walls of the monastery.

'There must have been a hundred monks living here once . . .'

She caught him by the arm, and held him back as they reached the corner. She peeped out from the wall, then stepped back into the shadows. 'Signor del Buono isn't all alone,' she said. 'You're the ranger, Cangio, what do you make of this?'

Cangio edged beyond the wall.

There was a fourth section to the convent, a large arched doorway in the centre, twenty or thirty windows set high in the ancient stone wall. Close to the door was an area which had been fenced off with wire mesh over two metres high. Inside the compound a large man was made to look even larger by the blue padded body-armour he was wearing on his arms and legs.

Three dogs lay stretched out on the grass in front of him.

They were full-grown Rottweilers, each one weighing up to forty kilos or more.

'Attack!' the man cried, and the three dogs bounded at him, two of them grabbing hold of his padded legs, while the third one sank its teeth into his padded right arm.

'Stay!' he shouted, and the dogs let go of him, and returned immediately to their positions of repose.

'What are the guard dogs for?' Cangio murmured.

'Protecting property, seeing off thieves? I bet they have some valuable equipment.'

'Well-heeled patients, too,' he said, pointing to the empty helicopter landing pad.

'Film stars with fat bums? Let's put a question mark next to this place.'

She turned and walked away quickly, saying, 'It's time to check out that list of yours, Cangio. I'd like to see where the ordinary mortals sleep in Valnerina.'

Scheggino, Valnerina

'Is *this* what you people do?'

Lucia Grossi pulled the ledger across the desk, and stared at it.

'Three one-week rentals, and spring just around the corner? What would you call it, Cangio? Cooking the books?'

Cangio remembered drinking coffee one day with Diego Rabitti in the company of Marzio Diamante, the senior ranger, who had known the rental agent a long time.

Rabitti was staring hard at Cangio now, a question burning in his eyes.

How dangerous is this woman?

Lucia Grossi had let Rabitti talk, spinning them a line about hard times, then she'd poleaxed him, and the casual conversation had suddenly flipped into a full-scale interrogation. Diego Rabitti, owner of Long & Short Term Lets, was walking on a bed of rusty nails.

'That *isn't* what I meant, signora . . .'

'Captain,' Lucia Grossi clarified. 'Captain Grossi of the SCS.'

'What's the SCS?' Rabitti asked her.

'The Special Crimes Squad.'

Cangio would have sworn that Rabitti's face changed colour, trying to blend in with the pale-yellow wallpaper at his back. Grossi noticed his discomfort, and pressed on mercilessly. 'Doesn't *anyone* in Valnerina keep honest accounts?'

'Your business doesn't concern us, Signor Rabitti,' Cangio put in, trying to pick up the pieces. 'We're simply trying to find the two men who appear in that photograph that we showed you. Any help in that respect would be appreciated.'

Rabitti ignored the peace offering

'Those names are all I've got,' he protested. 'There aren't that many holidaymakers about . . .' His face lit up like an exhausted swimmer who had spotted a life-raft. 'And the ones who *are* . . . you should try the hotels. Their prices are ridiculously low at this time of year. We can't compete, believe me. *Madonna santa!* I'd love to know how *they* get away with it.'

Rabitti was grabbing at sodden straws. He wasn't worried about a park ranger who kept a tab on newborn lambs and rampaging foxes. You could always spread a bit of dirt about the two-faced bastard in the valley. The problem was the female *carabiniere*. OK, a woman, but a senior one. She could get you into a cartload of trouble.

'Forget the hotels,' Lucia Grossi said. 'We've covered those already. Only the bigger ones are open this early in the holiday season. No sweat there, but no results, either.'

She sat back in her seat, and threaded her fingers into a mace, her thumb on her lower lip, the way she had done with Cangio six months before in Perugia, fully convinced that he had fired the twin-barrelled twelve-bore that had taken off Marzio Diamante's head.

Now she turned that stone-cold stare on Diego Rabitti.

'Did you rent a house or a flat to two English visitors last week?'

She seemed to give off sparks, seemed poised to slam a warrant down on the agent's desk and cart him off to serve a mandatory life sentence.

Rabitti was sweating, though the question had been innocent enough.

She hadn't asked him if he had murdered one or both of them.

She sat back in her seat and let out a loud sigh.

'If you are playing games with me, Rabitti, I swear to God, you'll never rent so much as a pigsty to a homeless pig for the rest of your life.'

'I've never seen them, I swear!'

'This is an important investigation,' Cangio said, trying to take the edge off Grossi's ire.

'If you didn't rent them a place,' Grossi insisted, 'then someone did. And you know who. You can help us, and help yourself at the same time.'

Rabitti looked from him to her, then he grabbed a pen, tore a sheet of paper from the Samsung printer on his desk, and wrote something. He folded the paper, folded it again, then let it fall on the desk in front of Lucia Grossi like a retriever dropping a dead pheasant at its master's feet.

'Keep my name out of it,' he said.

Jealousy and rivalry in Valnerina was working to their advantage, Cangio thought, first the restaurants and their claims to fame regarding truffles and cheese, now the letting agencies. Everyone had a knife out for someone else, and they were ready to use it.

Five minutes later in the car, Lucia Grossi latched her safety belt.

'Only one name, Seb. What do you think? Should I go back in and frighten him some more?'

'Why make him cry?' Cangio said. 'You got what you wanted.'

Luigino's All-In-One was further up the valley near Borgo Cerreto.

Carla Brunori was in her mid-forties, Cangio guessed. She was attractive, plump, and probably efficient. She ran the accommodation side of the business, she said. Her husband, Luigino, rented cars and minibuses out of a garage close to the railway station in Perugia. Anyone who fancied spending time in the national park could hire a car and rent a self-catering apartment without having to shop around too much.

She seemed ready to help, though she wasn't helping at all.

'I've never seen either of them,' the woman said, laying the photo face down on the table, pushing it back to Lucia Grossi as if she were dealing out cards in a casino. 'They didn't come to me, not even asking for information.'

'I think you're lying,' Lucia Grossi said, going straight for the jugular.

She'd been following the same line she had used with Diego Rabitti. She had told Carla Brunori about the two Englishmen, shown her the photo, asked the same questions, cranking up the pressure as denial followed denial.

'We are not the only agency in the valley,' the woman said, barely managing to keep her temper under wraps. 'We're smaller than the others,' she added, looking around the dusty room, taking in the shoddy desk, the aged computer, the sagging shelves behind her stacked with faded paper folders and file boxes. 'Our biggest competitor is Diego Rabitti down the road in Scheggino. Believe me, the competition's stiff . . .'

'I bet it is. And so you cut corners.'

Cangio sat back as Lucia Grossi lobbed in another hand grenade.

'Is all your business above board, Signora Brunori?'

'Of course it . . .'

'All I have to do is phone the Finance Police. They'd tear this place apart in minutes.'

The woman glared at her. 'It's that Rabitti, isn't it? He sent you . . .'

'No one *sent* us,' Lucia Grossi snapped. Then she put her elbow on the desk, and rested her cheek in the palm of her hand. Woman to woman, as if Cangio was nowhere to be seen. 'You've got a bad name, that's all.' There was nothing nasty about the way she said it. It was a fact, and it was useless to deny it.

When Lucia Grossi let herself off the leash, she was like a pit bull in the ring.

Carla Brunori stared back at her, then she stood up.

'I'll be back in a bit,' she said. 'I need to get the register for this month.'

She came back with a folder containing plastic envelopes.

'These are still pending,' she said.

Lucia Grossi pulled a sheet of paper from the top envelope. 'They haven't been registered. Isn't that what you mean?'

Carla Brunori nodded.

'You aren't paying tax on . . . what? Sixty, seventy per cent of the rentals?'

'You won't find the people you're looking for there,' the woman said. 'Those are long-term lets. It's still too early for the tourists.'

Cangio looked away.

There were photograph frames standing on the shelves, pictures of the Brunori family. One had been taken at the beach showing Carla and her husband, a teenage girl, and a little boy who was seven or eight years old.

Cangio recognised the tousled fringe of hair on his forehead. He was smiling in the picture, but there was no mistaking the look in his eye, shy but determined, the kid who told stories.

'Is that Sergio?' Cangio asked the woman, pointing to the photo.

Carla Brunori looked at him in surprise. 'My youngest. Do you know him?'

'I was talking to his class about the wolves in the national park a few days ago. Your son's a gifted storyteller, Signora Brunori.'

'He's bit of a handful at the moment . . .'

'He told us a story about a werewolf.'

'Oh, no,' she said, and let out a sigh. 'He's frightening the other kids. His teacher's not too happy . . .'

'Werewolves in Valnerina?' Lucia Grossi asked, a smile pulling at her lips.

'The place is overrun with them, if you believe Sergio,' Carla Brunori said. 'If he hears a noise at night, he's petrified. Still, last week . . . I must admit, we all heard that one. Me and Luigino heard it, too.'

'What noise was that?' Cangio asked her.

'A scream,' Carla Brunori said. 'Real blood-curdling, it was. On and on it went. Sergio came charging into our room, and dived in bed between us. Trembling like a leaf, he was. We both heard it, of course. It frightened me, I can tell you that . . . Luigino went out to have a look around the garden. He took his shotgun with him. There was something moving in the dark, he said . . .'

'In the garden?'

Carla Brunori looked at Grossi and shook her head. 'No, no. It was further up the hill. There's an empty farmhouse up there. That's where the screams were coming from.'

Was that the scream that had frightened Dino De Angelis? Cangio wondered.

'Did anyone else hear it?' Cangio asked her.

'The neighbours did. Said they did, anyway.'

Carla Brunori sat back, as if that was the end of the story.

'Had there been an accident or something?' Lucia Grossi asked.

Carla Brunori shrugged. 'Who can say? It's so dark up there. There are no lights at the Argenti house. It's empty, like I was saying . . .'

'I'm sorry, what is this Argenti house?'

'It's an old farmhouse,' the woman told Grossi. 'It's in a really pretty spot, what with the woods and the view, but it's been abandoned for years. We tried to rent it for the agency. Luigino wanted to do the place up, then let it out as holiday flats, but we couldn't trace the owners.'

'And that's where the screams were coming from?'

Carla Brunori nodded. 'A gang of kids, that's what we thought. You know what teenagers are like these days. What do they call them, rave parties? Drink and drugs, and who knows what.'

'And Sergio thought it was a werewolf,' Cangio concluded.

The woman let out a rasp with her lips. 'That's his grandad talking. He was in the Resistance during the war. Dead Germans, their bodies torn to bits by a werewolf near the Argenti house. That's what he always said. When his grandad died, Sergio started telling tales of werewolves all over the place.'

Lucia Grossi glanced at her watch, then nodded at Cangio. A signal, and an order.

Time to go.

'Thank you for your help, Signora Brunori,' she said.

'No trouble at all,' the woman said. 'Things are quiet around here until Easter.'

Apart from the screams of werewolves, Cangio thought, though he knew that Easter was when the tourist season started up after the winter lay-off.

Lucia Grossi was silent, concentrating on her driving as they headed south on the SS 209. It was a dangerous road, full of blind bends and occasional lumbering farm traffic, the only road in the valley that followed the meandering course of the River Nera.

'Hey, Cangio,' she said. 'What's your take on werewolves?'

'What do you think?' he replied with a chuckle.

'Yet they all heard screams coming from that farmhouse.'

Cangio turned to look at her. 'Are we hunting for werewolves now?'

She accelerated hard. 'I don't know . . . but we can't just ignore it. Those two men were *not* tourists, Seb. They were here for a reason. And whatever it was, it led to the murder of one of them when he went back to England.' She braked hard, slewing the car into a sharp bend. 'If they didn't stay in a hotel, or rent a flat, where *did* they stay?'

She dropped him off at the car park where he had left the Land Rover.

'I've got a meeting later in Perugia,' she said as he climbed out of the Alpha. 'But . . . I'd really like to take a closer look at that old farmhouse. Can you be here again tonight at midnight?'

He thought of Lori, and hesitated before replying.

'Well, if you can't come,' she was saying, as if she sensed his reluctance, 'I'll go there on my own.'

'No, no, that's OK,' he said quickly. 'I'll be here waiting for you.'

She accelerated out of the car park and left him standing there.

He heard her siren blaring as she disappeared into the Sant'Anatolia tunnel.

'*Midnight*?' he said out loud.

Did she have a ghoulish sense of humour, or didn't she?

SEVENTEEN

Borgo Cerreto, Valnerina

It was twenty minutes after midnight.

Away to the left, the farmhouse glimmered in the moonlight.

Cangio and Lucia Grossi were sitting side by side in the Land Rover.

She placed her hand on his shoulder, leaning forward to get a better view.

'A pity we're not a little bit closer,' she said.

He hoped that she was talking about the house.

She was wearing jeans and a leather jacket, which added a new dimension to her persona. She was wearing perfume, too, a fragrance which was sweet and spicy. *Sexy*, he might have said, if she had been anyone else. Every time she shifted in her seat, his head began to spin.

If Lori ever got to hear about this outing, he'd be in serious trouble.

'Just the place for a party,' he said, 'though no one's raving . . .'

She wasn't listening, her eyes fixed on the shadowy outline of the building.

The Argenti farmhouse seemed forlorn, forgotten, the windows broken, the paint faded, the wooden shutters rotten and crumbling. A footpath led to a flight of steps and the front door, the grass knee high, as if nobody had been there in a long time.

'This operation isn't authorised,' she said. 'It would be premature to involve an investigating magistrate at this stage. Then again, given what Carla Brunori told us, it seemed worth taking the risk.'

She didn't say a word about the risk that *he* was taking.

He had called Lori at work that afternoon, told her he'd be out watching the wolves that night.

'Why are you telling me?' Lori had fired back at him, her voice sharp over the phone.

'I wanted to warn you,' he said. 'Just in case I was late getting back . . .'

'What's so new about you chasing wolves, Seb Cangio?'

It sounded more like chasing whores, the way she said it.

'The female will be birthing soon,' he had told her. 'I'd like to see what happens next.'

Lori had taken it in her stride. 'The girls are going out for a pizza tonight. I was thinking of joining them, anyway. I would have phoned you. I'll sleep over at Rita's if we drink too much, so don't you worry about me.'

He *was* worrying now, but for the wrong reasons.

He was alone in a car with a woman who smelled like a jungle flower, wondering whether she'd been joking minutes before when she said, 'If anyone drives up here, Seb, pretend to kiss me, and I'll go along with it.'

She had laughed, but there was a lingering hint of something left unsaid.

He had to get a handle on the situation, take control, change the way the conversation was going.

'This afternoon you asked me if werewolves exist,' he said.

She turned to look at him, one half of her face palely lit by the moon. 'Do they?'

'Do you know what therianthropy is?' he asked her.

She shifted in the dark, her perfume wafting over him again.

'I've no idea,' she said, 'though I guess you're about to tell me.'

'It's a mental illness. Not very common, rare, in fact, but it exists. The sufferer believes that he is an animal, so he behaves like the animal he thinks he is.'

'How come you know so much about it?'

He felt better now, playing the expert, telling her something she didn't know.

'If you study wolves, you're bound to come across the syndrome sooner or later. The wolf is top of the wannabe list by a long way.'

'So, werewolves aren't just Hollywood crap. Is that what you're saying?'

'I once saw a man who exhibited the symptoms,' he said. 'If you'd been there, you wouldn't forget him.'

'How do you mean?'

'He was running around on his hands and knees, frothing at

the mouth, trying to bite the doctors and nurses as they put him
into a strait-jacket.'

'Thank God I've got my gun,' she said.

He wondered whether she was laughing at him.

'Do the *carabinieri* hand out silver bullets?' he asked.

Perhaps the word *carabinieri* triggered some conditioned
impulse in her brain.

'We're wasting time, Seb, sitting here and talking nonsense,'
Captain Grossi said.

Before he could say a word, she was out of the Land Rover,
moving fast towards the farmhouse. He had to follow her. It was
the basic rule of policing. Cover your partner's back; argue about
it later.

As he pressed himself against the wall of the house, he saw
a pistol glinting in her hand.

'Silver bullets?' she whispered. 'I don't believe Beretta manu-
factures those.'

She skipped up the stone steps to the front door, and he ran
up behind her.

They stood on either side of an ancient green door.

'Open it,' she said, pointing her pistol downwards.

He put his shoulder to the door, but nothing happened. It took
two more attempts before the door swung back with a loud creak.

'So much for silence,' she jibed, stepping past him, pulling a
torch from her pocket.

He might have said that rangers weren't housebreakers as a
general rule. Instead, he pulled out his own torch, and followed
her into what was evidently a big farm kitchen with low wooden
beams and a massive open fireplace. The room was entirely bare
except for a sagging sink-and-cupboard unit. Made of cheap
white laminate, it might have seemed prosperous fifty years
before, but now looked ready for burning.

'Tourists love these places. With the right furniture, and a
touch of paint . . .'

'The lap of luxury,' Grossi murmured.

She pulled open one of the cupboards, found nothing but
pellets of rat poison. 'Let's hope the tourists don't think everyone
lives like this in Umbria. Give me my nice modern flat in Perugia
any day of the week.'

'Someone's been here recently, though.'

She stepped close, standing at his shoulder. 'What makes you say that?'

He sniffed out loud. 'Can't you smell it? Bleach or something . . .'

'The house may not be as empty as it seems,' she said, and her gun came up in line with her torch.

'Snow White and the Seven Dwarves?' he suggested.

She didn't answer as she made for a door on the far side of the room.

She stopped there, as if uncertain whether to proceed.

'Do you want me to go first?' he asked.

'I'm the one with the gun,' she hissed back.

Was it humour, or tension that he heard in her voice?

'I'll cover your back, then, as they say in the movies.'

'Just keep out of my line of fire,' she said. 'That's what the police manual says. Hold that torch up high, Seb. No one will shoot if they think there are two guns pointing at them.'

The light from their torches danced off the walls as they entered a narrow hallway. There were four closed doors, two on either side of the corridor. She aimed her torch at one of the doors. 'Let's start here,' she said, waiting while he pushed it open, then walking past him into the room.

Her torch lit up a stained enamel bathtub, a plastic shower curtain, a toilet with no seat, and an old metal cabinet hanging on the wall beside a mirror.

'I wouldn't fancy stripping off in here,' she said.

He touched the plastic curtain with his hand. It felt damp, slick, but everything in the bathroom was damp. There were dark stains on the walls, green mold on the ceiling, a rank smell of closed, stale air.

'The Brunoris would need to spend a fortune before they could rent the house out.'

She opened the wall cabinet, looked inside. 'One block of soap, unused. One pack of cotton wool, empty. One razorblade, very rusty.' She might have been reading an inventory out loud. 'This stuff could have been here since the end of the war.'

The other rooms were full of junk, boxes bursting with mildewed books and yellow newspapers, old boots, broken chairs, sofas sprouting springs and horsehair.

'Let's try upstairs,' she said.

They tried to go quietly, but the wooden stairs creaked loudly beneath their weight.

There were four more doors on the floor above. The first two rooms were very small, the walls of no definable colour, the wallpaper faded. There was a smell of gloom, doom, and long neglect. Another room was packed with more miscellaneous junk, broken chairs, a stack of dated farmers' almanacs, boxes full of nothing that would ever see the light of day again.

'No sane person would sleep in here,' she said.

Had she ever seen the places where the homeless lived? He had stumbled on a few while studying the foxes in London's parks at night. The foxes' dens were cleaner than the tips where the alkies slept.

The fourth room at the end of the passage was the largest.

'The bridal suite?' she joked, pointing her torch at a double bed frame, the rusting rack on which a mattress had once been laid, and a thin mattress of no distinguishable colour which was folding under its own weight against the wall. There were rectangular stains on faded wallpaper where pictures had once hung.

'No one has lived here for ages,' Cangio said, looking around. 'Empty rooms, an abandoned house, there should be signs of mice and rats, as well.'

'You sound disappointed,' she murmured.

'Just surprised. When Man moves out, Nature moves in.'

'That smell you were talking about . . . It's weaker up here,' she said.

'No smell would drive them away. Bugs and mice would move to a different part of the house, and wait until the stink died down. We haven't seen a single spider, either.'

'What are you getting at?'

He looked around as if to confirm what he was thinking.

'You know what this place reminds me of?'

'No, I don't,' she said, a note of impatience rising in her voice.

'A den where wolves have been living. Even if the wolves abandon it, other creatures steer clear.'

She turned the torch on her face, turned her mouth down in derision.

'Come off it, Seb. This isn't Halloween,' she said. 'And we've found nothing. This is a waste of time. Let's get out of here.'

'Hang on a minute,' he said. 'This is a farmhouse, remember. There should be a cellar, a storeroom, a place to keep tools and things. Five minutes more won't hurt. We just stick our heads inside the door, see what's what, then we call it a night, OK?'

'If you insist,' she said.

They found a padlocked door outside beneath the stone stairway that led up to the kitchen.

One kick was enough to send the lock flying.

'*Santo cristo!*' Lucia Grossi covered her nose with her sleeve as they entered a cavernous chamber which ran from one end of the house to the other.

'Could this be the smell that Nora was talking about?' Cangio wondered.

'I'd shoot any man that smelled like this. My eyes are burning.'

Cangio moved the beam of his torch over a stack of chopped firewood, a rusty generator engine propped up on bricks, pyramids of broken furniture and farm tools piled in corners. An old tin bathtub had been used as a feeding-trough. A heavy old table stood in the centre of the space. The tabletop was scarred with cuts, the wood dark and unevenly stained. Cangio laid his hand on it, then held his palm to his nose and pulled a face.

Lucia Grossi bent close, then pulled back quickly.

'It's soaked with something,' she said. 'Acid, maybe . . .'

'These undercrofts are often used for butchering animals. Pigs, cows, sheep. The table was probably used to chop up the meat into manageable portions.'

'Is that what's been going on in here?'

'The Brunoris live close by,' he said. 'They and their neighbours heard screams from this direction. Pigs squeal when they see the butcher's knife. Could that be what Sergio and his parents heard?'

'No, no,' Lucia Grossi said impatiently. 'It makes no sense. Why would anyone butcher pigs in the middle of the night?'

He shrugged his shoulders.

'Whoever it was, they went to a lot of trouble to wipe the place clean.'

While he was speaking, her torch roved slowly over the flagstone floor.

'What's that down there?' she murmured, pointing towards the stack of firewood. 'Something flashed in the torchlight. Hidden gold, do you think? What are you waiting for? I thought you were a gentleman.'

Cangio dropped down on one knee, peering between the logs.

She squatted down beside him, sitting back on her heels.

'It looks like a tube of something, glass maybe,' he said, reaching out with his finger.

She put her hand on his arm and held him back. 'Don't touch it,' she said. 'See if you can pull it out with something. Don't park rangers usually go around armed with a Swiss army penknife? You know, with all the jiggly bits?'

'We carry these,' he said, pulling out his Land Rover key-ring, using the key as a probe.

'It isn't long enough,' she said.

'A twig might be better. Whatever it is, it's caught between the logs.'

She reached into her pocket, pulled something out, and held it up. 'I was reading a report before I came out of the house. I never like to throw the paper clips away. It's a silly hang-up, I know, but there you go.' She straightened it out, formed a hook at one end, then gave it to him.

He pushed the hook into the tube, and tried to pull it out.

'It won't budge,' he said. 'No, hang on a bit . . . it's . . . coming.'

A short glass tube rolled out on the floor, stopping centimetres away from his nose.

They both stared at it in silence for a moment.

'It looks like a vial for holding pills,' he said, pushing the clip inside the little bottle, holding it up. 'And there's a label on it . . .'

She brought the torch closer. '*The Old Pharmacy, Lamb's Con* . . .' she read in a whisper. 'There's something gooey blotting out the rest. Dirt, or mud . . .'

'It looks to me like congealed blood,' he said.

They stared at each other, an unspoken question hanging between them.

Is it human blood?

'Unknown Two?' suggested Cangio.

EIGHTEEN

Westminster, London, UK

'Is this where the Yard buys its ammo?'

Lucia Grossi was poking the peas that came with her battered cod and chips.

'Fire one of these things from a .38,' she said, 'you'd blow a hole in a wall.'

Hunger had grabbed her by the throat while they waited for Desmond Harris to arrive.

Things had been moving fast up to that point.

The decisions had been taken by Lucia Grossi, naturally. She had given the forensic lab in Perugia four hours to run preliminary tests on the bottle they had found at the Argenti farmhouse the night before. She had phoned him at six a.m. to confirm that it was human blood, telling him to be at the airport in Assisi by eight: they would be catching the first flight to London.

'If the mountain won't come to Mohammed,' she said.

The 'mountain' was still playing hard to get, dragging its heels, making things tough.

Cangio stared at his own pub meal, and thought of the restaurant where he had taken Desmond Harris. Black truffles, fresh trout, and *strangozzi* rolled by Nora's expert hands versus a congealed steak-and-kidney pie.

Talk about a no-contest.

'Maybe he'll take us to the Ritz for tea,' he said.

Lucia Grossi pulled a sour face. 'Tesco's would be better. The only decent thing I ate in London were their apple pies.'

Cangio popped a cold chip in his mouth. 'I got by OK when I was living here.'

'How did you manage that?'

'I stayed at home and cooked for myself.'

Lucia Grossi didn't react. She was in no mood for joking. She had come to London with one thing on her mind, and had talked about nothing else for most of the flight.

'I'll show Scotland Yard a thing or two,' she kept on telling him, clutching a leather document case on her knees all the way from Assisi to Stansted. 'This is just the sort of international operation that lifts a new department off the launching pad. From a PR point of view, it's a first-rate opportunity for the SCS to make its mark.'

He had settled down with his paperback and let her dream on.

The three-star hotel in Paddington where they had stopped just long enough to leave their bags was on the cramped side, the dark single rooms the size of the holding cages at the *carabinieri* command station in Perugia, but even that hadn't phased her.

'Small, but comfortable,' she had said. 'Next time, we'll be travelling in style.'

Cangio hoped that there never would be a next time.

She patted the leather document case that was sitting in her lap now, still chasing the hard green peas around her plate in the pub near Westminster. 'Without us, Seb, Scotland Yard would still be bumping their noses in the dark.'

When she said *us*, she wasn't talking about him and her, but her and her department.

'Maybe they know more than we do,' Cangio said.

'While we were risking our necks at the Argenti farmhouse last night, they were sound asleep in their nice, warm beds,' she said.

I wouldn't mind sleeping in my own warm bed tonight, Cangio thought. He wasn't sure what sort of welcome would be waiting for him when he got home. Loredana had hardly said a word to him before he left.

'You're going to London with *her*?'

'It's this investigation. I can't get out of it.'

Lori had looked him in the eye. 'Did she book one double room, or two singles?'

'She won't solve the case by sleeping in *my* bed, will she?' he had snapped back.

'Are you quite certain, Seb Cangio? London . . . *Dio mio*, any excuse to go back there! And you'd almost convinced me that you hated the place.'

For one moment he had almost told her about the photograph he had seen at Assisi Airport, the passenger with the salamander tattoo. If what he feared turned out to be true, he would have crawled to the South Pole with Lucia Grossi riding on his back to find out what was going on in Umbria, and to know how London tied in with it.

They had to be stopped.

Even if it meant arguing with Lori.

Even if it meant sitting next to Lucia Grossi on a crowded aeroplane, and facing up to Desmond Harris and his bosses at New Scotland Yard.

He hadn't said a word about the man with the tattoo.

Lori would have told him he was looking for trouble. Wasn't one gunshot wound enough of a lesson? He had almost bled to death twelve months before. The 'Ndrangheta had tried to kill him a second time just six months later. Why give them another excuse?

He hadn't mentioned the man with the tattoo to Lucia Grossi, either.

He wasn't going to tell her a thing until he was sure of it, though he still had no idea how to go about sounding out the British police on the subject.

The British police . . .

Now, *that* was a very sore subject.

'What did they say when you told them we were coming?' he had asked her on the plane.

She hadn't told them. 'Why should I?' she said. 'Harris barged in on me, asking for help. Now it's my turn. I mean to take the place by storm.'

Outside the windows, white clouds appeared.

A minute later, the plane began to shudder and bump.

The pilot's voice came over the intercom, asking passengers to return to their seats and fasten their seat belts.

'There's heavy turbulence over Paris,' he announced.

The turbulence turned out to be heavier in London when Grossi phoned Harris.

He only heard one side of the conversation, but he got the gist of it.

Lucia Grossi's face was more eloquent than a thousand words. She had come to a dead stop in the middle of the *Nothing to Declare* lane, passengers bumping into one another as they tried to steer their trolleys and suitcases around her.

'Oh, no car? Well, then . . . yes . . . yes, in that case.'

He watched her face, saw the changes. Like a summer day when a squall swept through the mountains. Sun, then shadows, dark clouds gathering, then the tempest breaking. She snapped her phone shut. 'A fucking pub? That's where we're going to meet our Mr Harris. And how the hell are we supposed to get there?'

They got to Victoria station by express coach, then took a taxi. 'Like plebs,' Lucia Grossi snarled, cursing all the way. He reckoned it was down to her military training in the *carabinieri*. Her vocabulary of insults outdid even Loredana's.

The Feathers was full of coppers, detectives by the look of them. The other customers might have been snitches or bank clerks. It wasn't easy to tell the difference. Dark suits, bright ties, scuffed shoes. The uniform of the working white-collar classes.

Grossi was seething, mashing the peas on her plate.

'We can't get in without a pass, he says. After all I've done for them!'

She turned to Cangio and stuck out her chin. 'Is this Brexit kicking in? If this is the future, the British cops are going to have a shit-hard time of it, I can tell you, Seb!'

Ten minutes later, the pub door swung open, and Desmond Harris walked in.

He smiled and raised his hand, as he approached the table.

'Excuse the gear,' he said. 'I came by bike.'

He was wearing one of those duck-tailed plastic helmets that racing cyclists favour. The helmet was red, white, and blue with a black leather chin-strap, his trousers jodhpurised by a pair of metal bicycle clips.

He looked more like a postman than a police inspector.

Cangio saw the disillusion on Grossi's face. Had she been expecting a Rolls Royce or the Coronation coach?

'I had to be somewhere,' Harris said, though he didn't say where, or why. 'The traffic was a nightmare coming back. So, then . . . well, yes, welcome to England! Er, did you . . . have a good flight?'

He glanced at the batter, chips, and peas on Lucia's Grossi's plate.

'Good choice,' he said. 'It's the best thing on the menu.'

Cangio looked away to avoid laughing. The expression on

Grossi's face was plain enough to a fellow Italian. *Is this guy nuts, or is he just pretending?*

'I have an omelette usually,' Harris was saying. 'Otherwise my ulcer kicks in.'

Lucia Grossi stared at Cangio with an air of desperation, seeking help.

Cangio picked up a table-mat and studied a picture of a partridge.

Her patience snapped. 'We didn't come to London for the food, Desmond. We've got important information which will definitely be of interest to Scotland Yard.'

Harris smiled, clenched his fist, then gave a thumbs-up.

'Sounds good,' he said. 'Now, just let me order some nosh, then I'll tell you how things . . . er, stand. Can I get you anything?'

Lucia Grossi shook her head.

'Not for me, thanks,' Cangio said.

Harris stood at the bar, chatting companionably with a pretty young barmaid who evidently knew him, while she tapped his order into a touchpad, then pulled him a pint of a beer the colour of mud.

'Is this some sort of delaying tactic?' Grossi murmured in Italian.

'It's a technique they used at the estate agent's when I was working in Islington. Play it cool, act as if you don't care whether the client buys the place or not. It's a test of strength, a bit like arm wrestling.'

Lucia Grossi nodded, never taking her eyes off Harris. 'Did the technique work?'

'In my experience, if they wanted the place, they bought it. If not, they didn't.'

'Let's see if we can break through his defences, then.'

Harris sat down, then tasted his beer. 'Ah, just what the doctor ordered! Look,' he said in the next breath, 'I hope you don't think I'm being ungrateful, dragging you off to the pub like this? It's the Yard that's the problem. It isn't easy to get in there these days, what with terrorist bomb scares, and so on. Of course, some folk have more trouble getting *out!*' He laughed at his own joke. 'I doubt you'll be able to discuss the case with anyone today . . .'

Lucia Grossi let out a yelp. 'When you turned up in Perugia, the *case*, as you choose to call it, was thoroughly investigated. We gave you all the help we possibly could.'

Harris sank his nose into his pint, then nodded.

'That's true,' he said. 'I . . . and my superiors, of course, we are very grateful. There will be an official letter of thanks in the pipeline, I shouldn't wonder.' He shifted in his seat, then looked at her finally. 'We had a meeting the other day, Lucia . . . As the murder took place on English soil, the powers-that-be – the bosses, in other words – they decided . . . well, they thought that . . .'

'*Number 34*,' a voice boomed out of a loudspeaker.

'That's me.'

Harris leapt from his seat like a whippet from a trap and made his way to the bar.

'A letter of thanks?' Her face was bright red. 'They know where they can stick it.'

Harris came back a minute later with an omelette, salad, and a bread roll.

'As I was saying,' he started, spearing a piece of omelette, popping it into his mouth, munching through the words that came out, 'they've . . . mm . . . decided to restrict . . . mm . . . the enquiry to the English part of the case.' He swallowed hard. 'The man who was killed near Stansted Airport. That's our priorit—'

'Don't give me that shit!' Grossi said sharply, bringing her hand down hard on the tabletop, turning heads as people looked to see what the commotion was about.

Harris stared open-mouthed at her.

'There were *two* men in Italy, Desmond. Two *English* men, remember? One of them was killed near Stansted. But I have evidence in this file that the second man, Unknown Two, was murdered in Umbria,' she said, patting the document case. 'That is why we came to London. Not to eat fish and chips and drink warm beer. I *demand* your full cooperation. We want to know everything that you know. And we want to know it *today*!' She narrowed her eyes and stared him down. 'If not, I promise you, I will knock your so-called "case" out of court!'

Cangio mentally applauded her.

Harris took a swig of beer, then stood up.

'I need to have a private word with the boss,' he said, as he ran for the door.

'Let's see what happens now,' Lucia Grossi said.

They watched Desmond Harris through the picture window, walking up and down the pavement, eyes on the ground, one ear clamped to his mobile phone. Then, suddenly, the phone snapped shut, he wiggled his finger at them, and he pointed up the busy road in the direction of New Scotland Yard.

'I think I see a white flag waving,' she said triumphantly.

NINETEEN

New Scotland Yard

Desmond Harris broke his tight-lipped silence as they passed beneath the revolving triangle and he took them through the security check.

'The building won't be ours much longer,' he said. 'This may be your last chance to see inside. An investment company from Abu Dhabi got their hands on it. They're planning to turn it into a five-star luxury hotel, I believe.'

'Where will you be going?' Cangio asked him.

'A smaller place on the Victoria Embankment. They'll probably call it *New* New Scotland Yard. There are staff cuts on the cards, too, apparently.'

Was Harris up for the chop?

Would Brexit downsizing start with him?

The aluminium doors slid open, and they took the lift.

Detective Chief Inspector Jardine's office was on the seventh floor.

Not so much an office, Cangio decided at a glance, more a place to dump things.

There was a battered old desk with a black Formica top, a computer long past its sell-by date, a narrow slice of the Thames just visible beyond an unwashed window that looked out on the other modern multi-storey buildings crowding close.

The man behind the desk glanced up at Harris. 'These are the Italians, I take it?'

The Italians . . . As if they were a gang of criminals planning to steal the family silver.

He didn't stand up, just waved his hand to a single chair in front of his desk.

Lucia Grossi sat down, Cangio and Harris standing behind her like prison guards.

'Mr Jardine, I take it?' she said tartly.

Cangio coughed to avoid chortling.

'Detective Chief Inspector,' Jardine specified. 'Inspector Harris tells me you've got something that might help us.'

It didn't sound like a question, and Cangio saw Lucia Grossi's reaction. Her head came up sharply, she stretched her back and seemed to grow in height. 'It would be more correct to say that we could help each other.'

Jardine slouched forward, clasping his hands in front of him on the desk. A tall man in a silver-grey suit, he appeared to be in his mid-fifties. He had the look of a fifties bit-player, too, black hair going grey at the edges, swept back over his ears, and a Presley-type quiff plopping down on a wide, unfurrowed forehead.

He pursed his lips, and a frown appeared. 'We are grateful for your . . .'

Lucia Grossi stood up and stretched her hand across the desk, waiting for him to shake it.

'I am Captain Lucia Grossi, *carabiniere*, head of the Special Crimes Squad in Umbria,' she told him. 'And this is my colleague, Ranger Sebastiano Cangio.'

Cangio nodded, but stayed well back.

This was Grossi's show, and he was curious to see how she would play it.

Detective Chief Inspector Jardine sat back in his chair, though he didn't look comfortable. 'As I was saying, we are grateful for your input in Italy, Captain Grossi. Desmond speaks most highly of the assistance he received there. We have managed to identify the man who was murdered at Stansted Airport, as he may have told you. Now we are looking for whoever killed him. An investigation is under way which should tie the case up once and for all.'

'You have half a case, Detective Chief Inspector,' Lucia Grossi said, 'but the other half . . . well, *I* have that.'

'Young lady . . .'

'Don't patronise me,' she warned him. 'I may have the answer to a murder that you are still investigating. And you know things which could be useful to me. We need to understand each other, and work together, Detective Chief Inspector. It is in the best interests of both our countries, it goes without saying.'

While she was speaking, she had taken a thin pink folder from her leather document case.

She laid it carefully on the surface of the desk in front of her, then spread her hand flat on top of the folder as DCI Jardine began to reach across to pick it up.

'This is what *I* have got,' she said. 'You can make a formal request to see the contents, of course. We call such a request a *rogatoria internazionale*. It may take weeks, even months, to be approved. Diplomats and ministers may be involved. Sometimes, a *rogatoria* request gets lost in the process. And Brexit may put the blocks on the free exchange of information between our police forces, as I am sure you are aware. However, I did take the precaution of making a paper copy of everything concerning my case before leaving Italy . . .'

'And in return?' Jardine had evidently drawn his own conclusions about Lucia Grossi.

'I want to know whatever you have got on the man who died near Stansted Airport.'

DCI Jardine let out a sigh, then rubbed his nose with his fist. 'There are two ways of doing this, Captain Grossi. I can go upstairs to my bosses, and tell them what's up. I may be there a very long time, and they mightn't like the idea.'

'British bureaucracy?' Grossi asked him with barely concealed sarcasm.

Jardine made no comment. '*Or* . . .' He looked at Desmond Harris. 'Des and I can pop downstairs to the canteen for a cup of tea, and I'll forget to switch off my computer.'

Lucia Grossi relaxed in her seat.

'A cup of tea sounds like an excellent idea,' she said, 'especially if the correct case happens to be up on the computer screen.'

'The correct case and all the related folders. That cuppa might take a little bit longer if we add a packet of crisps and take a look inside that nice pink file of yours.'

'Of course,' Lucia Grossi said, raising her hand from the file in question. 'There's one condition, though.'

Jardine stared at her.

'What's that?'

'You'll need to drink tea on your own, Chief Inspector. I want Inspector Harris here in case I can't find something, or something needs explaining to me.'

Cangio had to admire her pluck, dictating the law to a senior Scotland Yard police officer.

Jardine took a moment to think about it, then he stood up, a head taller than anyone else in the small room. 'I'll be off, then,' he said, sweeping up the file as he squeezed out from behind his desk. 'If anyone comes looking for me,' he said to Harris, 'you can tell them where to find me, OK?'

Carabinieri 1 – New Scotland Yard 0, thought Cangio.

As the door closed, Lucia Grossi swung the computer around to face her.

Harris grabbed his boss's chair. 'I can find you a stool,' he said to Cangio.

'It doesn't matter,' Cangio said, 'I can see well enough from here.'

'OK, Desmond. Take me through what you've got from A to Z,' Lucia Grossi said.

A to Z proved to be little more than they already knew. Kit Andrews, the man who had used a false passport as he entered Italy, then left it again, going home to be murdered, had been identified as Vincent J. Cormack.

'J stands for?'

'James. Born in Belfast thirty-eight years ago. We were able to identify him easily enough with NeoFace, our facial recognition database, using that photograph from the restaurant. This is his crime sheet,' Harris said, opening up an Excel spreadsheet. 'It's long, but it doesn't amount to much. Petty theft, a bit of dealing, then housebreaking – he got three years for that. He kept his nose clean afterwards, except for . . .'

He clicked on a passport image at the top of the document, filling the screen with the face and the profile of the man who had been enjoying truffles and trout in Valnerina the night before he was killed near Stansted.

Vincent Cormack had a long, narrow face – horsy, Cangio thought – greasy, slicked-back hair, a large nose, and large ears. Cangio read the description beneath the photo: height and weight, no birthmarks, scars, or tattoos.

Harris clicked on another document.

'This is his most recent file,' he said. 'He was arrested on suspicion last year of going armed with intent to rob. Unfortunately, nothing came of it. There was a whisper . . . a bank job, where and when it was going to happen, and who was likely to be involved. Vince Cormack was one of the gang. He was picked up near the bank as predicted, but he wasn't armed, and there was nothing incriminating in his vehicle. Probably an armourer was bringing the guns.'

'So he got away with it?'

'I'm afraid so,' Harris said. 'If he'd been in jail doing seven to ten years, he wouldn't have gone to Italy, and he wouldn't have got shot when he came back.'

'What *was* he doing in Italy?' Cangio asked. 'Have you any idea?'

What would a low-key criminal like Vince Cormack have to do with the 'Ndrangheta? That was what he was asking. For a start, Cormack wasn't Italian. He hadn't grown up in the shadow of a boss who told him who to kill, and rewarded him for each new notch on his gun.

Harris turned and looked at him. 'He was eating truffles, remember?'

Cangio smiled back at him. 'He wasn't only eating truffles, was he, Desmond?'

'We haven't gone too deeply into what he was doing there, to be honest. As I told you, we've been more concerned to find out what happened to him when he came back.'

'Somebody killed him,' Lucia Grossi said. 'But was he killed as a result of what he'd been doing in Italy? That's the question that we need to ask.'

'Something in that file of yours?' Harris asked her.

Lucia Grossi turned to face him. 'We think the man who was with Cormack in Nora's photo may be dead as well, Desmond. That's what we are working on. The problem is, he doesn't show up on any Italian database. We presume that he was English, too. We'd like you to run what we have got through your computers.'

'You'll have to ask the DCI,' Harris said, then curiosity kicked in. 'What have you got?'

Lucia Grossi took a moment to answer. 'Seb and I have found evidence of a possible crime scene. We've got a sample of hair, a sample of blood, and a DNA profile. The only thing we haven't got is a name.'

She didn't tell Harris about the medicine bottle they had found at the Argenti farmhouse. Nor did she mention the photograph that she had removed from the pink file, showing the label with a chemist's address in London. If this was a contest about giving away as little as possible, then Lucia Grossi seemed to be winning it hands down.

'Or the name of his killer,' Harris said. 'So, more or less, we're even.'

Not quite, Cangio thought, though identifying the man with the salamander tattoo would not be so easy.

'More or less,' Lucia Grossi agreed with Harris.

'DCI Jardine will be pleased,' Des Harris said, though he didn't say whether Jardine would be pleased because the Italian visitors knew so much, or because they knew so little.

As if on cue, the Chief Inspector arrived a moment later.

Harris jumped up and vacated the DCI's chair.

'How are you getting on?' Jardine asked, dropping into his seat like a fighter pilot.

'We've just about finished,' Lucia Grossi said. 'But there is one thing. This man, Vincent Cormack. I noticed that you searched his house.'

'We were looking for DNA evidence to confirm his identity,' Harris said. 'The usual things – toothbrush, comb, traces of blood on his shaving gear.'

'I didn't see that in your computer file,' Lucia Grossi objected.

'We haven't got that far updating the reports . . .'

'But you got confirmation?'

'That's right,' Jardine said quickly. 'His flatmate identified him from that photo.'

'Flatmate?' Lucia Grossi stood up. 'Someone who knows Cormack? That is good news. I want to speak with him, of course.'

'We've questioned him already,' Harris said.

Jardine backed him up. 'He didn't have much to say for himself.'

'I still want to speak with him,' Grossi insisted. 'That's another good reason for coming to London. We, too, have our jobs to do.'

Jardine set his elbows on the table. 'As you mentioned earlier, Captain Grossi, Brexit means respecting protocols, following the rules. So, please take note. Inspector Harris will ask all the questions. And second, I'd like to run your DNA profile . . . not *yours*, Captain, the other man's DNA, through our system.'

Lucia Grossi beamed a smile at him, and stood up.

'I was hoping you'd say that,' she said. 'Can we speak to the flatmate now?'

Jardine and Harris exchanged a glance.

'Don't you want to go to your hotel first?' Harris asked her.

Lucia Grossi glanced at her watch, then fixed Jardine with an expression of angelic innocence. 'Surely your officers haven't finished work for the day? It's only half-past two.'

Cangio saw the look that shot between Jardine and Harris.

Who the hell does she think she is?

TWENTY

South of the Thames

Desmond Harris wasn't the greatest driver in the world. 'I'm more of a dedicated cyclist,' he said by way of explanation as he swerved past a woman with a trolley on a zebra crossing.

Fortunately, he got them to Elephant and Castle without hitting anything, then heavy traffic on Tower Bridge Road slowed the car to a crawl. It took another ten minutes to get to Alice Street in Bermondsey.

'Are you sure he'll be at home?' Cangio asked.

'He'll be in bed, I bet,' Harris answered. 'He works all night as a bouncer.'

'What's a bouncer?' Lucia Grossi wanted to know.

'A hired thug,' Cangio told her.

'A doorman at a nightclub,' Harris amplified. 'Someone who stops people coming in, or throws them out because they've drunk too much.' He braked hard, turned left, then pulled the car into a parking slot. 'In our case, naturally, he won't be throwing anyone anywhere.'

Harris held his finger on the buzzer for longer than was polite.

A man opened the door in his vest and underpants, and Harris held up his warrant card.

'Police,' he said.

Eddie Murphy was a big man. Not tall, but big. There might have been muscles under the rolls of fat, but there was plenty of fat.

'Fucking hell, again?' he grumbled, leading them into what might have been a living room. The furniture comprised a three-seat brown-leather sofa, two mismatched armchairs, and a huge plasma TV on a sideboard along with a stereo unit. Everything else should have been thrown in a dumpster a long time ago.

He waded barefoot through a sea of empty pizza boxes, Chinese takeaway cartons, discarded clothes, empty fag packets, crushed beer cans, and an enviable collection of empty wine and whisky bottles, then flopped down on the sofa.

'Mr Murphy,' Desmond Harris began, 'I spoke to you last week about Vincent Cormack.'

'Now what a great pleasure that was,' Eddie Murphy murmured, reaching for a cigarette, then lighting up. 'You found him yet? He still owes me the fucking rent.'

In the car, Harris had told them that no official announcement had been made regarding the murder of Vince Cormack, just a one-liner in the papers noting that 'the body of a man had been found in woodlands not far from Stansted Airport.' As there were no known next-of-kin, New Scotland Yard had decided to say no more until they had a juicier bone to throw to the press. So Murphy still didn't know that his flatmate would never be coming back to settle his unpaid bills.

Lucia Grossi didn't wait for Harris, ignoring the pact with DCI Jardine. She started firing questions at Murphy like a tommy gun going off. Simple things at first, questions that the police had surely asked him. Where did Vincent Cormack work, what was his job, when had he last been seen at Alice Street, had he phoned Mr Murphy in the last two weeks, or sent any messages?

Eddie Murphy's answers came out pat.

'Dunno. Don't remember. Don't think so.'

'Just like the last time,' Desmond Harris murmured.

Lucia Grossi turned to Cangio, and said in Italian: 'Why didn't they beat the shit out of this devious arsehole?'

Eddie Murphy watched them, a smile on his lips.

'Where are you from, darlin'? You Spanish, or what?'

Lucia Grossi turned on him with a menacing glare. 'I come from Italy,' she said. 'You wouldn't like it there.'

'Ooo, spunky,' Murphy said, stubbing out his cigarette on the scarred window-ledge. 'I like my women tough . . .' Then he slapped the palm of his hand against his forehead. 'Oh, I get it now. Italian, right?' He scratched the hairs on his chest and smiled at Harris. 'So you finally made the connection, eh?'

'Connection?' Harris echoed.

He looked lost, Cangio thought.

'You want me to confirm it, I suppose?' Murphy pushed himself up from the sofa and crossed the room. He started opening the drawers of a sideboard, rooting around inside.

'What are you looking for?' Harris asked him.

Murphy didn't answer, spilling things out on top of the sideboard. Then he held up what might have been a postcard, glancing from Harris to Grossi, then back again. 'Who wants it, then?' he asked. 'Who's the boss around here?'

'Give it to Captain Grossi,' Harris conceded, nodding towards Lucia Grossi, whose hand was already stretching out to take it.

She glanced at the card, then looked at Murphy. 'An Italian nightclub? What was Cormack doing there?' she asked him. 'Was this where he was working?'

Murphy shrugged his shoulders. 'Beats me, doll,' he said. 'Me and him share the same flat, but we ain't living together. I don't ask him where he goes at night.'

'Why didn't you pull that card out when I came the last time?' Harris demanded.

It wasn't easy to say where his anger started and his embarrassment stopped.

'You didn't ask me what was hidden in Cormack's drawers,' Murphy laughed. 'And I *don't* mean his dirty underpants. I found this after you lot had gone. I haven't got the time to waste chasing after you. You should have got your own hands dirty and looked in there yourself.'

Cangio suppressed a smile. He would have said the same thing.

And clearly Lucia Grossi thought the same way, given the expression on her face.

'Yeah, all right, go on, then. You can keep it if you like,' Murphy said, as Grossi pushed the card into her pocket.

'Thank you for your help,' Grossi said over her shoulder, turning towards the door.

'Any time you wanna pay me back,' Murphy said with a smirk, 'you'll find me right here on the sofa, ready an' waiting.'

Out in the street, Harris asked if he could see the card.

Yet another point to Lucia Grossi, Cangio thought. She really did have it in for Scotland Yard. He wondered whether she would have shown it to him if Harris hadn't asked.

'Do you think you can get us to Brixton, Desmond?' Grossi asked him.

The Tarantella Club in Station Road

Brixton looked quiet and peaceful, a nice place to live, apart from the big, yellow, police warning signs telling people that there were dealers on the streets selling crack, cocaine, and other illegal substances.

Advertising, Cangio thought. If you needed anything, you knew you'd find it there.

'The streets look deserted,' Lucia Grossi said.

She was sitting in the passenger seat beside Harris.

'They come out once the sun goes down,' Harris said. 'A bit like vampires.'

The entrance door was open to let in fresh air, and a woman was inside cleaning the club. She was Caribbean, Cangio guessed, dressed in a floral cotton wrap-around apron, a red woollen ski hat on her head, a wet broom in her hand.

'Can we speak to the owner?' Harris asked her.

'He in't here,' she said.

'The manager, then?'

'He in't here, neither. Who a' you?'

'Police,' Harris said.

'Tha's wha' I thought.'

With each question, they took a step deeper into the club. It wasn't large. A basement room, maybe two adjacent basements knocked into one. A bar on one side, a dozen tables, chairs, a space for dancing, a raised platform for a band or a sound system at the far end.

'Do you know a man named Vincent Cormack?' Harris asked her.

'I don' know no one,' the woman said, shaking her head, and Cangio had the impression that she was telling the truth.

'So who does this place belong to?'

Cangio wandered away, leaving them to it. He ranged along the wall, looking at the photographs that were hanging there. There were pictures of parties, groups of people, people drinking, people dancing.

Harris insisted. He wanted to write down the name, address, and phone number of the club owner.

'I don' *know* who owns it,' the woman insisted back. 'Willy G jus' tol' me to clean it.'

'He pays you, does he, Willy G?'

'Tha's right.'

'So maybe he's the manager. Have you got a number for him?'

'Willy G's the one calls me.' The woman looked at him, and scowled. 'I don' know where to find 'im at this time o' day. I don' know no one. I wouldn' come in here at all if it wasn' for the dosh.'

Cangio was staring at a photo in a blue frame spotted with gold stars.

It was hanging in full view on the back wall near the bar. Three men were holding up brimming champagne flutes to the camera. Vince Cormack was sitting on the left, wearing a blue waistcoat and a red dickey-bow. Cangio had never seen the fat man in the middle, but he did a double-take when he saw the man on the right wearing dark glasses, his face turning away from the camera.

Was that a shadow on his neck? Or was it a tattoo?

Cangio glanced at Harris, Grossi and the cleaner, then he plucked the picture off the wall and tucked it inside his leather jacket.

A few minutes later, they were out on the street again.

'What now?' Harris asked.

TWENTY-ONE

Des Harris speed-dialled New Scotland Yard.

'DCI Jardine here.'

'It's me, sir. I've just dropped them off at the Elephant and Castle tube.'

'Seen enough for one day, have they?'

Harris breathed out noisily through his nose.

'Let's hope so, sir,' he said. 'Grossi said something about shopping, but I reckon they'll be heading back to their hotel for a kip.'

'So, Des, what happened at Alice Street?'

'That idiot, Eddie Murphy, pulled out an invite to that club in Brixton . . .'

'Didn't you search the flat thoroughly the last time?'

'He said he'd only just found it, sir.'

'And what did the Italians make of that?'

'Grossi wanted to see the place, of course. I had no alternative but to take them. Luckily, there was no one there who would have recognised me. I'd sort of banked on that, too. Mid-afternoon. The place was empty, apart from a woman who was tidying up.'

'Good work, Des. So Grossi doesn't know that we'd been asking questions there?'

'No, sir. She would have let on if she'd guessed. She's not the sort to keep her thoughts to herself.'

Detective Chief Inspector Jardine let out a sigh that might have been a groan.

'You can say that again! Did they manage to squeeze anything out of the cleaner?'

'Not a thing, sir. The woman didn't know what day of the week it was. She didn't even know who owned the place. They'll be going home very soon now, sir . . . Grossi and Seb Cangio, I mean. OK, they may start wondering how the Tarantella Club ties in with their dead man, but what will they make of it? For all they know, Vince Cormack may just be one of the regulars. They'll write it off as a dead end, I bet.'

'*I hope you're right, Des. We're at a crucial point in the investigation.*'

'We're well ahead of the race, sir. We can get them for conspiracy to murder, drug trafficking, money laundering. Whether the stuff they're selling comes from Italy or from Venezuela hardly matters, does it?'

'*It matters not a whit, not one tiny iota.*'

'I'm taking the Italians out to dinner this evening, sir. Is that all right with you?'

'*Good move, Des. You can charge it to expenses, obviously. No champagne, though. Just see if you can work out what's going on in that woman's head, then pack them off to bed.*'

'I was thinking of a place in Soho . . .'

'*Not the Imperial China, Des. We went there the last time, remember, Chas Bailey's farewell do? I don't want one of the waiters recognising you, and those two thinking that it's all a set-up. A quiet meal, a quiet chat, then get shut of the pair of them fast.*'

'Not to worry, sir. I was thinking along the same lines. The simpler we keep it, the less overseas interference there'll be. Once we've got the case tied up, the Italians will be left with just the crumbs.'

'*Phone me once you've put them in a taxi, OK?*'

'Yes, sir.'

'*Not too late, mind . . .*'

'Is this a good idea?' Cangio asked her.

They were on the Piccadilly Line heading north.

'Shouldn't we have told him what we're up to?'

'Why should I tell them a thing?' Lucia Grossi said. 'They aren't giving much away. Giving it away? They're keeping too damned quiet, if you ask me. I mean to say, they haven't even announced that Vince Cormack is dead. Murphy didn't know, and they had already spoken to him. And I would swear that Harris has been to the Tarantella Club, too. He drove us straight to the door, despite being such an abominable driver.' She tapped the side of her nose with her finger. 'You disappoint me, Seb Cangio. I thought park rangers had a sharper sense of smell?'

'What's that supposed to mean?'

'Something stinks,' she said. 'And our friend Desmond knows

what's causing the stink. Did you see the look on Jardine's face when I told him that I wanted to see Eddie Murphy? Like a little boy who'd been caught with his pants down. They're keeping something very close to their chests, Seb, and, until I know exactly what it is we are going to do a bit of sleuthing on our own account. If anything turns up, we'll decide what – if anything – we want them to know about it. End of argument.'

Determined was how Cangio would have described her. Bloody-minded, too. But Lucia Grossi's nose wasn't everything she thought it was. She didn't know what he was hiding in his leather jacket, and he wasn't going to tell her.

'End of argument,' he agreed.

The train began to rattle and shake, braking to a halt.

'Russell Square,' he announced. 'This is our stop.'

The address they were looking for was lost in a maze of streets a bit further south in Bloomsbury, so they had to walk some way to get there, cutting through side streets, skirting squares with neat, fenced-off gardens, and passing two or three hospitals along the way.

They came to a halt in Lamb's Conduit Street, and stared at the little green shop on the opposite pavement.

The Old Pharmacy.

'They need to vamp the old place up,' she said dismissively. 'It looks like the shop that time forgot.'

'It probably just serves local residents,' Cangio said.

'And the man that we are looking for, though *served* may be more accurate in his case, I fear.'

'Perhaps he lived around here, and someone knows him.'

'That would be a stroke of luck, wouldn't it?'

She stepped into the road taking care to look left, and a long-haired boy on a bicycle swung wide to avoid hitting her. 'Fucking arsehole!' he shouted back over his shoulder.

'*Vaffanculo, stronzo!*' Lucia Grossi muttered, as they crossed the street.

She was like a hand grenade with the pin pulled out. Cangio hoped she wouldn't explode in the shop.

A bell tinkled above their heads as they opened the door and entered.

Lucia Grossi marched up to the nearest assistant, a tall black girl in a white doctor's coat who was showing off some sort of an elastic girdle to a middle-aged woman. 'I'm with the Italian police,' she said. 'I need some information.'

The assistant looked at her, then at the customer.

Then both of them looked at Lucia Grossi.

'If you'd just wait your turn,' the girl said. 'I haven't finished serving this lady.'

Lucia Grossi reared up for an instant, and Cangio feared that he was going to witness one of those scenes where a foreigner complains and is given a talking-to about respecting the queue and other people's rights. It was a battle she was bound to lose, and Cangio knew it. Fortunately, Grossi had the good sense to back down. They were going to need all the goodwill they could get.

It took the assistant five minutes to ring up the till and send the lady on her way.

'Good afternoon. May I help you?'

The girl smiled as if the word *police* had never been mentioned.

Lucia Grossi opened her document case and pulled out a glossy photograph.

'I'm making enquiries about this label,' she said, handing the picture over the counter.

The young woman glanced at the picture, looked at Lucia Grossi, then handed it back.

'You'll need to speak to the pharmacist,' she said. She put her head through a door behind her, and called out: 'Dr Attar, it's for you!'

A small middle-aged man with a full black beard came flying through the door. He was wearing a long white coat, a large blue turban on his head. He looked over the counter at Lucia Grossi, who towered above him.

'What may I do for you, madam?'

She bent the truth a bit. She was an Italian policewoman, she said. She was working with Scotland Yard. 'Your label was found on a bottle at the scene of an accident,' she said, as she handed him the photograph. 'It may have belonged to someone you can identify.'

The pharmacist scrutinised the picture. 'It is definitely one of ours,' he said. 'The shop label is very, very dirty, but you can just see the address here at the bottom.'

'That's what brought me here,' Lucia Grossi said.

'It's a repeat request for Malarone . . .'

'And what is that?'

'Well, it's a medicine. Pills. They use them in places where malaria is common. The generic name is atovoquone or proquanil . . .'

'A repeat request, you said?'

The man smiled, showing off large white teeth. 'That's right, madam. A chronic malaria sufferer, perhaps, or someone who travels frequently in areas with a high risk of infection. Africa, India, or even my own homeland, Quetta, in Pakistan.'

Lucia Grossi threw back a warm smile of her own.

'Can you tell us the name of the patient?'

'Normally, it is printed on the label . . . but, well, these dark brown smudges . . .' He looked up, his eyes sparkling bright. 'Is it blood?'

'Dirt,' Lucia Grossi corrected him. 'Mud, or something similar. The bottle was left out in the rain. Is there any way of tracing back the . . . *Cazzo*, Cangio, how do you say *ricetta*?'

'The prescription,' Cangio helped her. 'Can you tell who issued it, Dr Attar? There's a date . . .'

'That is confidential information, I'm afraid,' the pharmacist said, shaking his head, his eyes fixed on the photograph.

'If you wish, you can clear it with Scotland Yard. Inspector Desmond Harris, or Detective Chief Inspector . . .'

'The man who took this medicine is missing,' Cangio piped up quickly. 'We don't know who he is, which is making things very difficult. If he has a wife or children, they're bound to be worried. We need to find them, too.'

'I can imagine,' the doctor murmured. He pulled a biro from his pocket, tapped it against his teeth. 'And it is a special case, it seems. An accident, you said, and the man is now missing? Please, give me a few minutes, and I'll see what I can do for you.'

Cangio smiled. 'It's very kind of you.'

'A patient of ours,' the pharmacist said. 'One feels a degree of responsibility.'

Five minutes later, they had much more than they had expected.

The address was on the better side of Harley Street.

Nothing had been done to mar the Georgian beauty of the terrace.

A midnight-blue door was topped by a dovetailed fanlight, the iron-work railings and balconies freshly painted black, a string of large new cars standing at the kerb beside the parking meters.

Cangio spotted two new Bentleys, and enough Jaguars to run a race.

'A ten-minute walk from the chemist's,' Lucia Grossi said, checking her watch. 'There and back on his lunch break.'

Cangio pressed the button on a name panel.

'N-R-I. Good afternoon. Do you have an appointment?'

Lucia Grossi hadn't been expecting that. 'Police,' she said loudly.

The door clicked open, and they stepped into a spacious reception hall with a crystal chandelier and a wide staircase. A youngish woman wearing a smart dove-grey suit with matching horn-rimmed spectacles came skipping down the stairs to meet them.

'N-R-I,' she said.

'Police,' Lucia Grossi said again, just in case anyone happened to be listening. 'And what does N-R-I mean?'

The woman's plucked eyebrows arched. 'The Neurological Research Institute,' she said.

'And you are?'

'The secretary. Mary Brown.'

Cangio was amazed at the way the British reacted when face to face with authority. This woman was an easier nut to crack than the pharmacist's assistant in Lamb's Conduit Street. The address made all the difference, of course. *Police* was a word that no one in Harley Street would ever wish to hear.

'I'm not sure who we need to see,' Lucia Grossi said. 'The director, perhaps?'

'Professor Cottrell? He's away in Germany, I'm afraid . . .'

'So, who can I speak to?'

The secretary glanced left and right. There were four doors leading off from the vestibule, each one with a brass plaque or a name panel.

'Well, look . . . you'd better come up,' she said.

She turned away and trotted up the white marble steps and bolstered red carpet ahead of them, then led them into a combined office and waiting room on the first floor, closing the door behind them.

'Professor Cottrell is travelling in Germany, as I said. There's no one else . . .'

'So, who's in charge here?' Lucia Grossi asked her.

Mary Brown took off her glasses. 'No one, as a matter of fact. Unless, that is, you count the humble secretary. We are a consultancy, you see. A wide range of specialists and surgeons work through us, but only on request. If we have a specific case which requires a particular consultant, we call in whoever is best qualified to make the diagnosis and carry out the follow-up procedures.'

Lucia Grossi took it in. 'So if I made an appointment, someone would be waiting here to see me?'

The woman put on her spectacles again, as if the worst part of this particular examination was over. 'That's right,' she said.

'And what about a . . .' She glanced at Cangio, then remembered the word. 'What about a chemist's prescription, if that were necessary?'

'It would be made out on the doctor's own prescription pad. It's their responsibility, you see. We just provide the contacts.'

'So, any prescription issuing from this address would be made out by . . . who?'

'Whom? Oh, Professor Cottrell, of course. It would be from his pad.'

'Will he have taken it with him to Germany?'

The secretary smiled, then shook her head. 'Oh no, he wouldn't need it there. He's doing a series of lectures and seminars on neurological . . .'

'If he hasn't got it,' Lucia Grossi said, 'where is it?'

'It will be in the safe, I imagine.'

'And the key?'

The secretary looked up timidly. 'He isn't in trouble, is he?'

Cangio wondered whether this might be termed *intimidation*. Lucia Grossi hadn't raised her voice, or made any threats, she just behaved as if authority came to her as a gift from the Gods which could not be denied.

Grossi smiled reassuringly. 'For doing his duty? Of course not. The fact is that a man has disappeared in Italy, and a medicine prescribed for him by Professor Cottrell was found in his room,' she lied, equally gently. 'We're just trying to identify him.'

'Thank goodness for that!' the secretary said. She was visibly relieved.

'We know which medicine it was, but we need to confirm the name of the patient, and inform his family of what has happened. They'll be worrying about him.'

'Why, of course,' the secretary said.

'Can you check if Professor Cottrell issued a prescription recently for Malarone? And if so, who it was for? Professor Cottrell doesn't even need to know,' Lucia Grossi said.

The woman pursed her lips and kissed her forefinger, as if thinking it over.

'It can't do any harm,' she said, 'and it may do some good.'

'Exactly,' Lucia Grossi smiled. 'It's in the patient's best interests.'

They hadn't been sitting on the big brown Chesterfield five-seater sofa for three minutes, when the secretary came back with a slip of paper. 'Professor Cottrell doesn't write very many prescriptions,' she said. 'Only five in the last three months, as a matter of fact. He lectures mainly, as I told you. And there's only one for Malarone.'

She handed the paper to Lucia Grossi.

Lucia Grossi read the name, then looked up. 'Do you remember Peter Hammond?'

'Peter?' the woman said. 'Well, of course, I do. He's one of our consultants. He didn't look too well, the last time I saw him. Ah, so *that's* why! Malarone's a malaria treatment. He had just come back from an assignment in . . . Egypt, I think it was. And now he's missing, you say? In Italy? Well, I wonder what he was doing out there. Professor Cottrell will be so concerned. You will let us know when you find him, won't you?'

'Do you have an address where I can ask for him?'

'Not his home address, no, but someone there will have it, I'm sure. It's only a ten-minute walk away. Do you know Queen Square?'

Cangio asked himself which English divinity was helping them out.

It was all there within the space of a quarter of a mile.

More like a village in Valnerina than a city of eight million people.

Valnerina, Umbria

Antonella was used to seeing things that turned her stomach.

She was a dentist with her own surgery. She spent five days a week peering into people's mouths, probing and repairing, extracting when there was no alternative, doing what she could to put things right, doing it with all the professional detachment she could manage.

Some of the things she saw in her job were truly revolting.

Decaying teeth were the cream on the cake.

There were lots of things worse than bad teeth, abscesses for a start, especially if you had to lance one. The stuff that came out . . .

She didn't like to think about it. She didn't like blood, or pus, and knew that she had made her career choice without giving it sufficient thought. Being a dentist was like facing up to your personal devils every day, hour after hour, as one patient followed another into the hot seat.

That day had been a bad one.

She had seen things she'd be having nightmares about for weeks.

A seventy-year-old man had been in first thing that morning. He hadn't been to a dentist in twenty years, he admitted, his black gums oozing watery blood whenever she touched them with a probe.

Then a teenage girl had come in with a sore tooth and a rusting 'silver' pin sticking up out of a big black patch in the middle of her tongue . . .

Antonella shuddered at the memory.

She had sent the girl to the hospital, suspecting that they would need to cut out the pin, and a piece of the girl's tongue, as well. Necrosis had set in. They ought to film it first, then put the film on YouTube and Facebook, and warn kids not to mess about with their delicate young bodies.

The rest of the day had been standard – teeth in various stages of decay or collapse, bad breath and nicotine fumes, minor infections, and, of course, the man who came in just after lunch and apologised as he opened his mouth.

'My wife always uses a lot of garlic,' he said.

'Does she really? I hadn't noticed.'

As always, she was glad to close the surgery door for the day and head off home.

Her cottage was outside Borgo Cerreto, looking down on the small town and the sparkling River Nera. Going home was always a pleasure. The cats would be waiting for her. There were fifteen at the last count, though an accurate census was out of the question. She kept her special pets inside the house: the Lords of the Manor. There were others that lived out in the woods, coming down to the cottage when she set out silver oven trays in the evening loaded with crunchy dry cat food. The renegades headed back into the woods again when they had eaten their fill.

They were hers, but they didn't really belong to anyone.

She didn't try to pet the cats from the woods, or even touch them, except when one looked ill. If she was able to catch it, she would take it down to the vet and get it treated, but most of them darted away, and, sooner or later, they didn't come back.

A cat's life.

You did what you could, but you couldn't do everything. All you could give them was food and respect. Some cats were wild, and you were never going to change them.

Even so, they must have felt some sort of feline gratitude.

Often, she would find a 'gift' on her doorstep.

She climbed out of the car and walked up the path.

A black cat was watching her from behind a geranium plant. She called him. 'Hey, Mishy!'

Mishy pulled back into the bushes, but he didn't go away. Mishy was always one of the first to start gathering for the evening feast. He'd be sitting there waiting for her, though he seemed to know that it wasn't feeding time yet.

As a rule, she would stop off at a supermarket on the edge of Spoleto, pick up whatever she needed, groceries and cat food, then drive through the Sant'Anatolia tunnel, heading for home.

'First things first,' she said out loud, as if Mishy might know what she was talking about. There was a bottle of wine to put in the freezer, other things to put in the fridge, then she would wash and change, start cooking dinner, feed the Lords of the Manor, then fill the trays outside with food for the renegades . . .

She let out a squeal and dropped the shopping bag.

Fortunately, it fell on the grass, so the bottle didn't smash.

One of the cats had left a gift. Coming home at night, or

leaving the house first thing in the morning, there was often something waiting for her on the doormat. It shows that they love you, everyone said,

She stared at the thing for some moments.

It was muddy, dirty, bent. It wasn't a vole or a mouse. It lay there, black, decomposing, the same length as a . . .

Then it hit her.

She couldn't take her eyes off it, scrambling for the mobile in her handbag.

The good thing about emergency numbers, they were short.

She pushed the digits 1-1-2.

'*Emergency. How can I help you?*'

'There's a finger on my door-mat. A human finger . . .'

'*We have localised your call and recorded your number,*' the voice came back. '*Do not move from the vicinity. Help will be there within five minutes.*'

Antonella sat down on the damp grass and waited.

Mishy pushed his head through the geraniums and watched her.

He was waiting, too.

He was getting hungry now.

Queen Square, London

The sign outside the red-brick building spoke of Neurology and Neurosurgery.

A notice board in the busy entrance hall listed the names of the various departments and the doctors who were working at the hospital.

Peter Hammond was a consultant oncological neurosurgeon in the Biological & Tissue Engineering Department.

Mr Hammond hadn't been seen for two or three weeks, the man in the porters' lodge reported. He might be off on an assignment abroad. He travelled a lot. All over the world, as a matter of fact.

'When is he expected back?' Lucia Grossi asked.

'I really couldn't say,' the porter told them.

Outside on the street, Lucia Grossi took Cangio by the arm.

'It seems we've found our man,' she murmured, purring like a cat.

Cangio was thinking of a different man, the man in the photograph that was nestling inside his leather jacket.

'What was Peter Hammond doing in Umbria?' he wondered.

TWENTY-TWO

Seven thirty

The bedside light was weak in his hotel room.

Fortunately, the bulbs surrounding the mirror in the white-tiled bathroom were brighter. He'd been in there for quite some time, sitting on the closed loo-seat, studying the picture he had lifted from the Tarantella Club and carried off beneath his jacket.

What had Vince Cormack been doing in the club?

And who were the two men he had been drinking with?

They were celebrating something by the look of it, raising champagne glasses to the camera, Vince Cormack on the left, an older man in the middle wearing dark glasses, and a younger man on the right who might just have a tattoo hidden in the shadow on the side of his neck.

Could it really be the same man?

He was thinking of the man at Assisi Airport who had stopped beneath the car-park camera to light a cigarette.

The man with the salamander tattoo.

Had he arrived on the same plane from London as Vince Cormack and Unknown Two – Peter Hammond, the Harley Street surgeon, as they had discovered that afternoon – or had he been waiting there in Assisi for one, or both, of them to arrive?

It would have helped if he had had the printout of the photograph that Lucia Grossi had handed over to DCI Jardine in the pink file, though there was no guarantee that a half-profile and a full-face portrait of the same man would match up.

And yet, there really was a distinct similarity . . .

Were his eyes playing tricks, letting him see what he wanted to see?

He looked at the photograph for the hundredth time.

He would – *almost* – have sworn it was the same man.

Were the 'Ndrangheta supplying gear to London dealers?

They were supplying drugs to Europe and the world. If coke was being smuggled into England, it was more than likely that the 'Ndrangheta were behind it.

But how did Peter Hammond fit into the scheme?

Was it merely a coincidence that he and Vince Cormack had been on the same plane, as Lucia Grossi had seemed to think? And how had that bottle of anti-malaria pills prescribed for Peter Hammond ended up in the cellar of the Argenti farmhouse?

Suddenly his mobile phone squealed in the bedroom.

He fumbled with the photo-frame as he jumped up, almost dropping it, though he managed to catch it before it hit the tiled floor, avoided breaking the glass.

He went into the bedroom, grabbed his phone from the bed, pushed the button.

'Hello, who is it?'

'What do you mean, who is it? Were you expecting Loredana?' Lucia Grossi asked. 'Desmond Harris will be here in ten minutes. He's taking us out to dinner, remember? He said he was going to pick us up at eight. A restaurant in Soho, he said. Some grotty place in Chinatown, I bet. Get moving, Seb. I'll be waiting for you down in the lobby.'

'Oh, yes, right . . . dinner,' he said.

'You've been dozing, haven't you? Well, screw your head back on, and get into gear.'

He put the phone down, looked around the room in a daze.

He might have been looking for his head and the screw.

He grabbed his jacket, thrust the stolen photo under his arm, and headed for the lift.

Valnerina, Umbria

It was dark in there, pitch-black, like an underground cavern.

The air was stale. It smelled of mould, rot, ancient straw, and animals long dead.

A voice shouted, 'Lights,' and switches were thrown.

Click! Click! Click!

Powerful arc lamps lit the scene starkly like a sound stage or a film set.

Scene 1: The Undercroft . . .

A long narrow room with a cracked floor of paving stones, a low and undulating ceiling, thick beams supporting a floor of narrow wooden boards above. The wood was so old, it had turned black long ago.

'Let's get started. Take it very slowly. If you spot anything, stop work and call me.'

They started by removing the paving stones near the rear wall.

There was something odd about the way they were laid down, something that didn't look quite right. As if they might have been pushed into place by hands that didn't usually do that sort of work. The others sagged, but these seemed humped.

They used crowbars for the paving stones, then metal picks and trowels, gouging a hole, brushing away the dirt, examining the hole up close before they made it any bigger.

'Take it off millimetre by millimetre, as if you were whittling wood . . .'

Four men in white nylon coveralls with zips, their faces masked like surgeons, their boots concealed by green plastic overshoes. A slow and dirty job, but a job that they were used to. *Avoid contamination.* That was the first rule of onsite excavation.

They hadn't been at it for more than five minutes when a voice said, 'Sir!'

Everyone stopped, put down their tools, gathering to see what had come to light.

The arc lamps on the left were refocused on their tripods, the ones on the right moved further back.

'What is it?'

'Here, sir, you see? It looks like fabric . . . the sleeve of a jacket, maybe . . .'

'Yes, sir, look. There's a button . . .'

'OK, brush it down. That's better. Now, take out another piece . . . just here.'

A rubber-gloved finger tapped the floor sixty centimetres away.

'That's it. Use a chisel, not the trowel. Prise the dirt away, rather than digging into it. Please, bring that airbrush over here . . . That's right. Keep the air jet fixed on the cutting edge of the chisel. Slowly now, *very* slowly . . . There's no rush . . . That's good, very good.'

Three minutes later, the first tooth appeared like a fossil embedded in a rock.

Ten minutes more with the airbrush and chisel, there was a full set coming out of the ground. Upper and lower teeth tightly clenched together.

Human teeth.

Eight thirty

Cangio caught the Underground to Brixton.

He was still amazed at the ease with which he had shaken off Lucia Grossi.

Or had it been the other way round? he wondered. Had she been glad to get rid of him, leaving her to dine tête-à-tête with Desmond Harris? He couldn't imagine any reason why she would have wanted to do that. Unless she was a man eater, and the one thing missing from her list was an English detective?

She'd been dressed to kill, that was for certain. He had found her waiting for him in the hotel lobby, taking a surreptitious glance at herself in a full-length mirror.

'Smart outfit,' he had said, meaning it as a compliment.

'This is the uniform I wear when I'm on parade, but not on duty.'

A light-blue blouse, a dark-blue two-piece suit. Only the silver braid and badge were missing. The suit was pinstriped, the blouse rough silk, the top three buttons left undone, but there was a slit up the side of her skirt which showed her knees and a tempting vision of nylon-covered thighs. Still, it was as close to a *carabiniere* uniform as you could possibly get. And she was wearing that sexy perfume again.

She had given him the once-over, then arched her eyebrows.

'Aren't you dressing for dinner?'

At that point, he had trotted out the tale he had made up in the lift. An old friend who lived in London, someone he owed a meal to. If they didn't meet tonight, they might never get a second chance, etc., etc.

'An old friend? What would Lori have to say about that?'

'This friend has a bushy beard and bad breath.'

'Pull the other one,' she had said with a laugh.

Still, the fact that she had let him off the hook so easily was rattling through his mind as he rode the Underground. Did she and Harris have things to tell each other that were not intended for a park ranger's ears?

Then he started thinking about the photo hidden inside his jacket.

There was a big chalk blackboard hanging on the wall outside the Tarantella Club.

TONITE ONLY – The Bashdog Squad, Hoagie James, & Big Kenny Young – back-to-back, whatever that meant.

A bouncer was guarding the door. Sharp suit, massive shoulders, a shaved head, a thick neck. His lips pursed in imitation of a smile as Cangio began to pull out his wallet.

'Free entry before ten on Thursdays. You're luck's in, mate.'

Cangio put his money away. 'Thanks,' he said. 'I need a bit of luck.'

He had already had his fair share: the bouncer hadn't bothered to pat him down, and discover what he was hiding under his leather jacket.

The club looked totally different at night.

Bigger, more exciting, less like a dusty cellar.

It was the light show that did it, the twirling mirror-ball overhead, the multicoloured strobing lights bouncing off it, shooting out dazzling flashes in all directions. The noise made a difference, too. A black guy with dreads and beads was testing his sound system, blasting out funk, house, soul, and an occasional oldie that Cangio recognised, then hip-hop, hip-hop, hip-hop.

Cangio knew what the music was because the DJ kept telling him.

'*Dis da massif hit o' Diddy, da hip-hop king . . .*'

And all the while, the bass thumped hard.

There were less than twenty people in the club. A group of girls on a hen night, maybe, were drinking hard, laughing loud, getting ready for what the night might vomit into their laps.

Cangio walked over to the bar.

The girl behind the counter was a punk maybe, pretty enough, but not his type: blue hair, rings in her ears, rings in her nose. He didn't like to think about the other possibilities.

'What you drinking?' she asked.

He surveyed the pumps. 'A pint of Foster's.'

'Tequila spritz is half-price tonight,' she said, pointing to a sign on the wall behind her.

'Foster's is fine.'

'Your choice,' she said as she pulled him a pint. 'That's seven quid.'

He couldn't stop himself. 'Seven pounds for a pint of Aussie piss?'

She chuckled, and nodded. 'Yeah, a rip-off, innit? Brewed in fucking Manchester, too. The tequila cocktail's cheaper, but it's too late now. There you go, lover boy.'

He took his beer to a table in the furthest corner from the music.

As he sipped, he looked around.

The hens were shouting louder now, two guys giving them the eye, ordering drinks at the bar while the punk went through her cheap drinks routine all over again. No one was paying any attention to him. Slowly, he unzipped his leather jacket and let the hidden photograph frame slide out onto the bench-seat beside him.

A couple strolled onto the floor and started dancing, stopping whenever the sound test stopped, starting up again when something else came blasting out of the speakers. They were really good, changing style and stance to match the noise, sometimes dancing close together, sometimes far apart.

Other people were slowly drifting in, but the place was still quiet.

'*We gonna kick off proper in fifteen minutes*,' the DJ announced. '*Dis is a part of the session we be playin' here come Sunday.*' He put on a tape, then headed for the exit, a tobacco pouch in one hand, a packet of Rizla papers in the other.

Cangio picked up the framed picture, and carried it over to the bar.

'You wan' a refill?' the barmaid said.

He held up the photograph.

'I found this over there,' he said. 'Someone must have lost it.'

The girl glanced at the photo in his hand. 'Some joker, more like. That pic's one of ours. They're always arsin' around in here, movin' things about.'

She took the picture from him, and propped it up against the back wall.

'What can I get you?' she said, reaching for a glass. 'Boy Scouts deserve a reward.'

Cangio sat down on a high stool at the bar. 'Not that crap from Manchester again.'

She winked, and ducked beneath the counter to open a fridge. 'Try this,' she said. 'Dead Pony. Important customers only.'

He looked over his shoulder. 'This lot don't look up to much.'

'Where are you from, then?' she asked him.

'Italy.'

'Yeah, I figured that much,' she said, glancing at the photograph behind her. 'The boss is Italian, too. That's him in the middle. Signor Franco Carnevale.'

'Which bit of Italy does he come from?'

The girl shrugged her shoulders. 'How should I know? Italy's Italy, innit.'

Cangio laughed. 'You're right about that. Still, if this is his place, he's done all right for himself, hasn't he?'

The girl smiled, then rubbed her index finger with her thumb. 'This is just one of his clubs,' she said, then mouthed the word *Money*. 'It can't buy you everything, though. Good health for starters.'

'At seven quid a pint, it can buy you a lot. That was quite a party they were having,' he said, nodding back at the picture. 'The champagne in this place must cost a fortune.'

'*You* pay a fortune,' she said, resting her elbows on the bar, 'but they drink free. It wasn't a party, though. Not a proper celebration, anyway. Can you imagine? They were toasting to the success of Jimmy's op. He was set to go into hospital the following week.'

'Which one's Jimmy?'

'Jimmy ain't in the photo. Just his dad, Franco, and a couple of mates.'

'What's Jimmy's problem?'

'Something up here,' she said, and tapped her temple with her finger.

Someone ordered a drink further down the bar, but she drifted back as soon as she had served the customer.

'What ya doing in Brixton, then?' she said.

'Temping. A few more days in London, then I'm flying back home.'

'A pity,' she said. 'I, er . . . I get off work at two tonight . . .'

She left the invitation hanging, waiting for him to pick up on it.

Cangio nodded back towards the photograph. 'None of them looks too hot,' he said. 'What's wrong with the other guy's neck? He looks as if *he* needs an operation, too. Was he burnt, or something?'

She glanced at the photo. 'Nah, that's a tattoo. A horrible, slimy-looking thing.' She showed him a red rose tattooed on her bicep. 'I like my ink, but that one? Like he had some sort of a lizard creeping inside his shirt.'

Cangio drank deep from the bottle of Dead Pony.

Champagne couldn't have tasted any better.

The man with a salamander tattoo . . .

'Hey, like I was saying, I get off work at two, if you wanna hang round.'

For a moment, he wondered what it would be like to fuck a punk, discover all the fancy silver rings and bizarre tattoos that were hidden in places yet to be discovered. Then he thought about Loredana, and his conscience kicked in.

He drained his glass, took out his wallet, laid a ten-pound note on the bar.

'Have a decent drink on me,' he said. 'None of that Aussie piss from Manchester, mind.'

'Are you off, then?'

She sounded disappointed.

'Afraid so,' he said. 'I've got to meet a man.'

'Oh, shit, another one,' she sighed.

The brush-off was as easy as that.

Valnerina, Umbria

Dino De Angelis stopped the car, and the engine died.

He didn't want to be seen, didn't want to be asked what he was doing there.

He pressed the button and opened the side window; the windscreen was clouding up with condensation from his breath.

What were those people doing at the Argenti farmhouse?

He could see figures moving about in the woods inside the curtain wall.

That was where he had heard the screams that night. The Brunoris had heard them too, though they lived further down the hill from his farm. And now, these folks wandering around in the woods at night, dressed in white like ghosts. He could guess who they were, but he didn't feel any better for knowing.

He was going home after spending the day on the mountainside with his cattle.

He wouldn't spend another night up there. Davud, the Albanian boy, was out of hospital now, and he had his brother, Zamir, up there to help him, too.

Dino had been too frightened to stay up there alone himself.

Three nights and no one looking after the herd . . .

It had cost him one stillborn calf, and he knew he'd been lucky to get off so lightly. But once the sun started going down, he had only one thing on his mind. He couldn't forget it. Never would. The noise the cows had made that night. And the noise that other . . . thing had made outside his . . . He started sweating just to think of it. *Cristo santo*, he wouldn't pass another night up there on his own for a million euro.

Davud and Zamir would cost him a hell of a lot less . . .

When he'd seen that figure in white step out on the road, he'd stamped on the brake in fright, and the engine had stalled.

What were they doing up here?

The figure in white bent low, pointing a torch at the ground, sweeping it back and forth, as if he was searching for something.

Suddenly, a second figure in white appeared from the bushes. They started to sweep the area with light. It was almost hypnotic, watching them from the growing darkness.

They were forty or fifty metres away, too busy to notice him.

Dino wondered why they were dressed like something out of a space movie, and whether the force of gravity was heavier where they were. It seemed to slow down their movements and gestures.

A gust of wind brought the sound of their voices.

He lowered the window a bit more to hear what they were saying, but he couldn't make much of it. Then a third figure in white came bursting out of the bushes, yelling, 'Hey, you two! Come up straight away. We've found a skull . . .'

Dino's hand was shaking as he twisted the ignition key, and the car sparked into life.

He accelerated hard down the road, sweeping past the people in white, heading in the direction of Borgo Cerreto.

Get away! Get away fast! That was what his head was telling him.

And while he pressed the accelerator to the floor, he wondered whether those creatures dressed in white were hunting down other strange creatures in the woods that night, and whether they might have found one.

We've found a skull . . .

He ran to his front door with his keys in his hand, jamming the key into the lock, opening the door in a rush, and closing it behind him even faster. Then he went from room to room, closing the shutters, and locking the windows.

'Is there a storm coming?' his wife asked, without taking her eyes from the television.

'Maybe,' he said. 'Who knows?'

Brixton, nine thirty

Outside, the air was warm and damp.

It would rain before long, he thought, but the weather was the last thing on his mind.

He was thinking about that photograph. Franco Carnevale, the Italian nightclub owner, with Vince Cormack, the man who had been murdered near Stansted. And the other man, the one who had a tattoo of a salamander on his neck.

Lucia Grossi would have said that he was paranoid.

He hoped to God he really was paranoid.

What the hell were they up to in Umbria?

A man stepped out of a doorway and zapped him in the face with a cosh.

Lights out, mental strobes.

Valnerina, Umbria

They were laid out on plastic sheets now.

It had been a very long day, but they'd got a result.

'Sir?'

He turned around. 'What is it?'

'We should start securing the scene for the day, *tenente*. It's getting on for eight o'clock. By the time they get the tarpaulins and the evidence trays back to Perugia and into the laboratory . . .'

'Of course, of course. So, what's the score?'

The pathologist smiled as if they might have been talking about football.

'The score, *tenente*? Two, so far, but who knows what tomorrow may bring. We haven't dug up half the floor, and . . . well, after what we've collected today, I have the feeling that there may be more. My team should be done by lunchtime tomorrow. Give or take a couple of hours.'

They watched the technicians folding up the plastic tarpaulins, each one containing a body.

'Can you tell me anything at all?'

His voice faded away.

The light was fading now. As dusk fell over the hillside, the forest seemed to take a step closer to the farmhouse, like sentinels moving in to guard the house and its secrets.

'Not a great deal,' the pathologist said. 'I need to reassemble the pieces, examine the bodies under bright lights, take X-rays, skin and fibre samples. The usual stuff. And yet . . .' She paused, looked up at the sky, the pink turning red, the upper folds of the clouds now dense and black. 'It seems so bloomin' peaceful here,' she said. 'It isn't the sort of place you'd think of as a dumping ground for dead bodies. I was wondering, well . . . you know, what brought them here. *Who* brought them here. That's what I meant . . . Two men with one thing in common, at least.'

'One thing?'

The pathologist smiled. 'They both have good teeth. They seem to be pretty much of an age, too. Not so young, but not too old. Middle-aged, let's say. Middle-aged men . . . with good teeth.'

'I don't follow you,' he said. 'Good teeth?'

'Good teeth, a good life. It's an axiom of forensic pathology. A regular dentist, regular care, a regulated life – that's the assumption until you find some counterindication. I'll probably stay at the lab tomorrow morning . . . Rather than come here, I mean. My men can handle it without my interference. I'd like to get started on the analysis straight away. If anything unexpected turns up, of course, just call me. I'll be here within an hour.'

'Thanks,' he said. They were closing the vans, putting *no entry* seals on the undercroft doors. The local police would be keeping watch that night. 'If you find anything unusual under the micro-scope, you've got my number.'

The pathologist turned away, walked towards her car, lit a cigarette before she climbed into the driver's seat.

Funny, he hadn't imagined that she was a smoker.

Then he got on the phone to Lucia Grossi in London.

Brixton, ten o'clock

A bucket of cold water woke him up.

He was sitting in a barber's chair, his wrists tied tightly to the porcelain arms. He couldn't move his feet on the footrest, some-thing pulling at his ankles when he tried. His head was cushioned at the back with something hard. It might have been the headrest old-time barbers used when they pulled out the cut-throat razor and started to strop the edge on a leather strap.

He hoped there wouldn't be a razor.

He prayed there'd be no shaving done tonight.

He looked up and saw two men. One was Franco Carnevale. The other one looked like a boxer – too old for the ring, but still a bruiser. The bruiser grabbed hold of Cangio's broken nose, gave it a twist, waited until he stopped screaming, then said in a quiet voice: 'Who the fuck are you, then?'

Cangio tried to remember what he had in his pockets. The electronic key to the hotel bedroom, his wallet, his mobile phone. He had left his passport in the drawer of the bedside table in his room.

'Antonio . . . Antonio Benedetti,' he said, his father's first name, his mother's maiden name.

The man flicked the end of Cangio's nose with his nail, which made him cry out.

'We haven't started yet,' Franco Carnevale said, pushing the other man aside, 'so you'd better get your story straight.'

Did they know who he was?

'What story?'

'You tell me. What were you doing with that picture in the club?'

Cangio thought of the girl behind the bar.

Had she told the boss that he had been asking about the photo?

'That picture? I found it,' he said, his fright spiralling out of control. 'It was lying there on the bench when I sat down with my drink. I thought someone had lost it. I . . .'

They must have been watching the scene at the bar from a hidden camera.

'So you gave it to Sandy?'

'The barmaid?'

'And you started asking her questions.'

'I was trying to . . . to chat her up.'

Franco Carnevale leant close, looking into his face, peering at his nose, examining the damage the cosh had done.

'You won't be chatting anyone up ever again if you fuck around with me,' he said in Italian. Cangio tried to place the accent. Maybe London had taken the edge off Carnevale's native tongue. He wasn't Calabrian, that was for sure.

'*Ch' cazz' sta' facenda cà, guaiò?*'

Cangio's blood ran cold. *What are you doing here, my friend?*

That dialect was from the bay of Naples.

Franco Carnevale was running nightclubs in London, drinking champagne with Vince Cormack who was dead, and the man with a tattoo that branded him as an 'Ndrangheta soldier. This was dangerous shit he had got himself into.

'Listen,' he said, desperation kicking in. 'Sandy, the barmaid . . . I wanted to chat her up. Like I said . . . What's the harm in that? A nightclub in London? I was cruising, looking for a girl. She was working late, she said. I couldn't wait . . . I . . . I was going to try somewhere else . . .'

'Where are you from, *guaiò*?' Franco Carnevale hissed in his face.

Calabria was out, and so was Naples.

'*Jo so' de Roma*,' Cangio said, moving his tongue, rounding out his vowels.

'From Rome, you say?' Franco Carnevale turned to the boxer, and said in English, 'Gimme them pliers.'

A hand came out of the darkness holding a pair of spring-loaded pliers.

Carnevale twitched them twice in his hand, then prodded the prongs on either side of Cangio's nose. 'This is your last chance, son. Why the fuck were you asking about that picture?'

The pliers began to squeeze.

'Spit it out!'

He managed to resist for a couple of seconds, then he screamed until his throat ached.

'*Fica, fica fica!* I . . . I wanted to fuck her!'

Panic welled up in his chest. The pliers blocked his breathing. He started to retch. Then the pliers eased off a fraction.

'Your first time down the club, was it?'

Cangio nodded, tried to breathe, felt blood bubbling out of his nose, running into his mouth, and down his chin. Had the CCTV been recording that afternoon when he had gone there with Lucia Grossi and Desmond Harris? Had the cleaner told the boss that the police had been there?

'I came to Brixton hoping to score . . .'

'Burning a fucking hole in your pants, was it?' Franco Carnevale sneered, pressing hard on the pliers, leaning close to see the pain that he was causing.

Carnevale didn't know that he'd been there with Grossi and Harris.

The pliers eased, the pain eased, too.

Franco Carnevale narrowed his eyes, then turned away.

'Get shut of this wanker,' he ordered.

The boxer stepped out of darkness, holding something that flashed in the half-light.

Cangio caught a whiff of ether, petrol, something chemical and nasty.

The needle plunged into his neck, and the lights went out again.

TWENTY-THREE

London

He couldn't make out where he was.

Couldn't figure out if he was dead or alive.

His head was spinning, each thought crowding out the last.

Waves of panic swept over him, though what he was frightened of, he couldn't say. Nor did he know what to do about it.

His jaw ached, his nose ached even worse.

The corners of his mouth were cracked, and it hurt when he tried to speak. It was such a small word, but he couldn't get it out. He could see what he wanted, see it running down a hillside, rolling through a river valley, gurgling into a pipe, then coming out of a metal tap, hitting hard on a porcelain sink, then splashing into the air, and making bright rainbows in the sunlight.

'Water,' he heard a voice say. 'Water.'

He felt a warm hand slide beneath his neck, his head being lifted, then something cool being poured onto his tongue, dribbling wet and fresh down his chin. He tried to turn his head to catch the liquid with the corner of his mouth, which made him groan, then retch.

A voice that didn't belong to him said, 'It was really massive . . .'

He remembered the Tarantella, the DJ with the dreadlocks. *Diddy, the hip-hop king . . .*

'. . . a massive dose. He's lucky to be alive.'

Then he closed his eyes and slept.

He could hear a murmur of voices . . . Like bees. Three of them at first, then two. A low, constant murmur. Then a different voice breaking in, saying more loudly, 'You'll have to wait outside please, we need to change him.'

Change him?

He felt himself being moved and shifted, first one way, then the other, then patches of dampness on his body, then some rough material grating against his skin which made him moan with pain.

'There, there, dear. You' quite safe now. Just be a good boy.'

'He shoulda been a goo' boy before . . .'

He must have blanked out.

When he opened his eyes again, Lucia Grossi was sitting next to the bed, staring out of a window, her face as dark as the clouds beyond the window.

He felt his legs twitch, his chest was aching, pulsing, his muscles like Plasticine.

'Where am I?' he groaned.

She turned her face and looked at him. 'That was quite a night on the town,' she said. Her voice was hard, disapproving. 'I should never have let you out of my sight.'

'Where am I?' he said again.

'Hospital. An emergency admission. What the hell did you take, Seb?'

'I don't know,' he managed to say, feeling exhausted, his chest pumping harder, faster, now. 'I didn't . . . take . . . anything. *They* . . . they gave it . . . to me.'

Next thing, Lucia Grossi was on her feet screaming for a nurse.

Valnerina, Italy

Sergio heard his parents whispering.

He couldn't see them from his bed, but he could hear them.

They must have opened the window in their bedroom.

He could feel the cold air coming through the open door from the corridor.

The numbers on the digital clock reflected off the ceiling, flashing, off and on. Four red numbers and a dot in the middle – *02.35.*

He was frightened by the fact that they were up so late.

The fact that they were whispering frightened him even more, his mother's voice, hoarse with terror, saying: 'I don't want to hear that word again. Ever . . .'

What was she talking about?

His father said something that Sergio couldn't make out.

'What are they doing up there, Luigino? At this time of night, I mean?'

'They're doing what they always do,' his father said, 'in cases like this . . .'

His father sounded gruff and tense, as if he had a sore throat.

Sergio lay still in bed and listened. He didn't say a word, didn't make a sound.

He knew what they would tell him if he went into their room. *Be a good boy, Sergio. Go back to sleep. Mamma just needs a bit of fresh air. It's the asthma . . . you know the way she sometimes has trouble breathing.*

But he knew what they were talking about.

He knew that they were scared.

His mother had said . . .

There were shadows in the doorway.

'Sergio . . .' his mother whispered. 'Are you awake?'

'He would have called, or come running to us.'

Sergio didn't move, or say a word.

'He's fast asleep,' his father murmured after a while.

'Thank goodness for that. I mean . . . what would you tell him? How could you explain a thing like that?'

He heard the window close a short time later, heard the creak of the mattress as they got back into bed. He couldn't stop himself from shivering. He would have liked to climb in bed with them, but that meant getting out of bed, crossing the room in the dark, running down the corridor, then into their dark room.

And anyway, they were scared, too . . .

He remembered what his father had said.

They're digging up what Evil has devoured.

DE-VOUR-ED . . .

Sergio pulled the sheet up over his head.

He didn't sleep again that night.

'Heart failure,' Grossi told him an hour later.

She was sitting in a chair beside the bed, eating a sandwich, and swigging Coke from a bottle. 'I thought I might be taking you home in a box,' she said. 'You suddenly went blue in the face. Your girlfriend wouldn't have been too happy, would she? Then again, you're not the easiest man to live with, if this is anything to go by. That girl of yours, Seb. What's her name?' she said, and it might have been a test.

'Lori . . . Loredana.'

'OK, that's fine. Now, tell me what happened.'

His head was lighter now, his memories clearer.

'I didn't meet up with a friend . . . We didn't hit the town . . .'

Lucia Grossi stopped in mid-bite. 'Where *did* you go, then?'

He buckled beneath a wave of pain, felt nausea, wanted to throw up.

She didn't notice how ill he was, hardly seemed to expect an answer to her question.

'I went to a club . . .'

She didn't ask him which club, or why he had gone there, didn't seem to be listening.

'I have to get back home without delay,' she thundered on. 'Oh, what a mess you've caused! If you can't make it, Seb, I'm going to leave you here. The . . .'

He pushed himself up against the pillow, thought that he was going to die.

'That's . . . exactly what . . . I was thinking,' he said. 'Help me, will you?'

She glanced at her wristwatch. 'We've got five hours. Do you think you can manage? Will you be able to travel?'

He swung his legs off the side of the bed, felt giddy, felt pain. He gritted his teeth, and fought against the nausea. Why this sudden haste to go back home? Had something come out of her dinner date with Desmond Harris the night before?

'What's going on?' he said, his lips cracked and painful.

The face of Harris appeared like a full moon rising over Lucia Grossi's shoulder.

'Things are moving, Seb. Lucia will give you the details when you're feeling better. For the moment, you have to stay as calm and quiet as you can. Otherwise they'll never let you out of the hospital.'

'What's he doing here?' he asked Lucia Grossi.

'We're lucky he *is* here,' she said. 'Thank goodness he was with me last night. We were having a nightcap in the hotel lobby when the manager came over. The railway police had been on the phone. They'd found you wandering on the Kent Coast Line in a daze, with trains whizzing past every couple of minutes. You'd tried to stop a couple with your bare hands, they said. Luckily, you had the hotel key card in your wallet, so they knew where to phone. Otherwise, we might have had another unidentified corpse to add to the list.'

She glanced at the Englishman.

'Maybe you should tell him,' Desmond Harris said.

'Tell me what? What's happened?'

'Lucia told me that she had discovered the identity of Unknown Two.'

That she had discovered?

That was why she'd been glad to let him go off alone. Old friend, old flame, it made no difference to her where *he* was going. She'd wanted Harris all to herself. It wasn't hard to imagine the look of triumph on her face as she told him that *she* had done what Scotland Yard had been unable to do.

'You told him?'

'Yes,' she said, 'but there's more. They called me from Perugia

while we were eating. Yesterday, I ordered my men to start
digging at the Argenti farmhouse. They've found some teeth,
human remains. Two men for the moment. One of them may
well be Peter Hammond. Unknown Two, let's say, until we can
verify his DNA. I've no idea who the other man may be. That's
why we need to get back to Umbria as fast as possible.'

Cangio pushed his arm into his shirt, trying to take it all in.

'A third man dead?' he said, thinking of the man with the
tattoo. 'Unknown Three?'

TWENTY-FOUR

Valnerina, Umbria

Cangio enlarged the face on the computer screen.

'Gotcha!' he murmured, more of a groan than a word.

His jaw was aching. His teeth were aching. He felt as
if he was sucking air through a wet sponge. But that hadn't
stopped him booting up his laptop the minute Loredana left for
the late shift at work. He had typed in the search term *Tarantella
Club + London*, and Google had done the rest. Working his way
through the list of items the computer spewed up, he had found
what he was looking for on the third page.

As he read the article, everything fell into place.

It spelled bad news.

Bad news for London, but even worse for Umbria.

How would Lucia Grossi take it? he wondered. The information contained in the article would certainly lend weight to the
Italian investigation, but would it be enough to convince her to
go back on whatever arrangement she had worked out with
Desmond Harris over dinner in London?

Grossi hadn't spoken much that morning on the way to
Stansted.

The truth of it was that they had hardly spoken at all. He had
been in no fit state to talk, and she had only one thing on her
mind.

'We have to catch that plane!'

It was leaving at 8.30, he had to get up, get dressed. She had helped him into his shirt and his trousers, even tied his shoelaces for him. His bag was packed, she had brought it from the hotel. They'd made a fuss about releasing him from the hospital at four o'clock in the morning, but Desmond Harris had explained the situation to the doctor on duty. Even so, they had forced him to sign a voluntary discharge sheet before letting him go.

Grossi had a minicab waiting to take them to the airport.

She'd been sitting up front in the passenger seat, talking with the Bangladeshi driver to keep him from falling asleep at the wheel.

Cangio didn't remember the journey.

He had slept on the back seat in a drug-induced oblivion.

On the plane he had managed to drink a cup of coffee, complaining about the pain in his nose and jaw.

'This should help,' she had said, and had handed him a pill. 'Just consider yourself lucky, Seb. If you can feel the pain, you're still alive.'

Then she had turned away, and closed her eyes.

He had had no idea whether she was sleeping or not. One thing was certain: she wasn't talking. As the plane swooped down on Assisi Airport, he had tried to break the barrier of silence.

'So, what will happen now?'

'A joint investigation is inevitable,' she said. 'I'll be working shoulder to shoulder with New Scotland Yard.'

'That's a feather in your cap.'

She hadn't been able to suppress her glee. 'And *what* a feather!'

'You and Harris?'

She had turned to look at him as if he had just said something very foolish. 'Harris? I hardly think so. Detective Chief Superintendent Jardine will want the lion's share of the glory, I imagine.'

She was staring out of the porthole as she said it, a transfixed look of satisfaction on her face. Floating out there on Cloud Nine, if he was any judge, imagining the bright future that was opening up before her, a female *carabiniere* who had shown New Scotland Yard a trick or two.

The plane had hit the tarmac with a jolt, the engines screaming as the thrust reversers opened, and the jet had rolled slowly towards the terminal building.

'As soon as we get off this crate,' she had said, 'I'll put you in a taxi.'

That was the moment.

That was when he had decided not to tell her what he had discovered at the Tarantella Club. Lucia Grossi thought she had it all sewn up. She thought that she was one step ahead of everyone. But what he had just discovered from the Internet put him many steps ahead of Lucia Grossi.

She still had no idea who was behind it all.

The photo filling his computer screen showed a man in his mid-twenties whose face had appeared on the front page of the *Daily Mail* the year before. Giacomo Carnevale – known as Jimmy to his friends – had been arrested after a prostitute accused him of maiming her. The woman had told the court what had happened in shocking detail, and the story had run under the front-page headline *THE BEAST BIT OFF MY NIPPLE.*

The article cited a plea which had been made on the defendant's behalf by his lawyer:

'My client denies the accusations made by Miss Jennifer Reilly. The teeth marks on the lady's breast may well be his, but I submit this declaration made by a competent medical expert who avows that Mr Carnevale is suffering from a long-term clinical psychosis, a severe form of schizophrenic disorder, which renders him unfit to plead. He was not aware of any aggression, either during or after the sexual act. Nor can he recall it now. If a crime was committed, then my client was unaware that he was committing it.'

Jennifer Reilly had been awarded a quarter of a million pounds in damages.

Jimmy's father, Franco Carnevale, a 'well-known nightclub entrepreneur', had paid it.

On impulse Cangio had entered the name *Giacomo Carnevale* and the word *morso* in an Italian search box to see if the news had filtered back to Italy.

The Internet had taken him far from London, back to another time and a different place.

Twelve years earlier, an Italian newspaper had reported a story that featured Giacomo Cannavolo, the teenage son of a 'well-known businessman' from Naples whose name was Franco Cannavolo. The Cannavolo family had gone on a Mediterranean cruise aboard the good ship SS *Costa Lucente*, where a fight had broken out between Giacomo and an English boy. The father of the English kid – a lawyer, as the article reported – had been so outraged by what had happened, he insisted that the captain put the Cannavolos off at the next port or face a legal action for damages. Father, mother, and teenage son had been marooned on the island of Crete, and all because young Giacomo had taken a huge bite out of the other kid's shoulder. The journalist had ended the piece by asking whether Giacomo 'Jimmy' Cannavolo would be known forever afterwards as 'Jaws'.

It didn't take much to guess that the Cannavolo family had changed its name to Carnevale, and moved to London. The 'well-known London entrepreneur' was likely importing drugs on behalf of the 'Ndrangheta, distributing and selling them through the chain of nightclubs that he ran in south London, while keeping his son out of trouble.

Cangio took a sip of coffee.

It was the third cup he had got through since sitting down at the computer.

It was time to print out the articles he had cached.

But then he hesitated.

Giacomo Carnevale had an operation . . .

That was what the barmaid at the Tarantella had told him.

He typed the word *dottore* into the search engine, then followed it with *sparizione*.

The icon twirled for a second or two, then a page appeared. He checked the list, and felt the need to drain the last of the coffee. The liquid was cold, but it didn't matter. He didn't even taste it. He glanced at his watch. It was twenty to eight.

Would Lucia Grossi still be in her office?

The phone was picked up on the second ring.

'Cangio?' she said. 'Shouldn't you be resting?'

He didn't bother to answer the question. 'I was surfing the net,' he said. 'I came across something you'll want to know about.'

She let out a groan that almost ripped his ear off.

'*Cristo santo*, it's late! You should get some sleep.'

'You think so?' he said, and a smile hurt his face. 'Let me ask you a question.'

Lucia Grossi blew a raspberry into the phone.

'Do you know how many doctors have disappeared this year?'

'What the heck . . . Have you lost it completely?'

'Give me a number.'

'A thousand? A million . . .'

'Five,' he said. 'Five doctors have disappeared without trace this year.'

'So what?'

'Five doctors walked out of the door and were never seen again. Not alive, at any rate. One of them was an ophthalmic surgeon from Catanzaro in Calabria. Guess where they found his corpse.'

'Will you stop this fucking quiz?' she growled.

'In the nearby Aspromonte mountains buried beneath a pile of rocks.'

'That's what happens in the mountains,' she said. 'It's called an avalanche . . .'

'His wife was puzzled. He never goes near the mountains, she said. He wasn't dressed for the outdoors. But you know what's really strange?'

Lucia Grossi took a deep breath. 'You tell *me*,' she said.

'The post-mortem reported multiple fractures, a pulverised skull, yet *every* contusion on the body was exactly the same shape. *Perfectly round* was the phrase . . .'

'I don't see where this is leading!'

'You know the name of one of the doctors the computer coughed up.'

'*O Cristo* . . .'

'We know where he disappeared, and we know that it wasn't an accident.'

She was silent for a while.

'I want you in my office first thing tomorrow morning,' she said.

The line went dead before he could speak.

There was one thing he wanted to check before he went to Perugia.

TWENTY-FIVE

Villa San Francesco

Cangio staggered up to the front door.

He had ripped off the bandages that were covering his face.

His eyes were black and blue, his nose was puffed up, his lower lip was split.

He looked a sight, and he knew it.

He held his stomach as if he'd been shot, then pressed the intercom button, holding his finger there, looking up into the lens of the CCTV camera fixed high above the door on the right.

Beyond the door, he heard nothing, only the echoing whine of the electronic buzzer.

He stared hard at the camera lens, showing all the pain that he could muster, letting out a tortured groan, still pressing hard on the button.

The seconds stretched out. Almost a minute, and still the door remained closed.

If this was a hospital, they couldn't ignore an emergency cry for help . . .

'*Yes?*'

He held on to the button, let out a groan that sounded hideous to his own ears.

'*Yes?*' the metallic voice said again, more sharply this time. '*What is it?*'

'Help me . . . please,' he moaned. 'I . . . feel . . . so . . .'

He let go of the button, and collapsed on his knees, still holding on to his stomach.

As he heard the bolts being drawn and the door was opened, he closed his eyes, fell forward flat on his face, groaned with real pain, then lay there like a dead man.

'Jesus Christ!' he heard. 'What the fuck . . .'

'Bring a trolley,' another voice said. 'We'd better bring him in. Be quick about it.'

Hands rolled him over onto his back. A finger lifted an eyelid, saw an eye that had rolled upwards in its socket.

'He's out cold by the look of it.'

He felt himself being lifted onto a gurney which began to move quickly into the clinic. A minute later, he was being lifted again, and laid on what felt like a hard bed.

'Off with those shoes. Raise his legs on a pillow.'

He felt his shoes being pulled off, a pillow or two being bundled beneath his feet.

'Can you hear me?' a voice said, and he felt warm breath on his ear. 'Bring in the ECG. You, roll up his sleeves and his trouser legs.'

He felt a finger pressing hard on his neck beneath his left ear, and a minute passed. Then his shirt was pulled open and he felt a cold metal disc pressed hard against his chest above his heart. He heard the same voice saying, 'Hm,' three or four times. 'The heart's beating fast, and the pulse is strong. Nurse, we ought to check his blood sugar. Have you got a test-strip handy?'

Some moments later, he felt his hand being turned to expose the palm, then a quick jab with something sharp in the fatty tip of his middle finger. It took all his concentration not to react as a drop of blood was squeezed from his fingertip.

'Well?'

'It seems quite normal, Doctor. Seventy-one mg/dl.'

Nurses, doctors. Cangio felt better, though he still didn't move or open his eyes, not even as he felt a cold hand resting flat on his stomach.

'Not a diabetic coma, then. There are no signs of insulin injections here. It isn't epilepsy, either. And his breathing seems regular, so we're not talking about a collapsed lung. Take a good look at the veins in his arms, will you? Maybe he's a user . . .'

'No track marks, Doctor,' the other voice said.

That hand was still on his stomach, moving slowly over his skin. Suddenly, a second hand pushed down hard on the first hand, and Cangio let out a groan, though he managed not to open his eyes.

'Peritonitis, Doctor?'

'A burst appendix, probably. The one thing that surprises me is . . . well, this faint. I mean to say, two or three minutes would fall within the safety limit, but this has been going on for . . . what, five minutes now? Hand me that, will you?'

Whatever *that* was, Cangio had no idea.

And whatever was in *that*, it acted so fast as the needle slid into Cangio's arm that he didn't have time to open his eyes and tell them that he had been testing them.

He went out like a light.

'We've got a window of about three hours . . .'

'Only three?'

'We could stretch it out a bit, maybe. It depends how long we can keep him subdued with "twilight" anaesthesia. I don't want to go too heavy on the sedation and knock him out cold. I could do the job now, of course, and keep the stuff on ice in the fridge until you get here, but, as a rule, I prefer to work with fresh tissue. I'm sure that you do, too?'

The silence at the other end of the telephone stretched out too long.

'Did you hear me?'

'Yeah, I heard. I'm looking at logistics, organising my departure. It's not an easy thing to do at such short notice.'

'He took us by surprise, as well. I didn't expect to see him here again so soon, and not in that condition. But I couldn't turn him away. I had no choice but to let him in. And then I thought, well, who actually knows he's here? The more I thought about it, the more the situation seemed perfect . . .'

'You done good.'

There was that silence again, the merest hint of voices beneath the surface.

'OK . . . OK. I'll be on the jet in twenty-five minutes max. Send the chopper to meet me at Assisi. I should be there in just over an hour. Phone the control tower, they'll give you the IFPS flight plan with the time of arrival, OK?'

'That puts us well inside the three-hour threshold. The surgeon's less than an hour away. He lives in Terni. Now, remember, please, do not eat or drink anything from this moment on.'

'Naturally.'

They were both silent, then the question came that everyone asked.

'OK, so I arrive . . . and then what happens?'

'We've been over this a number of times, Don Michele. It shouldn't take more than forty minutes, and at the end of that time, you'll have the immense satisfaction of killing two birds with one stone. You'll remove a nuisance from the face of the earth at this end of the line, and you'll get a pair of brand-new eyes into the bargain. We've been waiting a long time for the right occasion to come along. This one, believe me, is absolutely unique.'

'If everything works out as it should, we'll be drinking champagne tonight. And then I'll tell you how it *really* feels . . .'

His patient seemed to be in the highest of spirits.

The medical director waited a moment for him to explain, then he asked: 'How does *what* really feel? In what sense, I mean?'

'I was thinking of the priest who says mass in my private chapel each Sunday.'

The laugh that followed those words raised the hackles on his neck. He couldn't help but wonder how a man who laughed like Don Michele would react to the idea of things *not* working out well.

'What does the priest say?' he asked nervously.

'The same advice. Every Sunday, the same damned line. "See the world through the eyes of your enemies." That's what he tells me.' He laughed that frightening laugh again. 'We're gonna put the priest's words into practice. So, tell me this, Doc, how should I answer him *next* Sunday?'

It was like a curdled dream.

A nightmare, fading in and out of consciousness, aware and unaware, hearing, not hearing, as the sedative swept over him in waves.

'. . . should be arriving soon . . .'

'. . . we'll worry about that when the time comes.'

'What the hell was he doing . . .'

'. . . he's been here before . . .'

'But these are fresh . . .'

'You can bet on it . . .'

Then he heard no more – for how long, he had no idea.

Yet even as he drifted away, he knew that there was something wrong.

Very wrong . . .

Apart from a broken nose, there was absolutely nothing wrong with him.

Something woke him.

A noise, perhaps. Or something in the air.

He tried to open his eyes, but they were already open.

It was the drug-induced darkness that was passing away.

Like a blind being drawn, a curtain being slowly lifted, his sight began to fill with blinding light from overhead. An arc light with reflecting mirrors, a light so strong it burnt his eyes like the noonday sun in a desert.

He tried to close his eyelids, but they wouldn't close. Something was holding his upper and lower lids in a tight grip. Pins or clamps, perhaps, cold and metallic, were holding his eyes wide open.

An eyelid speculum . . .

He knew the name. He had used the tool – seen it used, at any rate – while still a student, attending an operation on a wolf that had a thorn impaled in its eye. The speculum was a device that pulled back the lids and kept the eye immobile, a window locked open for easy access.

What was going on?

'Prepare the trephine,' a voice said, somewhere behind his ear.

What was a trephine?

'We need to increase sedation, Doctor. He's coming round. His heart is racing . . .'

'In a moment,' the voice said. 'Just a moment . . .'

Were they waiting for something? For someone?

Who or what were they waiting for?

He tried to move his arms without success.

He tried to bend his legs, then shift on his hips.

He wanted to move his body, to stand up, but he couldn't do anything.

He was strapped by the wrists and the ankles to a cold unyielding table. The table was made of hard planes, strange bumps and angular ridges where he didn't expect them. It was damned uncomfortable. An anatomical table. The sort that a surgeon used.

He wanted to say, 'This is a mistake. There's nothing wrong with me. I was play-acting. I'm as well as you are,' but he couldn't. He wasn't able to form the words, couldn't get them out of his throat.

'He's getting agitated,' a voice said behind his head.

'Give him a touch more Propofol,' a soft voice answered. 'That'll keep him quiet.'

'The other patient's being prepared,' a third voice said. 'Tell me when to bring him in.'

Something loomed over him, cutting out some of the light. A dark shadow that wore a surgical mask, a white plastic cap, and glasses with drooping telescopic lenses.

'It won't be long now,' the voice said. 'Not long . . . not long . . . not . . . long . . .'

With the fading echo came total darkness.

He woke up with a chemical jolt.

The blackness dissolved, and he was staring at a different face.

This face was big and bloated, strangely disproportioned, not hidden by a surgical mask.

It loomed closer and closer, coming so close he could smell the man's breath, peering into his eyes, as if the man had trouble focusing or seeing him.

'Seb Cangio?'

He couldn't answer, not even if he tried.

He heard a growl that might have been a laugh. 'You don't know how long I've been waiting for this moment, you fucker. This is the first and the last you'll ever see of Don Michele Cucciarilli. You won't be seeing anything again, you bastard. I need those eyes of yours. I'll be looking out of them for the rest of my life, and you won't have a life to look out of. You've fucked with me too many times, but you never will again.'

Then blinding light came back as the head bobbed away, and Don Michele said to the surgeon, 'OK, Doc, I'm ready. Let's get this over and done.'

Who was Don Michele Cucciarilli? Cangio wondered in a daze.

A Calabrian by the sound of it.

A clan boss, maybe . . .

What had he ever done to offend the Don?

He was awake in an instant.

His eyes were still wide open, held open by the medical clamps.

Eyelid speculums . . .

The term came back to him, and so did his memory – being prepared for surgery, the arrival of Don Michele Cucciarilli, the threats and insults, then his own final terrifying thought: *I will never see again.*

Staring up, he could see three things: a large piece of white enamelled medical equipment with a silver tube at the centre which blocked out most of the view, a segment of the head of a person wearing a surgical mask and a cap, and what looked like the end of a pistol being pressed against the surgeon's head.

'What's this thing called?'

'An ocular trephine . . .'

'Get rid of it!'

A motor whirred, and the medical equipment moved upwards, growing smaller, enlarging his field of vision, exposing his eyes to the light.

'Those things on his eyes?'

The voice was that of Lucia Grossi.

'Speculae . . .'

'Is it safe to remove them? OK, get rid of them.'

Gloved fingers closed in on one his eyes like enormous spiders.

Then something went *click*, and his right eye was free.

His eyelid closed as he blinked.

And in that instant, a sharp explosion shattered the silence. He saw the snub-nosed pistol shift from the side of the surgeon's head. Now, it was directly above him, sixty centimetres from his face. He saw a forefinger jerk backwards, heard a loud bang, saw a brilliant flash of light, then a trace of smoke. Then the gun turned, and was gone.

He heard, but didn't see, the rest of the gunfight.

It must have lasted five or six seconds, seven or eight shots, echoing and reverberating around the room, then Lucia Grossi was leaning over him, saying, 'Are you all right, Seb?'

The surgeon's hands were shaking as he released the second speculum.

'What's a trephine?' Cangio managed to say, as the surgeon leant close.

'It's a . . . a medical instrument . . .'

The gun was pointing at his head again.

'Tell him,' Lucia Grossi said.

'It's a . . . a drill and circular saw combined. We . . . *It* is used to remove the cornea . . .'

'That Don Michele would have got,' Cangio said.

'They were going to bore your eyes out,' Lucia Grossi said, 'then bury what was left of you with Peter Hammond.'

The anaesthetist was ordered to wake up Don Michele.

'The operation did not go well,' Lucia Grossi told him. 'You're under arrest for . . .'

She didn't know where to start, the list was so long.

TWENTY-SIX

Perugia, Umbria

A *carabiniere* standing guard saluted Cangio as he entered Room 23.

Desmond Harris was propped up in bed on a pile of pillows, his right shoulder held in a plaster cast. A plastic tube fed fluid into his left hand from a drip. He looked happier than he ought to have looked, given that a bullet had grazed his right lung before shattering his collarbone. Did the presence of Lucia Grossi on the far side of the bed have anything to do with it, Cangio wondered. He would have sworn that she'd been holding Harris's hand when he opened the door.

'How's the patient?' Cangio asked.

Harris groaned. 'My shoulder's killing me.'

Cangio understood the feeling. He was still limping a year after taking a bullet in the thigh, still in pain on days when it was cold or damp. Most days of the year, if he was honest.

'It's like a ton weight pressing you down,' Harris said.

If he was fishing for sympathy, he seemed to have found it.

'The important thing is that you're alive,' Lucia Grossi said, her words sounding all too familiar to Cangio's ears. 'Other people didn't get off so lightly. One of the nurses was hit by a stray bullet. She died in the line of her mistaken duty, I suppose you might say. And so did Don Michele's right-hand man. Rocco Montale was the one who started trying to shoot his way out of there. He got what was coming to him . . . The papers will make a hero out of you, Desmond.'

'What about the Don?' Cangio asked her.

Lucia Grossi smiled. 'He won't be giving you any more trouble, Seb.'

That was easy to say, Cangio thought, though not as reassuring as she intended. Don Michele Cucciarilli ordered other people to kill you. And knowing that you had put him in a cell, he wouldn't wait too long before taking his revenge.

The door burst open and a man as bulky as an aircraft carrier came bustling in, carrying a briefcase. He might have been an overgrown baby with red hair, a red beard, and bulging red-ringed eyes.

'Sorry I'm late,' he said wheezily. 'The traffic here beats Mexico City's!'

Alberico Rondini was the magistrate who would be handling the case in Italy.

That was how Lucia Grossi had described him to Desmond Harris.

The magistrate seemed to fill the room with his physical presence, and he seemed to drain it of air each time he took a breath. He headed straight for the only vacant chair and lowered himself into it.

'I have called this preliminary judicial hearing to clarify the facts as we know them,' he announced. 'Fortunately, Inspector Harris is here to represent New Scotland Yard. You had a lucky escape this morning, I believe, Inspector?'

Harris smiled at Lucia Grossi. 'Captain Grossi was in the right place at the right time.'

'You can say *that* again,' Cangio seconded.

Lucia Grossi tried to look blasé, though she was evidently flattered.

'I tried to tell you not to come to Perugia this morning, Seb,' she said. 'Desmond had phoned to say that he was arriving in Assisi, so it would have been easier for us all to meet in Valnerina. But you didn't answer your phone . . . I had the feeling something was wrong, so I called your girlfriend. Loredana really *should* join the police force, Seb. Her built-in lie-detector system is second to none. You told her you were going to Perugia, but you didn't bother to don your uniform! She guessed that you were up to something . . . *unofficial*, let's say. Given what we'd learnt in London about Peter Hammond and Jimmy Carnevale, I guessed that you might be at Villa San Francesco. I had ordered a raid, in any case. *Cristo*, Seb, that was a risky thing to do. They were keeping you under sedation, waiting for Don Michele to arrive by helicopter . . .'

Alberico Rondini held up his hand for silence.

'I declare this court open,' he said in excellent English. 'I will ask the questions from now on, and no one will speak without my permission. Is that understood?' He was silent for a moment. 'It is the sequence of events which concerns me in particular. We need to decide whether this investigation belongs to England or to Italy . . .'

'The story starts near Stansted Airport,' Harris said without waiting to be asked.

'It begins with a murder in Italy some months earlier,' Cangio corrected him.

'Cangio is right,' Lucia Grossi insisted.

Rondini let out a snort, and shifted in his seat. 'Where *exactly* in Italy?'

'Catanzaro, Calabria,' Cangio went on. 'Michele Cucciarilli, an 'Ndrangheta boss, was going blind. He turned for medical help to a local eye specialist. When the treatment failed, the doctor was punished. His body was found in the Aspromonte mountains beneath a pile of rocks, so it seemed like an accident . . .'

'Can this be proved?' Rondini asked.

'No conclusions were reached at the time,' Lucia Grossi chipped in, 'but we believe that he was stoned to death . . . maybe with billiard balls. The first *scena criminis* certainly took place in Italy.'

The magistrate shuffled through his notes. 'And how does this relate to the murder near Stansted Airport?'

'Vincent Cormack was a low-ranking member of a London gang . . .'

'Low-ranking, Lucia?' Harris pushed himself up on his pillows. 'He murdered Peter Hammond . . .'

'Please, ladies and gentlemen, no bickering. One thing at a time,' Rondini protested. 'We have got two deaths so far then, the first in Calabria, the second one near Stansted. That is, two murders committed in two different countries.'

Italy 1 – England 1, Cangio thought, though he knew the game wasn't over yet.

'But Cormack killed Hammond in Italy,' Harris insisted. 'Then *he* was killed in England to keep the story under cover. We're talking about two dead Englishmen . . .'

'Which story?' the magistrate asked him.

Lucia Grossi laid her hand on Desmond Harris's thigh. 'As Inspector Harris just said, Dr Hammond was murdered in Italy, together with his patient, Jimmy Carnevale. So we're talking about *three* deaths in Italy now, and only one in England . . .'

'Three dead *Englishmen*,' Desmond Harris insisted. 'Two here, and one there.'

'Surely you aren't claiming that Jimmy Carnevale is English, Desmond?'

'He may have been *born* in Italy, but . . .'

'No, no! This will not do!' Magistrate Rondini exploded. 'The European guidelines on cross-border murder investigations assigns the case to the country which is most intimately involved, and which has the strongest likelihood of carrying the investigation to a successful prosecution. Until I know the simple facts of the case, or cases, I cannot assign anything to anybody.'

He looked around the room.

'Ranger Cangio,' he said at last, 'you seem to have been involved from the very start. Please, tell me how you see things.'

Cangio gathered his thoughts for a moment. 'The basic factor in all of this,' he said, 'is Michele Cucciarilli. Don Michele became interested in Umbria after the last earthquake. He was involved in the reconstruction, trying to siphon off money from the rebuilding fund, I imagine. He made many investments in Umbria, and one of them was Villa San Francesco in Valnerina. When Don Michele started to lose his sight, he came up with a bright idea.'

Rondini might have been an owl, his eyes fixed on Cangio. 'Go on.'

'He turned Villa San Francesco into an exclusive private clinic, and he made his enemies an offer that they couldn't ignore. These men are hunted criminals,' Cangio said. 'If they fall sick, where can they turn for help? Villa San Francesco was the answer. The patient could fly in by helicopter, protected by his own bodyguards. No one would know that he had been there. Doctors and surgeons, the world's top specialists, could be bought. Money was not a problem for these people.'

Rondini held up his hand. 'Some of the doctors didn't go home, it seems. Captain Grossi?'

'We don't know how many Mafia big-shots may have used the clinic,' Lucia Grossi said. 'Not just members of the 'Ndrangheta, but the Camorra and Cosa Nostra, too. No register of names has come to light, but we do know that a number of highly qualified specialists have disappeared since the clinic opened its doors. At least four Italian doctors are dead, as well as the brain surgeon who flew here from London to operate on a man whose remains have also been found at the Argenti farmhouse, which lies inside the boundary wall of Villa San Francesco.'

'Do you think there will be more bodies?'

'There could be *many* more,' Lucia Grossi confirmed.

'There may be other English doctors, too,' Harris threw in, clutching at straws.

'My men are working to crack the computer codes,' Lucia Grossi said. 'I'm sure we'll have a better idea of the scope of the clinic very soon, the names of the doctors and their patients. The doctors may not have known who their patients were. My feeling is that the majority did not. The ones who did . . . I imagine they put the squeeze on for a larger fee, and they paid for it with their lives.'

Rondini shook his head, a glum expression on his face.

'The idea that these doctors *knew* what they were letting themselves be dragged into,' he said. 'There'd be a frightful scandal.'

'We already have a scandal,' Lucia Grossi said. 'One of Italy's leading urologists was arrested this morning. It is believed that he may have operated on a very big name from Palermo, a Cosa Nostra boss, one of the top dogs. The doctor carelessly forgot his fountain pen at Villa San Francesco. He denied ever having been there, of course, but there wasn't much to deny. His name was engraved on the barrel of the pen. His daughter collapsed when her father was taken into custody . . .'

'Thank you, Captain Grossi.'

'I was about to say that we also arrested two surgeons and the anaesthetist this morning, sir. They knew that there was nothing wrong with Cangio, yet they prepared him for an operation. They *knew* what was going to happen, and that it was strictly illegal.'

Cangio knew what would have happened. Don Michele would have stolen his eyes, and buried his body with the others in the Argenti farmhouse. He shuddered at the memory of the trephine drill, the mechanical whir of the blades closing in on his eyes. He imagined the viscous *pop* as a cornea was extracted, and Don Michele gloating as he saw again through eyes which had once belonged to the park ranger who had caused him so much trouble.

Fortunately, Magistrate Rondini turned to him again.

'Tell me about the English patient,' he said.

'Jimmy Carnevale had a problem. A malformation of the brain, a tumour, perhaps. His father, Franco, knew about Villa San Francesco, and he managed to find a top surgeon in London who was willing to perform . . . well, a lobotomy, I suppose you might call it. Jimmy had been flown to Italy by air ambulance, and Vince Cormack brought Doctor Hammond to Umbria on a Ryanair flight. But something went wrong at the Villa. Jimmy escaped, and he had to be eliminated. Maybe the operation didn't work the miracle they were hoping for. At that point, Peter Hammond was killed to keep him quiet, and the bodies of the surgeon and his patient were buried in the Argenti farmhouse.'

'We have dental evidence in both cases,' Lucia Grossi told the magistrate.

'Then, Cormack was killed when he got off the plane at Stansted on his way home,' Desmond Harris went on. 'Franco Carnevale wanted no living witnesses. That's how New Scotland Yard sees it playing out.'

'Only the man with the tattoo is missing,' Cangio said.

Magistrate Rondini stared at him. 'Who?'

'The man with the salamander tattoo,' Cangio said more boldly now, looking at Lucia Grossi. 'While we were watching security videos in Assisi Airport, I spotted a man on one of the CCTV cameras. The image wasn't clear, and I couldn't see his face, but I was pretty sure that he was wearing a distinctive 'Ndrangheta tattoo . . .'

'Cangio was shot last year by a member of the same clan,' Lucia Grossi explained to the magistrate. 'The younger thugs wear a special tattoo as a sign of their membership.'

'It's a badge,' Cangio added. 'It means that they've killed someone.'

The magistrate stared at him. 'That sounds silly. Why tell the world you're a killer?'

'They want the world to know,' Cangio said. 'The police can't arrest a man for having a tattoo, but everyone in Calabria knows what it means. And the message is simple. Watch out, or you're dead.'

Lucia Grossi was on her feet now. 'Why didn't you tell me?'

Cangio held up his hands in surrender. 'What could I tell you? It was only when we got to London that I made the connection. There was a photo on the wall in the Tarantella Club in Brixton: three men drinking together, the Camorrista, Franco Carnevale, a man with what may have been an 'Ndrangheta tattoo, and Vince Cormack, who turns out to be a killer.'

'If only we had that photograph,' Rondini said.

Cangio pulled out his mobile phone.

'I took a snap of it,' he said, 'before I handed it over to the barmaid at the club.'

Rondini beamed at him. 'Excellent! That should give you something to start work on, Captain Grossi.' The magistrate stood up, gathered his coat and briefcase. 'I'll expect your written reports at the earliest opportunity.'

He might have left the room, but a voice from the bed stopped him.

'I brought copies of documents relating to Cormack and Hammond from London,' Harris protested. 'And I'm expecting a summary of the interrogation of Franco Carnevale at any time now. He's been arrested on suspicion of the murder, or conspiracy to murder, Vincent Cormack. I need to take back copies of the Italian documentation. Franco Carnevale will be standing trial in London, obviously. We'll need to know what *you* know, magistrate.'

Rondini sat down again.

The chair creaked under him.

'This affair is complicated, and modern politics makes it no simpler. We still don't know how Brexit will affect relations between our countries. I mean to say, sir, you are no longer a part of Europe.'

'We haven't left it yet,' Desmond Harris objected.

'I'll need to take legal counsel on this matter,' the magistrate said. 'We aren't in a state of war, after all.'

Not in a war, Cangio thought, but there was plenty of aggression on display.

'If the 'Ndrangheta can work with the Camorra,' Cangio said. 'I don't see why Scotland Yard and the Special Crimes Squad shouldn't collaborate.'

He might have been the little boy who said that the Emperor was wearing no clothes.

All eyes turned on him. And silence reigned.

Then, Lucia Grossi shattered the silence by clapping her hands.

'I have a proposal to make,' she said.

TWENTY-SEVEN

Valnerina

Cangio saw the outcome of Grossi's 'proposal' the following week.

It was the second item on the eight o'clock news on *Canale 5*, the evening round-up that everyone in Italy watched. The first item was the newly elected American president. Next up, Captain Lucia Grossi.

The press conference had taken place that morning at New Scotland Yard. DCI Harold Jardine, Inspector Desmond Harris, and other members of the London team were seated shoulder to shoulder at a long table, while Grossi stood in front of a projection screen, holding court for the journalists, video cameras, and TV reporters who filled the room.

She was wearing full-dress uniform with silver tabs and golden